THOSE JENSEN BOYS!

Center Point
Large Print

Also available from Center Point Large Print
by William W. Johnstone with J. A. Johnstone:

Sidewinders Series
The Butcher of Bear Creek
Bleeding Texas

The Family Jensen Series
Helltown Massacre
The Violent Land
Massacre Canyon
Hard Ride to Hell

**This Large Print Book carries the
Seal of Approval of N.A.V.H.**

THOSE JENSEN BOYS!

William W. Johnstone

with

J. A. Johnstone

CENTER POINT LARGE PRINT
THORNDIKE, MAINE

This Center Point Large Print edition is published in the year 2015 by arrangement with Kensington Publishing Corp.

PUBLISHER'S NOTE
Following the death of William W. Johnstone, the Johnstone family is working with a carefully selected writer to organize and complete Mr. Johnstone's outlines and many unfinished manuscripts to create additional novels in all of his series like The Last Gunfighter, Mountain Man, and Eagles, among others. This novel was inspired by Mr. Johnstone's superb storytelling.

The text of this Large Print edition is unabridged. In other aspects, this book may vary from the original edition. Printed in the United States of America on permanent paper. Set in 16-point Times New Roman type.

ISBN: 978-1-62899-594-7

Library of Congress Cataloging-in-Publication Data

Johnstone, William W.
Those Jensen boys! / William W. Johnstone with J. A. Johnstone. —
   Center Point Large Print edition.
      pages cm
Summary: "Ace and Chance Jensen find their skills put to the test when two young ladies ask them to protect their struggling stagecoach line from a ruthless, bloodthirsty mine owner with money, power, and enough hired killers to slaughter half the territory"
   —Provided by publisher.
ISBN 978-1-62899-594-7 (library binding : alk. paper)
1. Large type books. I. Johnstone, J. A. II. Title.
PS3560.O415T49 2015
813'.54—dc23
                                                        2015010052

THOSE JENSEN BOYS!

Chapter One

Wyoming Territory, 1885

The atmosphere in the saloon was tense with the potential for violence. All the men around the baize-covered poker table sat stiffly, waiting for the next turn of the cards—and the trouble it might bring.

Except for one young man. He sat back easily in his chair, a smile on his face as he regarded the cards in front of him. He had two jacks and a nine showing. He picked up some greenbacks from the pile next to him and tossed them into the center of the table with the rest of the pot. "I'll see that twenty and raise fifty."

Most of the other players had already dropped out as the pot grew. The bet made them look even grimmer.

The player to the young man's left muttered, "Forget it," and shoved his chair away from the table. He stood up and headed for the bar.

The game had drawn quite a bit of attention. Men who had been drinking at the bar or at other tables drifted over to see how the hand was going to play out.

The young man said, "Looks like it's down to you and me, Harrington."

"That's *Mayor* Harrington to you," said his sole remaining opponent.

"Sorry. Didn't mean any disrespect, Mr. Mayor." The young man's slightly mocking tone made it clear to everyone around the table and those standing and watching that disrespect was exactly what he meant.

One patron who seemed to be paying no attention at all stood at the bar with the beer he'd been nursing. He was a man of medium height, dressed in range clothes, with sandy hair under his thumbed-back Stetson. At first glance, not much was remarkable about him except the span of his broad shoulders. He took another sip of his beer and kept his back to what was going on in the rest of the room.

Harrington's pile of winnings was considerably smaller than that of the young man. He hesitated, then picked up some bills and added them to the pot. "There's your damn fifty." He was a dark-haired, well-dressed man of middle years, sporting a narrow mustache. "Deal the cards, Blake."

The nervous-looking dealer, who happened to be the owner of the saloon, swallowed, cleared his throat, and dealt a card faceup to the young man. "That's a three," he announced unnecessarily, since everybody could see what the card was. "Still a pair of jacks showing."

With expert skill, he flipped the next card in the

deck to Harrington. "A seven. No help to the mayor, who still has a pair of queens."

"We can all see that, blast it," Harrington snapped. "Who the hell bids up the pot like that on a lousy pair of jacks? It's not good enough to beat me and you know it."

"I thought we'd already been introduced," the young man said as his smile widened into a cocky grin. "The name's Chance."

He was in his mid-twenties, handsome, clean-shaven with close-cropped brown hair. The brown suit he wore had been of fine quality at one time. It was beginning to show some age and wear, but the ivory stickpin in his cravat still shone.

"I know who you are," Harrington said coldly. "A damn tinhorn gambler who should have been run out of town by now."

The grin on Chance's face didn't budge, but his eyes turned hard as flint. "I think everybody here knows this game has been dealt fair and square, Mr. Mayor. They've seen it with their own eyes." He put his hand on the pile of bills and coins and pushed it into the middle of the table. "And I reckon I'm all in."

Before Harrington could react, another man pushed through the batwings into the saloon and started across the room toward the poker table. He was the same age as Chance but bigger and huskier, with a thatch of rumpled dark hair. He wore denim trousers and a pullover buckskin shirt. His black hat hung behind his head from its chin strap. A Colt Peacemaker rode in a holster on his right hip.

A couple hard-looking men got in the newcomer's way, but a flick of Harrington's hand made them move back.

"I need to talk to my brother for a second," the dark-haired young man said.

"Ace, you know better than that," Chance drawled. "You don't go interrupting a fella when he's in the middle of a game."

"It's all right," Harrington said. "Those cards stay right where they are, though."

"Of course," Chance said smoothly. He stood up, and he and his brother Ace moved a few feet away from the table. Chance continued to smile and look relaxed, but his voice was tight and angry as he asked under his breath, "What the hell are you doing? I've got the mayor right where I want him!"

Ace kept his voice low enough that only his brother could hear him. "I heard over at the general store that you'd gotten into a game with him. The mayor is crooked as a dog's hind leg! Those are his hired guns around the table. You can take that pot off him, but he'll never let you leave town with it."

Chance tried not to appear as shaken as he felt. "How'd you find that out?"

"The fella over at the general store likes to gossip. Seems like Harrington's got everybody around here under his thumb, and some folks don't like it."

"Well, that's just too bad," Chance insisted. "I haven't done anything wrong, and I'm not gonna throw in my hand now. That's what you want, isn't it? You want me to quit? What would Doc think if I did that?"

"Doc wouldn't want you getting killed over a poker game."

"I don't know about that. Seems like he always knew what was important in life."

From the table, Harrington said, "Are you going to play or jaw with your brother all day?"

Chance was as self-confident as ever as he turned back to the table. "Why, I'm going to play, of course, Mr. Mayor. I believe the bet was to you." Chance settled back into his seat while Ace stood a few feet away, looking worried.

"And I'm going to call, you impudent young pup. I'm not going to let you bluff me." Harrington pushed his remaining money into the pile at the center of the table. "I'll have to give you a marker for the rest."

"Well, I don't know. . . ." As Harrington's men loomed closer to the table, Chance went on. "Of course I'll take your marker, Mr. Harrington."

The mayor turned over his hole card, which was an eight. "My queens beat your jacks."

11

"But they don't beat my jacks *and* my threes," Chance said as he flipped over his hole card, which was the second trey. "Two pairs always beat one pair."

Harrington's face was bleak as he stared at the cards on the table.

Chance said, "I believe you mentioned something about a marker. . . ."

Harrington's breath hissed between his clenched teeth. He shoved his chair back and stood up abruptly. "You think you're so damn smart." He looked around. The two men who had tried to stop Ace from talking to his brother had been joined by three more big, tough-looking hombres. "Teach these two a lesson and then dump them somewhere outside of town. Make sure they understand they're never to come back here."

"Wait just a minute." Chance's right hand moved almost imperceptibly closer to the lapel of his jacket. "Are you saying you're not gonna pay up, Harrington?"

"I don't honor debts to a cheater," Harrington snapped.

"It was a square deal," Chance insisted. "What'll your constituents think of you welshing like this?"

Everybody in the saloon had started edging away. The feathered and spangled serving girls headed for the bar where they could duck behind cover. In a matter of moments, nobody was anywhere near Ace and Chance to offer them help.

Harrington smirked at the two young men. "Why in the hell would I care what they think? Nobody dares do anything about it. They all know I run this town." He gestured curtly, and his hired toughs started closing in around Ace and Chance.

The sandy-haired man who'd been standing at the bar, seemingly paying no attention to what was going on, turned around then. "Hold it right there, gents."

Harrington stiffened. "You don't want to get mixed up in this, stranger."

The man ambled closer, thumbs hooked in his gun belt. "You're right. I'm a stranger here. So I don't care if you're the mayor and I don't care if these hombres who think they're tough work for you. I don't like to see anybody ganging up on a couple young fellas."

One of Harrington's men said, "We don't just think we're tough, mister. We'll prove it if we have to."

The stranger stood beside Ace and Chance. "I reckon you'll have to."

"Get them!" Harrington barked.

Five men charged forward. Two headed for the stranger, two for Ace, and one lunged at Chance and threw a looping punch.

Chance ducked under the blow and stepped in

13

to hook a left into his opponent's belly. His punch packed surprising power. As the man's breath gusted out and he bent over, Chance threw a right to his jaw that landed solidly. The man's head jerked around and his eyes rolled up. His knees unhinged and dropped him to the sawdust-littered floor.

A few feet away, Ace had his hands full with the two men who had tackled him. One of them grabbed him around the waist and drove him back into the bar. He grunted in pain. Stunned, he couldn't stop the man from grabbing his arms and pinning them. Grinning, the other man closed in with fists poised to deliver a vicious beating while his friend hung on to Ace.

As his head cleared, Ace threw his weight back against the man holding him and raised both legs, bending his knees. He straightened them in a double kick that slammed into the chest of the man coming at him. The kick was so powerful it lifted the man off the floor and sent him flying backwards to crash down on a table that collapsed underneath him and left him sprawled in its wreckage.

The move also threw the man holding Ace off balance. His grip slipped enough for Ace to drive an elbow back into his belly. As the man let go entirely, Ace whirled around and planted his right fist in the middle of his opponent's face. Blood spurted and the man's nose flattened as he reeled against the bar. Ace finished him with a hard left that knocked him to the floor.

While that was going on, the broad-shouldered stranger dealt with the two men attacking him. Moving almost too fast for the eye to follow, his hands shot out and grabbed each man by the throat. With the corded muscles in his shoulders and arms bunching, he smashed their heads together with comparative ease—about as much effort as a child would expend to do the same thing to a pair of rag dolls. The two toughs dropped as limply as rag dolls, too, when the stranger let go of them.

Clearly furious at seeing his men defeated, Harrington uttered a curse and clawed a short-barreled revolver from under his coat. He started to lift the gun—only to stop short as he found himself staring down the barrels of three revolvers.

Ace, Chance, and the stranger each had drawn a weapon with breathtaking speed, Chance's gun coming from a shoulder holster under his coat. All it would take to blow Harrington to hell was a slight bit of pressure on the triggers.

Harrington's hand opened, the pistol thudded to the floor, and his eyes widened in fear. "P-Please, don't shoot. Don't kill me."

"Seems pretty foolish for anybody to die over a stupid saloon brawl," the stranger said. "Why don't you kick that gun away?"

Harrington did so.

The stranger went on. "I was watching in the bar mirror, and as far as I could tell, this young fella beat you fair and square, mister. I'd like to hear you admit that."

"O-of course," Harrington stammered. "He beat me."

"Tell him, not me."

Harrington swallowed and looked at Chance. "You won fair and square."

"That means the pot's mine," Chance pointed out.

"Certainly."

He replaced his gun in the shoulder holster, then began gathering up the bills and stuffing them in an inside pocket of his coat.

"I-I'll make out that marker," Harrington went on.

"Forget it. What's here on the table is good enough. My brother and I are leaving, and I'd just as soon not have to come back to this burg to collect."

"That's very generous of you."

The stranger said, "I'd advise you fellas to saddle your horses and ride on out as soon as you can. I'll hang around here for a while just to make sure the mayor doesn't get any ideas about sending his men after you to recover that money."

"I wouldn't do that," Harrington insisted. His

face was pale, making his mustache stand out in sharp contrast.

The stranger smiled. "Well, a fella can't be too careful, you know."

Ace and Chance looked at each other.

Ace asked, "You ready to go?"

"Yeah." Chance turned to the stranger. "We're much obliged to you for your help, Mister . . . ?"

"Jensen. Smoke Jensen."

That brought surprised exclamations from several people in the room. Smoke Jensen was one of the most famous names in the West. He was a gunfighter, thought by many to be the fastest on the draw who had ever lived, but he was also a successful rancher in Colorado, having put his notorious past behind him, for the most part. His reputation was still such that nobody in his right mind wanted to cross him.

Ace and Chance exchanged a glance when they heard the name, but they didn't say anything else except for Ace expressing his gratitude, too, as they made their way around the unconscious men on the saloon floor. When they left the place, they headed straight for the livery stable in the next block. They had already gotten their gear from their hotel room and settled the bill, since they'd planned on leaving town, anyway. Their restless nature never let them stay in one place for too long.

Quickly, they saddled their horses, a cream-colored gelding for Chance and a big chestnut for Ace.

Chance tossed a silver dollar to the hostler and smiled. "Thanks for taking care of them, friend."

The brothers swung up into their saddles and headed out of the settlement.

When they had put the town behind them, Chance said, "Smoke Jensen. How about that? We had an honest-to-goodness legend step in to give us a hand, Ace."

"He's mighty famous, all right," Ace agreed. "We've talked about him, but I never really figured we'd run into him someday."

Chance grinned. "You reckon we should've told him that *our* last name is Jensen, too? Shoot, we might be long-lost relatives!"

"I doubt that," Ace said dryly. "You really think a couple down-on-their-luck drifters like us could be related to the famous Smoke Jensen?"

"You never know," Chance replied with a chuckle. "Stranger things have happened, I reckon. Anyway, we're not down on our luck right now." He slapped the sheaf of money through his coat. "We're as flush as we've been for a while. Let's go see what's on the other side of the mountain, brother!"

Chapter Two

Denver, Colorado Territory, 1861

"Jacks over tens, gents." Ennis Monday laid down his cards. "I believe that takes this hand."

"Dadgum it, Doc!" one of the other players exclaimed. "You're just too good at this game."

Monday smiled slightly. "That's how I make my living, Mr. Tucker—being good at what I do."

"Well, I don't begrudge you." Alfred Tucker slid a small leather pouch full of gold nuggets across the table to the gambler. "Everybody in Denver knows that Doc Monday is a square player."

"I appreciate that." Monday tucked the pouch inside his coat and gathered up the cards to shuffle them. "Another hand, gentlemen?"

One of the other players nodded toward a woman across the room. "Looks to me like you might have something more interesting to turn your hand to, Doc. That lady over there's been watching you mighty keenly for the past few minutes."

Monday had been concentrating on his cards or he would have noticed the woman. As he met her eyes across the room, she started toward him.

She was a little on the short side, dark-haired,

and curvy. Most of the females who ventured into this establishment in Denver's red-light district were no better than they had to be, but this young brunette had a certain air of respectability to her.

Alfred Tucker chortled. "She's comin' over here, Doc. You got an admirer, all right."

"Or else she's looking for someone who loved and left her, eh, Doc?" another card player gibed.

"I believe I'll sit out the next hand." Monday gathered up his winnings. "Best of luck."

"Oh, it'll improve once you're gone," one of the men said.

Monday's eyes narrowed. "You wouldn't be implying anything by that, would you, Clete?"

Quickly, Clete held up his hands and shook his head. "Not a thing, Doc, I swear. Just that you're too good at this game for the likes of us."

"In that case . . ." Monday gave the men at the table a friendly nod, then moved to meet the woman coming toward them.

"Excuse me," she said as she looked up at him. "Would you happen to be Mr. Ennis Monday?"

He touched the brim of his hat. "You have the advantage of me, ma'am. I am indeed Ennis Monday. But my friends call me Doc."

"I'm pleased to meet you, Mr. Monday." Her voice was a bit pointed as she addressed him formally. "My name is Lettie Margrabe." She paused, then added, "Mrs. Lettie Margrabe."

Something about the way she said that struck

him as being off, but he didn't press the issue. "It's an honor, Mrs. Margrabe. What can I do for you?"

"Perhaps if we could sit down at a table where it's quiet . . ."

"We're in a saloon, ma'am. There's only a certain level of privacy and decorum we can hope to attain. However, that said"—he gestured toward an empty table in the corner—"let's try over there."

Once they were seated, Monday took a better look at the woman. She was dressed in a decent traveling outfit, but it wasn't anything fancy or expensive. A waiter came over and Monday asked her if she'd like anything to drink, but she shook her head.

"Bourbon," Monday told the waiter, who left to fetch it. "Now, you obviously know who I am. Were you given a description of me?"

"That's right," Lettie Margrabe replied. "An old friend of yours told me to look you up. Belle Robb."

"Belle . . ." The memory brought a smile to Monday's lips under his neatly trimmed mustache. "I haven't seen her in a long time. How is she? As lovely as ever?"

"Yes, I suppose so. She, ah, provided me with a letter to give to you."

"A letter of introduction, eh?" Monday cocked an eyebrow. "Are you in the same line of work as

Belle? Looking to get into that game here in Denver? I must say, with all due respect to Belle, you don't really look the sort."

In fact, even in the shadowy confines of the saloon, he could tell that Lettie was blushing furiously at the suggestion she might be a lady of the evening like Belle.

"We were friends, back in the town where I come from in Missouri," she said. "That's all. I . . . I taught school there and helped Belle by tutoring her with her own reading."

"I see. Belle always did enjoy improving her mind," Monday said with a sardonic smile. "About this letter . . . ?"

"Of course." Lettie reached in her handbag and brought it out. "Here."

Monday unfolded the paper. As he read what was written in Belle Robb's extravagant hand, his expression grew more solemn. He looked up from the letter and said, "My apologies, Mrs. Margrabe, and my sympathy, as well. I didn't realize your husband was dead. And to be killed in the very first battle of the war that way."

"Yes, it was . . . tragic," Lettie agreed. "You can understand why I wanted to leave. I had to get away from all those . . . bitter memories. Belle suggested I might come to Denver and make a fresh start."

"She thought I could help you with that?" Monday murmured.

"She said you were a good man, Mr. Monday. She said you would treat me well."

His eyebrows arched. "My God. You're not thinking that I'll marry you, are you? Not even Belle would suggest—"

"No. No, marriage isn't necessary. I just need a place to stay, perhaps a job . . ."

"I spend practically all my time in saloons," Monday growled. "All the jobs I know of for women aren't what you'd call respectable. They're not anything a former schoolteacher would want to do."

"Perhaps a former schoolteacher who is desperate enough would," Lettie said.

Monday studied her in silence for a moment. "You're plainspoken. I like that in a man, and I find that I appreciate it in a woman, too. I'll tell you what. I have a room in a boardinghouse where the landlady doesn't ask many questions. You can stay there for now." He held up a hand to forestall any protest she might make. "I'm not suggesting anything improper. There are plenty of other places I can stay for the time being."

"With other women, I suppose."

Monday laughed. "You go beyond plainspoken to blunt, but I don't mind. It's a pretty refreshing attitude, to be honest. Anyway, you can stay there, and I'll ask around and see if I can find something for you to do. Agreed?"

Lettie hesitated, but only for a second. Then

she extended her hand across the table. "Agreed."

"We'd drink to it," Monday said as he shook her hand, "if you drank . . . and if that slovenly waiter had come back with my bourbon. At any rate, we have a deal. I hope you knew what Belle was letting you in for."

"Salvation," Lettie Margrabe said.

Ennis Monday was good as his word, for which Lettie was exceedingly grateful. He allowed her to stay in his room at the boardinghouse without ever making any improper advances, and he found her a job keeping the books for a store on Colfax Avenue. Her knowledge of arithmetic gained from being a teacher came in very handy.

Within a few weeks of her arrival in Denver, however, two things began to be obvious. One was that Ennis, or *Doc* as he preferred to be called, was smitten with her.

The other was that Lettie was with child.

The letter from Belle Robb had given her a perfectly reasonable excuse for that, of course— the dead "husband" who tragically had lost his life at the Battle of Bull Run. In truth, Lettie had never been married, and while it was certainly possible the father of her child had been killed in battle, she didn't know that. It was just as possible that Luke Jensen was still alive. She hadn't seen him since he'd joined the Confederate Army and gone off to war.

That blasted war had played a part in her current predicament. The night before he left, Luke had come to Lettie's room to say good-bye, and their passion for each other had caused them to get carried away. Luke had spent the night and was gone the next day without ever knowing that he had planted new life inside her.

Once she'd discovered it, she hadn't written to tell him. He had enough to do, trying to stay alive in the madness of war. He didn't need anything distracting him. Someday, when the terrible times were over and if he came home safely, she would let him know he was a father.

When her belly had swollen enough that only a blind man could miss it, she finally said something to Doc when they were out to dinner one evening. Two or three times a week, he took her to dinner in one of Denver's better restaurants. As he was chewing a bite of steak, she leaned forward on the other side of the table. "Mr. Monday, there's a subject we should discuss."

He swallowed. "Let's discuss why you still resist calling me Doc. It's what my friends call me, and I think we're friends by now, don't you? You don't object when I call you Lettie."

"I could hardly object. You've been so kind to me—"

"So you really do mind, is that it?"

She shook her head and reached out to rest her

hand on his. "No, I don't mind. In fact, I like it . . . Doc."

"Good. That's settled," he said with a grin.

"But that's not what I want to talk about."

His grin disappeared and was replaced by a frown. "Blast it, you sound serious. You know I'm not fond of serious matters. That's why I spend most of my time in saloons, playing cards."

"You spend most of your time in saloons playing cards because you're a rapscallion."

He inclined his head in acknowledgment of her comment. "Guilty as charged, ma'am."

Lettie drew in a deep breath. "What I'm talking about is that I . . . I'm in the family way, and you know it, Doc."

He shrugged, but Lettie wondered if he truly felt as casual as he was trying to act.

"You were a married woman until recently. There's nothing unusual or unexpected about a married woman being with child."

"I know that. It's just—" Her hand still rested on his.

He turned his hand over and gripped hers. "Do you think it really matters to me, Lettie? I'll be honest with you. I've grown quite fond of you in the time we've known each other. Why, if I had anything to offer you other than a wastrel's life — No, best not go down that path, I suppose. The facts are what they are. But the fact that you're expecting doesn't change the way I feel about you. Not one bit."

Her fingers tightened on his as she smiled. "You are a dear man, Ennis Monday."

"Don't let my enemies hear you say that. They'll laugh themselves silly." He took her hand in both of his. "Let's just put this behind us, shall we? When the child is born, I'll be there for you. Whatever you need, I'll provide, if it's in my power to do so."

"All right," she whispered. "Thank you."

She knew she ought to do something to express her gratitude in a more tangible manner. He had hinted that he wanted to marry her. In many ways, that would be a good thing to do. Her child could grow up with a father and would never have to know the truth . . .

But what about Luke? If he lived through the war, didn't he have a right to know about the child? Besides, in many ways she still loved him. Luke Jensen was a good strong man from a decent family. Back in Missouri, Luke's younger brother and sister, Kirby and Janey, had been in Lettie's class. Janey was a bit of a flirt but a decent girl at heart, Lettie believed, and Kirby was a fine young man. Lettie would have been quite happy to be part of the Jensen family by marriage . . . if only the rest of the world hadn't gotten in the way.

But as Doc had said, the facts were what they

were. Luke was gone and might not even be living. Lettie was in Denver, growing larger by the day, and Ennis Monday's friendship had proven to be the salvation for which she had hoped.

That night when he took her back to the boardinghouse, she took hold of his hand as he started to turn away at the door and told him that he didn't have to leave.

"You can stay if you like," she told him.

And so he did.

Not many more weeks passed before Lettie knew that something was . . . well, not *wrong,* exactly, but not the way she expected it to be.

Doc, despite his nickname, had no medical training whatsoever. He found a good physician for her, and after an examination, the man told her, "It's my considered opinion, Mrs. Margrabe, that you're carrying twins."

"Twins!" Lettie gasped. "But that's . . . I started to say impossible, but I suppose . . . Are you sure, Doctor?"

"As sure as I can be at this point in time." The man frowned. "It's a bit worrisome, too. Let me phrase this carefully. You're somewhat of a . . . delicate woman. Giving birth to one baby may be rather difficult for you. If we're talking about two . . ." He spread his hands. "But we'll give you the best of care, you have my word on that.

Do everything I tell you, and there's every chance that in a few more months you'll be the proud mother of two infants."

"Sons," Lettie said, surprising herself.

"Well, there's no way to know that until the time comes, of course."

She knew it, though. Somehow she knew that the babies inside her were boys, and she didn't question it.

Winter had settled in on Denver, bringing with it cold winds and blowing snow. Doc leaned against the wall just outside the door of his room in the boardinghouse and smoked a cigar. He heard the pane in the window at the end of the corridor rattle as the howling wind struck it, but he was really listening for something else.

He was waiting to hear a baby's cry.

The sawbones had run him out of the room, making some excuse about how the place wasn't big enough for the doctor, the nurse he had brought with him, Lettie, and Doc. He knew the man just wanted him out because he was afraid Lettie was going to have a hard time of it.

Judging from the screams that had sounded earlier, that was what had happened. The cries had twisted his guts. Even worse was the knowledge that he couldn't do anything to help her. Being one of the best poker players in the territory didn't mean a damn thing.

Doc puffed anxiously on the cigar. Over the past six months, he had grown closer to Lettie than any woman he had ever known. He had done his best to talk her into marrying him, but she steadfastly refused. She said she couldn't marry another man until after the babies were born. That didn't make any sense to him, but he hadn't been able to get her to budge from her decision.

Now it might be too late. He tried not to allow that thought to sneak into his brain, but it was impossible to keep it out.

He straightened and tossed the cigar butt into a nearby bucket of sand as a wailing cry came from inside the room, followed a moment later by another. Doc's heart slugged hard in his chest. He was no expert, but to him it sounded as if both babies had healthy sets of lungs. That was encouraging.

But he still didn't know how Lettie was doing.

After a few minutes that seemed like an eternity, the door opened. The doctor looked out, and the gloomy expression on the man's face struck fear into Doc's heart. "You can come on in, Mr. Monday, but I should caution you, the situation is grave."

"The babies—?" Doc asked with a catch in his throat.

"That's the one bright spot in this affair. Or rather, the *two* bright spots. Two healthy baby boys. I think they'll be fine."

Doc closed his eyes for a second. He wasn't a praying man, but he couldn't keep himself from sending a few unspoken words of thanks heavenwards.

But there was still Lettie to see about. He followed the doctor into the room.

She was propped up a little on some pillows, and her face was so pale and drawn that the sight of it made Doc gasp. Her eyes were closed and for a horrible second he believed she was dead. Then he saw the sheet rising and falling slightly over her chest.

There was no guarantee how long that would last, however. When the doctor motioned him closer, he went to the bed, dropped to a knee beside it, and took hold of her right hand in both of his.

Her eyelids fluttered and then opened slowly. She had trouble focusing at first, then her gaze settled on his face and she sighed. A faint smile touched her lips. "Doc . . ." she whispered.

His hands tightened on hers. "I'm here, darling."

"The . . . babies?"

"They're fine. Two healthy baby boys."

"Ahhhh . . ." Her smile grew. "Twins. Are they . . . identical?"

Doc glanced up at the physician, who spread his hands, shook his head, and shrugged.

"They look alike to me," Doc said to Lettie,

although in truth he hadn't actually looked at the babies yet. They were in bassinets across the room, being tended to by the nurse. Of course, to him all babies looked alike, Doc thought, so he wasn't actually lying to Lettie.

"That's . . . good. They'll be . . . strong, beautiful boys. Doc . . . you'll raise them?"

"We'll raise them. You've no excuse not to marry me now."

"No excuse," she repeated, "except the best one of all . . ."

"Don't talk like that," he urged. "You just need to get your strength back—"

"I don't have . . . any strength to get back. This took . . . all I had." She paused, licked her lips, and with a visible effort forced herself to go on. "Their name . . ."

"We'll call them anything you like."

"No, I mean . . . their last name . . ."

"Margrabe," Doc said. "Your late husband—"

"No," Lettie broke in. "I'm ashamed to admit it . . . even now . . . but I was . . . never married to their father. His last name is . . . Jensen . . . I want you to name them . . . William, after my father . . . and Benjamin, after my grandfather . . . William and Benjamin . . . Jensen."

"If that's what you want, my dear, that's what we'll do," Doc promised. "I give you my word."

"You'll take care . . . of them?"

"We—"

"No," she husked. "You. They have . . . no one else . . ."

Lord, Lord, Lord, Doc thought. This couldn't be. He'd barely spent time with her, barely gotten to know her. She couldn't be taken away from him now.

But he couldn't hold her. He sensed she was slipping away. A matter of moments only. He felt a hot stinging in his eyes and realized it was tears—for the first time in longer than he could remember.

"Take . . . take care . . ." she breathed.

He could barely hear the words. Her eyes began to close and he gripped her hands even tighter, as if he could hold on to her and keep her with him that way. "I will. I'll take care of the boys. I love you, Lettie."

"Ah," she said again, and the smile came back to her. "And I love . . ."

The breath eased out of her, and the sheet grew still.

Doc bent his head forward and tried not to sob.

The doctor gripped his shoulder. "She's gone, Mr. Monday. I'm sorry."

"I . . . I know," Doc choked out. He found the strength to lift his head. "But those boys. They're here. And they need me."

As if to reinforce that, both babies began to cry.

"Indeed they do," the doctor agreed. "Would you like to take a look at them?"

Gently, Doc laid Lettie's hand on the sheet beside her and got to his feet. He turned, feeling numb and awkward, and the doctor led him over to the bassinets. Doc had seen babies before, of course, and always thought of them as squalling, red-faced bundles of trouble.

Not these two, though. There was something about them . . . something special.

"William and Benjamin. Those are fine names, but . . . so formal. I'm not sure they suit you. We'll put them down on the papers because that's what your mother wanted, but I think I'll call you"—he forced a smile onto his face as he looked at the infant with darker hair—"Ace. And your brother . . . well, he has to be Chance, of course. Ace and Chance Jensen. And what a winning pair you'll be."

Chapter Threee

Wyoming Territory, 1885

Ace and Chance kept a close eye on their back trail for several days after their run-in with Mayor Harrington's men, but eventually it became obvious that the corrupt politician hadn't sent any of his hired hardcases after them.

It wasn't really a surprise. Nobody wanted to be on the wrong side of Smoke Jensen. If even half the stories told about him were true, making an enemy out of Smoke would be a good way to wind up dead in a hurry.

One night as they sat next to their campfire in some foothills butted up against a range of low but rugged mountains, the subject of the famous gunfighter came up again.

Ace sipped coffee from his cup. "You know, I've been thinking about Smoke Jensen."

"Well, you might as well forget about that," Chance said. "He's not our pa."

"I never said he was!"

"You know my theory."

"Yeah, I do," Ace said with a nod. "But don't you think that if Doc was really our father, he would have told us?"

Chance shrugged. "Maybe. Maybe not. What if he promised our ma that he wouldn't?"

"Why in the world would she ask him to do that?"

"Hell, I don't know. We never met her, so we can't really say what she would or wouldn't have done, can we?"

It was a question that had haunted the brothers their entire lives. Never knowing their mother had left a big hole. All they knew of her was what Doc Monday had told them . . . and the one photograph that he had of her, a small portrait that showed a pretty, dark-haired woman in her twenties and revealed absolutely nothing else about her.

Ace peered into the darkness. He knew better than to stare directly into the fire. The glare from the flames would ruin a fellow's night vision quicker than anything. If trouble broke out, that momentary blindness would be a distinct disadvantage. Maybe a fatal disadvantage. They had found themselves in enough scrapes over the years that both brothers had gotten into the habit of being careful.

"I've always had my doubts about Doc being our pa," Ace mused. "Neither of us really looks like him."

"Yeah, well, we don't really look alike, either, and that doesn't stop us from being brothers. Twins, at that."

It was true. There was a certain family resemblance, but no one would ever have any trouble telling the two Jensen boys apart. As Doc had explained when they were old enough to understand it, they were what were called fraternal twins, instead of identical. They had looked a great deal alike when they were infants, but as they grew older they began to take on more distinct characteristics.

They shared one quality common to most twins, however. Often, they seemed to know what the other brother was thinking, and if they weren't together and one was in trouble, the other one knew it, somehow. That had come in handy on more than one occasion.

"I never said I thought Smoke Jensen was our pa," Ace went on. "I don't think he's really old enough for that. But he *could* be a distant relative."

"I suppose. Next time we're down in Colorado maybe we ought to pay a visit to that big ranch of his. What's it called? The Sugarloaf? Just ride up and say, 'Howdy, Cousin Smoke. Remember us? We're your long-lost cousins Ace and Chance.'"

Ace grinned, picked up a stick from the pile of branches they'd gathered for firewood, and threw it across the fire at his brother. Chance ducked easily.

"Now you're just bein' loco. Smoke Jensen would never claim a couple of fiddle-footed saddle tramps like us, even if he *was* related to us."

"Speak for your own self." Chance straightened the lapels of his coat. "I may be fiddle-footed, but I'm not a saddle tramp. I'm a gambler."

"Yeah . . . a tinhorn gambler, to hear most folks tell it."

"Honest as the day is long," Chance said with a grin.

"I hear tell that up in Alaska, the days only last about four hours."

"I can manage to be honest for that long," Chance said. "If I really work at it."

Ace laughed, shook his head, and finished off

his coffee. They had been on the trail for a while, and he thought they ought to be coming to a settlement soon. That would be good, because their supplies were running a little low. It might be nice to spend a night in a hotel, too. Sleep in a real bed again.

Most of the time when they were young, he and Chance had lived in cities. Doc Monday wasn't what anybody would call a frontiersman. He liked his creature comforts, as he called them. A soft bed, a fire in the grate, a good meal, a glass of bourbon to sip, a fine cigar . . . For Doc, those were the things that made life worth living. That was why he had adopted the profession of gambler.

It was only when Ace and Chance were nearly grown, when Doc had gotten sick and gone off for a rest cure, that they had started drifting. All their lives, they'd had restless natures, and now they could indulge those urges. For several years, they had ridden a lot of lonely trails, supporting themselves with odd jobs and Chance's poker playing ability, sending money back to the sanitarium where Doc was staying whenever they could.

They assumed he was still there. It had been quite a while since they had been to see him. It had been too painful to witness what the ravages of age and illness had done to the once vital man who had raised them.

Neither of them thought any more about Smoke Jensen that night, and the subject was pretty well forgotten as they moved on the next day, following a trail that led higher into the mountains.

Riding next to a creek that bubbled and sang along a little valley, Ace suddenly reined in and pointed up at the slope that rose to their left. "Look up there," he told Chance with worry in his voice.

Chance looked and let out a low whistle of surprise. "That jehu better be careful or he'll drive that stagecoach right off that blasted mountain!"

From down in the valley, they watched as a stagecoach careened along the road above that zigzagged back and forth down the pine-dotted slope. It seemed that the man was taking the hairpin turns too fast. The coach had stayed on the road so far, but the way it leaned over on each turn showed that it was in danger of tipping over.

"He's going to wreck if he doesn't slow down," Ace said with alarm in his voice.

"Yeah, I reckon you're right, but there's not a blasted thing we can do from down here," Chance said.

It was true. The stagecoach was several hundred yards away and still a hundred yards above the valley floor. Three sharp turns remained to navigate before the vehicle would reach the relatively level terrain of the valley.

"There!" Ace exclaimed as he pointed again. "That's why the driver's running his team so hard!"

Several men on horseback had come into view as they pursued the stagecoach. The way the road twisted back and forth, they were above it, and they fired down toward the coach with six-guns. The booming reports echoed back and forth between the mountains that loomed on either side of the valley.

"They've got to be outlaws," Ace went on as he pulled his Winchester from the sheath strapped to his saddle.

"Maybe not," Chance argued. "What if bandits held up the stage and stole it, and those are lawmen chasing them?"

"Stole the whole stage, not just the express box? Why in blazes would anybody do that?"

"I don't know! I'm just saying we can't be sure those fellas on horseback are up to no good."

While they were talking, the stagecoach hurtled hell-bent for leather around another hairpin turn, with the team running full blast to stay ahead of the speeding coach. Ace didn't figure the horses or the coach would be able to make the next turn if they kept going that fast. He levered a round into the rifle's chamber, raised it to his shoulder, and fired, aiming above the galloping riders.

The whip crack of the shot joined the other echoes. He saw dirt and rock fly up from the slope where his bullet hit. He levered the Winchester and fired again.

"Oh, hell," Chance muttered. He hauled out his rifle and joined in the fusillade.

Both brothers cranked off a handful of rounds in a matter of seconds, spraying lead over and around the men on horseback.

That got the riders' attention. They hauled back on their reins and twisted in their saddles to return the fire. The range was too great for handguns, though, so their shots fell well short of the Jensens. Ace and Chance renewed their efforts and peppered the edge of the road just below the horses' hooves with slugs. The dirt and gravel that sprayed up made the mounts dance around skittishly.

One of the riders waved an arm and probably shouted something, but with the racket from the earlier shots Ace and Chance couldn't hear anything else. They saw the results, though. The men wheeled their horses around, not as easy as it might sound on the narrow road, and charged back up toward the pass.

The brothers let them go.

Ace lowered his Winchester and looked to see how the stagecoach was doing. It was still dashing down the mountainside. Holding his breath, he watched it sway around the next-to-last turn.

"The brake must be broken," Chance said. "Otherwise that driver would have slowed down by now."

"He would have if he has any sense," Ace said. "Look, there's a guard on there, too."

It was true. A second figure clung to the driver's box on the front of the stage, hanging on for dear life to keep from getting thrown off.

"That jehu's doing some mighty fancy driving," Chance said. "Some of the best I've ever seen, in fact. Most fellas would have piled up that coach already."

Ace looked up at the pass. The men who had been chasing the stagecoach were gone, although a haze of dust hung in the air at the top of the pass where they had disappeared. "Let's go meet that coach," he suggested. "Those fellas might need some help."

They followed the creek that led in the direction they wanted to go, keeping their horses moving at a fast clip. Up ahead, a wooden bridge came into view.

The echoes of the gunshots had died away, and Ace and Chance were close enough to hear the hoofbeats from the team, along with the rattle and squeal of the coach's wheels and the squeaking of the broad leather thoroughbraces underneath the coach. As they reached the bridge, the driver successfully negotiated the last turn.

Once the coach was on level ground it began to slow down. It wasn't crowding the team, anymore. The driver hauled back on the reins and slowed the vehicle even more.

"Look at the long hair on that shotgun guard," Chance commented as he and Ace reined their horses to a halt at the edge of the road at the west end of the bridge. "Must be ol' Wild Bill Hickok come back to life."

Neither of them had ever met or even seen the so-called Prince of Pistoleers while he was alive, but Doc Monday claimed to have sat in on a poker game with Wild Bill one time in Cheyenne. Ace and Chance never knew how much credence to give that story. At one time or another, Doc claimed to have met almost every famous person on the frontier.

While Ace didn't believe that the shotgun guard on the approaching stage was the reincarnation of Wild Bill Hickok, the man did have long hair tumbling over his shoulders. A broad-brimmed brown hat was crammed down on the curly mass. He wore a buckskin jacket and had the butt of a coach gun resting on the seat so that the barrels pointed upward.

Ace frowned as he studied the guard. Something about that fella just didn't look right. . . .

"Wait a minute. Are you seeing what I'm seeing? Look at the way that jehu is built." Chance had noticed the same thing his brother had, although he was looking at the checked flannel shirt the stagecoach driver wore, rather than the guard's buckskin jacket. But the vehicle was close enough to see that the shapes underneath those garments definitely weren't masculine.

That stagecoach was being driven and guarded by a couple women.

Chapter Four

Young women, at that, the brothers saw as the coach came to a stop about thirty feet from them.

The guard with the thick, curly blond hair lowered the coach gun until the barrels were pointed at them. "You two better not be a pair of road agents," she called to them in a clear, sweet voice.

"I told you, they helped us." The driver's voice was musical, too. "They ran off Mr. Eagleton's men. You saw that with your own eyes, Emily."

"Maybe so, but that doesn't mean they ain't road agents who want to hold us up them-selves."

"Well, I suppose you're right about that," the driver admitted.

Chance started to move his horse forward.

The young woman called Emily lifted her coach gun even more and trained the weapon on him. "That's far enough, mister, until you tell us who you are and what you want!"

Chance made sure both hands remained in plain sight. He didn't want to risk making her trigger-happy. He put a smile on his face and thumbed back his brown hat, being careful not to move too fast about it. "You've misjudged us, ma'am. We saw those fellas chasing you and just wanted to help. That's why we drove them back over the pass."

Emily snorted. "If you really wanted to help, you should've ventilated a few of them. I don't reckon Eagleton would've missed a couple gun-wolves. He can always hire more."

Ace said, "We're not in the habit of gunning down anybody when we don't really know what's going on. I reckon they must have been bandits?"

The driver said, "They didn't want to rob us, exactly, although I don't doubt they would have looted whatever they could find on the stage after we crashed. What they really wanted was to wreck us."

She was more slender than the blonde, with short, dark hair under her hat. She wore baggy denim trousers, high-topped boots, and a flannel shirt. The butt of a revolver stuck up from an old holster attached to a gun belt around her waist.

Chance said, "Why in blazes would anybody

want to wreck you? That doesn't even make any sense."

"It does if you work for Samuel Eagleton," the driver said. "Emily, put down that gun. These men don't mean us any harm."

"Well, if that turns out not to be true, it's on your head, Bess," Emily muttered. She lowered the shotgun until the barrels were pointed at the floorboards of the driver's box.

Ace and Chance eased their horses forward. The two young women watched them closely but didn't seem spooked, even after that harrowing run down the mountainside. Both of them were so self-possessed, Ace had a feeling it would take a great deal to spook them.

He reached up and tugged on his hat brim. "My name is Ace Jensen, ladies. This is my brother Chance."

"Ace and Chance?" Emily repeated, a look of amused disbelief on her face. "Really? Those are your names?"

"Well . . . that's what we're called, anyway." Both brothers knew their real names, of course, but Doc had always called them by the nicknames he had given them and that was how they had thought of themselves ever since they were old enough to understand such things.

"Those are perfectly good names," Bess said. "I'm Bess Corcoran, and this is my sister Emily."

"A pair of brothers and a pair of sisters,"

Chance said. "That's mighty cozy."

"No, it ain't," Emily snapped. "And don't go thinkin' it is, Jensen. Now, if we're all through jawin', my sister and I have a schedule to keep. The Corcoran Stage Line has the mail contract between Palisade and Bleak Creek, and the government's a mite picky about things like bein' reliable and prompt."

Ace had already noticed the Corcoran name painted on one of the stagecoach's doors. "You ladies own the stage line?"

"Our pa does," Bess said. "We just work for him."

"Because nobody else will do it," Emily said with a bitter note in her voice. "Eagleton's scared off everybody else with his hired guns."

Chance said, "From the sound of it, I don't like this Eagleton fella, and I never even met the gent."

"You will if you go on to Palisade," Bess said. "He owns practically everything in and around the town."

"Except the stage line," Ace guessed. He was starting to see how things were laid out.

"And a few other small businesses," Bess agreed with a nod. "He'll get around to the others sooner or later, I suppose. Right now, he's got his eyes set on our father's operation."

Chance pointed up at the pass. "So this Palisade place is higher up in the mountains?"

"That's right. It's a mining town, and I suppose it's no surprise Mr. Eagleton owns just about everything, since he's the one who made the first strike around here. There wouldn't be a settlement if it wasn't for him and his mine."

Emily said, "That doesn't give him the right to run roughshod over everybody who came after him."

"No, it doesn't," Ace agreed. "And you're headed for someplace called Bleak Creek?"

"That's right," Bess said. "It's on the other side of those mountains to the east. There's a railroad spur there that connects up with the Union Pacific. We deliver the mail there and pick up any mail bound for Palisade."

Emily regarded the Jensen brothers with a suspicious glare. "You boys are mighty curious about our business."

"You have to be curious to learn anything," Chance pointed out.

Ace said, "I was just wondering about Eagleton. If he sent men after you to try to wreck the coach as you came down from the pass, could he have sent other men ahead to set up an ambush in case the first bunch failed?"

Emily and Bess glanced worriedly at each other.

Ace thought the possibility he had just brought up probably hadn't occurred to them. But now that he had mentioned it, they didn't like the idea.

"We do have to go through Shoshone Gap," Bess said.

"And it's a good spot for a bushwhackin'," Emily agreed. "We'll have to be careful."

"And we'll ride along with you," Chance said, "just in case of trouble."

"Nobody asked you to do that."

"Nope," Ace said. "That's why we're volunteering."

Even though it was Chance's idea, it was a good one, Ace thought. There was at least a chance something else might happen on the way to Bleak Creek, and although the Corcoran sisters seemed plenty competent, it wouldn't hurt for them to have some allies along.

Of course, they didn't know the full story behind the clash between the Corcorans and this mining magnate named Eagleton. Things might not be as clear-cut as Emily and Bess made it seem.

It was possible, Ace mused, that he and his brother were jumping into this mess feetfirst simply because the Corcoran sisters were a couple mighty pretty girls. Well, there were worse reasons for doing things, he supposed as Bess got the team moving again and the stagecoach lurched into motion.

He and Chance turned their mounts and fell in alongside it, one on each side.

"You girls don't happen to be twins, do you?" Chance asked after they had gone a mile or two across the valley. He rode on Emily's side of the coach.

"Do we *look* like twins?" Emily responded.

"Well, Ace and I are twins."

Bess said, "I wouldn't have guessed that."

"Fraternal twins, they call it," Ace said. "We look alike, but more like regular brothers would."

"Yes, I can see that. Emily and I are two years apart, though."

"I'm the oldest," Emily said. "That means I'm the boss."

"That's what you've always thought, anyway," Bess said sweetly.

Ace chuckled. It sounded like these two scrapped about as much as he and Chance did, even if they weren't twins. "Is this the first trouble you've had with Eagleton?" he asked as they continued toward the mountains on the other side of the valley.

"No, he made an offer to Pa to buy out the stage line almost a year ago," Bess said. "Pa turned him down, of course. Mr. Eagleton warned him then that he didn't like being said no to."

"That wasn't the smartest tack to take with Pa," Emily put in. "Once he gets his back up, he's about the stubbornest old pelican you ever saw."

"Emily!" her sister scolded her. "That's no way to talk about our father."

"It's true, ain't it?"

"Well, yes, but . . ." Bess took a deep breath and went on. "Anyway, after Pa refused Mr. Eagleton's offer, things started happening. Breakdowns with the coaches. Shipments of grain for the horses that got lost. Damaged harnesses. Even a few shots out of the blue. That scared some of our drivers. Others got jumped and beaten up. It's gotten bad enough that nobody wants to work for us, so Emily and I have been taking the runs through ourselves."

"Sort of odd to find a couple gals driving a stagecoach and riding shotgun, isn't it?" Chance asked.

"Our father's worked on stage lines all of our lives," Bess said. "We were raised around them."

"You ought to hear her cuss when she gets mad." Emily grinned. "She can put a lot of those old jehus to shame."

Bess's face turned pink under her hat. "Sometimes I think that sort of language is the only thing those horses understand!" She tried to change the subject by looking at Ace again and asking, "What about your father? What's he like?"

"I couldn't tell you," Ace answered honestly. "We never met him. Or our mother, either."

"That's terrible! I'm sorry. Were you raised by relatives?"

Chance said, "We were raised by a gambler named Doc Monday. He's as close to a pa as we've ever had. In fact, it wouldn't surprise me if he *was* our pa."

"I don't think so." Ace didn't want to have the old argument again, so he did some subject changing of his own by asking the young women, "What's this Shoshone Gap you mentioned?"

"It's the pass through the mountains on this side of the valley," Bess explained. She pointed. "You can see it up there, a couple miles ahead. It got the name because the old Shoshone Trail goes through it. It's a lot easier than Timberline Pass back the other way, between here and Palisade. It's lower and the slopes aren't nearly as steep, but there are a lot of rocks and trees on the sides of the gap."

"A perfect spot for an ambush, in other words," Emily put in.

"Maybe Ace and I should ride ahead and do a little scouting," Chance suggested. "You know, make sure it's safe to take the coach through there."

"Or to set up an ambush yourself, if you've been lying to us all along and planning a double cross," Emily said caustically.

"We haven't lied to you." Ace was getting a mite tired of the blonde's suspicions, but he kept his voice calm and level as he went on. "We just want to help, but if you don't want us to scout ahead—"

"No, I think it's a good idea," Bess said. "Go ahead. We'll follow along behind you."

"Keep an eye on your back trail," Ace warned as he heeled his horse to a faster pace and pulled ahead of the stagecoach.

Chance's mount matched his. "Eagleton's men might have doubled back after we chased them off."

As the coach fell behind them, Chance glanced back over his shoulder. "Maybe one of us should have stayed with them."

"One of us meaning you, of course."

"They're just a couple gals. Wouldn't want anything to happen to them."

"Did you see the way Emily handled that scattergun? And Bess put that team through its paces like she'd been driving a stagecoach for forty years. I don't think they're exactly what you'd call helpless or defenseless." Ace chuckled. "Anyway, Emily doesn't seem to have much use for either of us, and Bess strikes me as too levelheaded to fall for any line of bull that you might try to put over on her."

"I think I'm offended."

"Fine. Just keep your eyes on the sides of that gap up ahead."

As they neared Shoshone Gap, Ace saw that

Bess's description had been accurate. The mountains loomed on either side, but the trail between them wasn't too steep or rugged. The slopes were covered with boulders and clumps of pine trees. Plenty of places where bush-whackers could hide, he thought.

However, nothing happened as he and his brother entered the gap. No shots rang out, and there was no sign of trouble. Ace waved a hand toward the slope on the right and told Chance, "Take a closer look over there. I'll check out this side."

They split up. Ace rode up the incline, his big, sturdily built chestnut picking its way across the slope. He drew his rifle from its sheath and rode with it resting across the saddle in front of him. His keen eyes searched every hiding place he came to.

Looked like they had gotten skittish for nothing, he decided. Shoshone Gap was deserted. Nobody was waiting to ambush the Corcoran sisters and their stagecoach.

That thought had barely had time to pass through his brain when shots blasted from the other side of the gap.

Chapter Five

Chance was approaching a clump of boulders when he heard a rock rattle somewhere close by and then the clink of metal against stone. It was the only warning he had before somebody thrust a rifle barrel over the top of a big slab of rock and opened fire on him.

He was already diving out of the saddle when the slugs sizzled through the space he had occupied a heartbeat earlier.

He hit the ground hard, narrowly avoiding some cactus, and rolled over. The gun he carried in his shoulder holster, a .38 caliber Colt Lightning, was in his hand as he came back up on one knee. He triggered the double-action revolver twice at the rock where the bushwhacker was hiding, then surged up and dashed toward some nearby trees. His shots had made the hidden gunman duck momentarily, giving Chance enough time to reach cover, although a couple bullets kicked up dirt near his feet as he ran.

He darted into the pines, twisted so that he was behind one of them, and pressed his shoulder against the rough-barked trunk, making himself as small a target as possible. Some of that bark leaped in the air as lead thudded into the tree.

The ambusher's bullets searched through the pines for Chance but failed to find him.

That hombre probably thought he had him pinned down, Chance mused, but there was a wild card in this game. An Ace, to be precise, and he was taking a hand. Chance heard the sharp crack of his brother's rifle from across the gap.

Bullets smacked into rocks and spanged off as ricochets. The bushwhacker returned Ace's fire. All of it blended together into a racket painful to the ears.

Since Ace was keeping the rifleman busy, Chance risked moving up to the edge of the trees where he could see better. Gun smoke still rose from behind the rock where the bushwhacker was hidden. Chance thought that from his new location, he might be able to bounce a few slugs behind that slab of rock. He sighted carefully and squeezed off three swift rounds, emptying the Lightning.

He drew back into better cover and reloaded the revolver with fresh cartridges from his pocket. He heard hoofbeats and looked up. A man on horseback, bent low in the saddle, was lunging up the slope toward some trees. The bushwhacker was lighting a shuck.

Chance sent a couple bullets after him, but the horse never broke stride and the rider was still slashing at the animal with the reins as they disappeared into the trees. Chance didn't know the terrain and wasn't going to give chase on foot. It looked like the bushwhacking son of a gun was going to get away.

As Chance was replacing the cartridges he had just fired, he heard another horse rattling up the slope.

Ace shouted, "Chance! Where are you?"

Chance stepped out of the trees and called, "Up here!" He saw that Ace had caught the cream-colored gelding and was leading it. "Be careful! That no-good bushwhacker might double back."

Ace had his Winchester in one hand as he rode on up the slope toward his brother. "We'll make him sorry if he does."

Chance holstered the Lightning and looked around for his hat, which had flown off when he dived out of the saddle. He spotted it, picked it up, and flicked several pine needles off before he settled it on his head. By that time, Ace had reached him.

Chance took the reins and swung up into the saddle. "I reckon you didn't run into any trouble over on your side of the gap."

"Peaceful as can be over there, but as usual, you seem to have a way of attracting trouble."

Chance snorted in disgust. "Getting ambushed wasn't my idea. I promise you that."

"Was there just one man?"

"Only one that I saw, and I never heard but one

gun shooting at me. You think he was one of the men who work for that fella Eagleton?"

Ace shook his head. "No telling, but he sure might have been. He could have been posted here to ambush Bess and Emily if they made it past those other varmints. Or he might have been just a run-of-the-mill owlhoot looking to rob you."

"Either way, he's gone now. Let's take a look at the place where he was holed up. He might've left something behind."

They rode over to the slab of rock where the bushwhacker had been hiding and dismounted to look around. Chance found some empty cartridges from the man's rifle and the butt of a slender black cigarillo, but that was all. The ground was too hard to take boot prints.

Ace said, "He had his horse over here behind this other boulder, but the ground's too rocky for there to be any tracks."

"Same here." Chance studied the cigarillo for a moment, then tossed it away. If he ran across a man who smoked stogies like that, it might be worth remembering, but it wouldn't really prove anything. "We'd better get back to the girls and let them know what happened. They must've heard all the shooting."

That proved to be the case as Ace and Chance rode out of the gap. They found the stagecoach stopped in the road near the entrance. Emily held her coach gun ready to fire, and Bess had drawn the old pistol from her holster. The young women visibly relaxed as they saw the Jensen brothers riding toward them.

"Are you two all right?" Bess called.

"We heard a lot of gunfire," Emily added.

Ace and Chance reined in beside the coach.

Ace said, "Somebody was waiting in the gap, all right. Whether he was there to ambush you or was proddy for some other reason, we don't know. But after we'd traded some lead with him, he took off for the tall and uncut."

"Did you get a good look at him?" Bess asked.

Ace shook his head. "He was just an hombre on a horse, riding away from us as fast as he could."

"So you think it's safe to go on through the gap?" Emily wanted to know. "You cleaned out anybody who might want to stop us?"

Ace and Chance exchanged a look.

Chance shrugged. "That fella's gone, and nobody else took a shot at us. We didn't see anybody else, but I don't suppose we can guarantee anything."

"Well, all life is a risk, I guess. Sometimes you've just got to take a—" Emily glanced at Chance, stopped short, and frowned. "Get that damn grin off your face, Jensen."

"Yes, ma'am. You're right, though, about life being a risk."

Emily blew out an exasperated breath and told her sister, "Let's get this rattletrap moving again."

Nobody shot at the coach as it rolled through the half-mile-long gap. Ace and Chance had their rifles out, ready to return any fire that came their way, but nothing happened.

"Plumb peaceful," Emily muttered as they came out the other side and started down a long, fairly gentle slope onto some flats that stretched for miles to the east.

Still high enough, Ace was able to spot the settlement several miles away. A dark line cut across the flats beyond the town and he figured that was the railroad Bess had mentioned.

It took only a half hour for the stagecoach to reach Bleak Creek, named, Ace supposed, for the little stream that meandered past it. It was a decent-sized town with a business district that stretched for several blocks along the main street and quite a few houses on the cross streets. The redbrick railroad station at the far end was the largest building in town.

"The stage line has an office in the depot, so that's where we're headed," Bess explained to the Jensen brothers. "There's a stable next door where we keep the coach and the horses."

"You should be safe enough here in town," Ace said. "Chance and I need to pick up some supplies."

"So do we," Bess said. "Why don't we meet you at the general store once we've handled our mail business?"

Ace nodded "Sure. We'll be there for a while. When do you start back to Palisade?"

"First thing in the morning. We always spend the night when we make this run. There are a couple cots in the office at the depot."

Chance said, "I see a hotel on the other side of the street. I suppose Ace and I can get a room there for the night."

Emily frowned. "Wait a minute. You're making it sound like you're going back to Palisade with us."

"We thought we would," Ace said. "If Eagleton wants to ruin your father's company as much as you say he does, he's liable to have his men try something else."

"We don't have anyplace where we have to be," Chance added. "Palisade is as good as any."

"Drifters usually don't have anywhere they have to be," Emily said, still wearing a disapproving frown. "But I suppose it's a free country and if you want to ride in that direction, we can't stop you."

"Better be careful," Chance told her. "Keep talking like that and folks might think you're warming up to us."

"Fat chance of that!" Emily said with a disgusted glare.

The coach rolled on toward the railroad station while Ace and Chance turned their horses toward a building with MERCANTILE painted in

61

big letters across its front above the entrance. They tied their mounts at a hitch rack and climbed the steps to the high porch.

The store was fairly busy. They had to wait a few minutes for an apron-wearing clerk behind the counter at the rear to ask how he could help them.

Ace gave the man the list of what they needed —staples like coffee, flour, beans, and bacon— while Chance roamed around the store looking at the various displays of merchandise. He leaned over a glass-topped case and studied several nickel-plated, ivory-handled derringers. He was particularly taken with a two-barreled, over/under model. According to what somebody had written on the piece of cardboard beneath it, the weapon was a .38 caliber, so it would take the same ammunition as his Lightning.

Ace came up beside him and asked, "What are you looking at?"

"I want that derringer," Chance said, pointing at the little gun. "Never can tell when it might come in handy."

"There's nothing wrong with the gun you've got."

"Yeah, but didn't you ever want something just because you wanted it? And we can afford it. We've still got a good stake from that poker game."

"We won't have if we waste it."

"Buying a gun's not wasteful," Chance argued. "That little beauty might save our lives someday."

Ace shook his head. "I'm not going to be able to talk you out of it, am I?"

"Probably not," Chance replied with a grin.

"Well, I told the clerk we'd pick up those supplies before we ride out in the morning, so I reckon if you're still bound and determined to have it then . . ."

"Oh, I will be."

"I don't doubt it for a second," Ace said.

They walked toward the front of the store and stepped out onto the porch to wait for the Corcoran sisters. The stagecoach was still parked in front of the depot, but there was no sign of Bess and Emily, who were probably still inside tending to their business.

Ace and Chance had been standing there for only a few minutes when Ace said quietly, "Badge coming."

A man in a black frock coat and string tie was crossing the street toward the general store. He had a clean-shaven, hawk-like face and iron-gray hair under his black hat. A holstered pistol with walnut grips rode on his right hip. As Ace had said, a lawman's badge was pinned to his vest.

The star-packer might be going to the store or just headed in their general direction on some other errand, but as he drew nearer it became obvious that his intent, steely-eyed gaze was fixed on the Jensen brothers. They straightened from their casual stances as the man climbed the steps to the porch and approached them.

Without preamble, the lawman said, "You boys are new to Bleak Creek, aren't you?"

"Just rode in a little while ago," Ace confirmed.

"What are your names, and what's your business here?"

Chance said, "Do you ask those questions of every stranger who rides into your town, Marshal . . . or do you have some reason for picking on us?"

"I'm not picking on you," the lawman snapped. "And I ask what I want of whoever I want. I expect answers, too."

"My name's Ace Jensen. This is my brother Chance. As for what brought us here, we're friends of Bess and Emily Corcoran. We came in with them."

Claiming that they were friends of the Corcoran sisters might be stretching it a bit, since they'd only been acquainted for about an hour.

"You rode in on the stagecoach?" the Bleak Creek marshal asked.

"No, we were on horseback. We just rode with them."

"Through Shoshone Gap?"

"Well, that's just about the only way to get here from the other side of the mountains, isn't it,

Marshal?" Chance drawled. His insolent tone made the lawman get more stiff-necked.

"Those are your horses?" he asked as he jerked his head toward the two mounts tied at the hitch rack.

Ace didn't like the way this conversation was going, but he didn't see any way to get it on another track. Before Chance could frame some sarcastic response, he said, "That's right."

The lawman nodded in apparent satisfaction. "Then I reckon I've heard enough." He stepped back, pulled his gun, and leveled it from the hip at the brothers. "You two are under arrest."

Chapter Six

The marshal's draw wasn't very fast. Either of the Jensens could have beaten it, but Ace's hand shot out and closed on Chance's arm to keep him from reacting. He wasn't sure what was going on, but getting in a shoot-out with a lawman was bound to just make things worse. "Hold on, Marshal. You don't have any call to be arresting us."

"Yeah," Chance said, his face flushed with anger. "We haven't done anything."

"I'd say ambushing one of the leading citizens of this town and trying to kill him warrants being thrown in the hoosegow," the marshal responded as he kept his revolver leveled at them.

"Now shuck your guns and any other weapons you're carrying."

"You're loco!" Chance burst out. "We never ambushed anybody."

"But somebody *did* try to bushwhack us a little while ago, out in Shoshone Gap," Ace added. "Sounds to me like you've been sold a bill of goods, Marshal."

"Being impertinent is not going to get you anywhere." The lawman gestured with the revolver he held. "I told you to drop your guns. You'd damn well better do it now, before I lose my patience."

Chance glanced over at Ace and muttered, "You should've let me wing him."

"Too late for that now." Ace reached for the buckle of his gun belt, unfastened it, and lowered it to the porch.

"You, too, smart mouth," the marshal told Chance.

Carefully, Chance reached inside his coat and removed the Lightning from his shoulder holster. He bent and placed it on the porch next to Ace's Colt.

"Step back away from 'em," the marshal ordered. "Keep your hands where I can see them."

"I still say you're making a mistake," Ace insisted. "We haven't done anything wrong." An idea occurred to him. "You can go down to the depot and ask the Corcoran sisters.

They'll tell you we were just trying to help them."

"Maybe I'll do that," the marshal said, "after you two are behind bars where you belong."

He didn't have to wait that long. At the end of the street, Bess and Emily emerged from the depot building and stopped in stunned surprise at the sight of Ace and Chance being arrested. A second later both young women started toward the general store in a hurry.

Ace saw their reaction. "Here they come now," he told the marshal.

Under the circumstances, the lawman couldn't do anything other than wait for Bess and Emily to get there. A crowd had started to gather, since any excuse to break the monotony in frontier settlements was always welcome.

"What's going on here?" Emily demanded as she shouldered her way through the press of townspeople with Bess close behind her. They reached a spot just in front of the porch where they could look up and see Ace, Chance, and the lawman. "Marshal Kaiser, are you arresting these men?"

"Yes, miss, I am," the marshal said.

"Why?" Bess asked as she stepped up beside her sister. "They haven't done anything wrong."

"How do you know that?"

Emily said, "Well, they haven't done anything wrong in the past hour, anyway. They were with Bess and me that whole time—unless they caused some sort of ruckus in the store just now, I guess, while we were up at the depot."

"There's a vote of confidence for you," Chance said dryly.

"They ambushed Jacob Tanner out in Shoshone Gap and tried to kill him," Marshal Kaiser said.

Ace and Chance looked at each other, and Ace said, "Now I'm sure there's some sort of mistake, Marshal. We don't know this fella Tanner. Never heard of him. We wouldn't have any reason to try to hurt him."

"Maybe you don't know his name, but he sure as hell knows you. Described both of you right down to a *T*."

That statement told Ace that Tanner likely had been the bushwhacker who'd tried to kill Chance. Tanner had to have been in the gap or he wouldn't have been able to describe them.

Ace looked down at Bess and Emily. "Who's Tanner?"

"He works for the railroad," Bess said. "He's some sort of surveyor or engineer."

"Not the kind that drives a locomotive," Emily added.

"All right, we've all flapped our gums enough," Kaiser said. "You two come with me."

Bess said, "Marshal, these two men came through the gap with us. They couldn't have attacked anybody."

She was smart, Ace thought. She hadn't said anything about how he and Chance had been ambushed, and how the man who did it must have been Jacob Tanner. That would just muddy the waters. They could figure out later what was going on, but the first order of business was to stay out of jail.

Kaiser frowned. "Were they with you the whole time, from when you met them until you got into town?"

"Well . . . not the *whole* time," Emily said. "They scouted ahead for a little while." She looked at her sister, who was frowning at her, and went on, "What? I'm not going to lie to the law for a couple hombres we just met."

Kaiser gestured with the gun and said to Ace and Chance, "Come on. You can tell your story to the judge . . . when he gets here on his regular circuit in a couple weeks."

Chance groaned, and Ace knew why. The prospect of spending the next two weeks cooped up in a small-town jail cell was more than Chance could stand, especially since there was no guarantee they would be released after that. Actually, since their accuser was well-known around these parts and they were strangers, it was a real likelihood they would be found guilty and sentenced to prison.

They couldn't let that happen. For one thing, the Corcoran sisters needed help. They might run into trouble on the way back to Palisade. It didn't seem like anybody else was willing to help them.

Normally, Chance was the impulsive, reckless, even hot-headed brother. But before he had an opportunity to think about it too much, Ace decided he wasn't going to be locked up for something he hadn't done and leaped into action.

His left hand shot out and closed around the wrist of Marshal Kaiser's gun hand. He thrust the lawman's arm in the air.

Kaiser yelled, "Hey!" and jerked the trigger. The gun boomed and sent a slug whistling high over the false fronts of the buildings across the street.

At the same time, Ace lifted a punch to the marshal's jaw, hitting Kaiser hard enough to stun him without doing any permanent damage. The lawman sagged and would have fallen if not for Ace's grip on his wrist.

The shot made the townspeople gathered in front of the general store scatter. A couple women screamed, and several men shouted angry curses. A few of them moved forward as if they intended to climb onto the porch and tackle the young strangers.

Chance grabbed his Lightning from the porch and barked, "Stay back, boys! I don't want to hurt anybody."

Ace wrenched the revolver out of Kaiser's hand and gave the marshal a shove that sent him sprawling. "Let's go!" he snapped at his brother.

The crowd really cleared out as the Jensen boys charged down the steps, each brandishing a gun. Two who didn't flee were Bess and Emily. Bess caught hold of Ace's sleeve and said anxiously, "What are you doing? Now you'll be fugitives!"

"Better than being locked up," Ace told her.

Chance told Emily, "Maybe we'll see you girls later."

"And maybe you'll get yourselves lynched, you damn fools!" she responded. Her angry attitude eased a little as she added, "Go on. Get out of here while you've got the chance."

Even under the extreme circumstances, Chance summoned up a grin for the pretty girl as he jerked the reins loose and swung up in the saddle. Ace was right beside him. They wheeled their horses away from the hitch rack and urged them into a run, streaking through an open space in the thinning crowd.

Behind them, Marshal Kaiser recovered his wits enough to sit up on the mercantile porch and bellow, "Stop them! Somebody stop them before they get away!"

The weapons of the men on the street began to boom as the townies tried to bring down the fleeing brothers. Ace and Chance leaned forward over their horses' necks and galloped west out of Bleak Creek.

The settlement's name was certainly appropriate, Ace thought as they rode past the creek. Their luck had been nothing but bleak.

They rode hard until they reached Shoshone Gap, then slowed down or risk having their mounts give out. The horses hadn't had much time to rest while they were in the settlement. As they reined in, Ace and Chance turned to look back toward Bleak Creek.

"I don't see any dust," Chance said. "It appears there's no posse coming after us . . . yet."

"Kaiser's probably mad as hell, but according to his badge he's just the town marshal, not the sheriff," Ace pointed out. "He didn't really have the authority to arrest us for something that happened outside the town limits. So he'd probably have trouble convincing enough men they ought to risk their lives by coming after us."

"Wait a minute. Why didn't you point out that business about his jurisdiction before you grabbed his gun and walloped him?"

"It didn't occur to me until now," Ace admitted with a sheepish smile. "Anyway, I don't think it would have done much good. Kaiser was dead set on arresting us. He would have thrown us behind bars and promised to look into the jurisdictional issues, then left us there to rot."

"You're probably right about that. Why was he being so mule-headed, do you reckon?"

"Probably because he wants to stay in the good

graces of that fella Tanner. Bess said he works for the railroad. That makes him an important man. Bleak Creek wouldn't amount to much of anything without that spur line."

"Tanner's the fella who was waiting to ambush those gals when they took the stagecoach through this gap."

Ace rubbed his chin and frowned in thought. After a moment, he said, "That's what I figured, but maybe not. He could have been out here earlier and seen the ambush, but not been the one who was doing the shooting."

"Yeah, I suppose," Chance said grudgingly, "but either way, he lied to the marshal about what happened, and damn if I can see why."

"It doesn't make any sense to me, either, unless there's some connection between Tanner and Samuel Eagleton, and he doesn't want us helping the Corcoran girls."

Chance shook his head and sighed. "It's too damn complicated for me. Let's get out of here, just in case the marshal decides to come looking for us after all."

After everything that had happened, they were wary as they rode through the gap and into the valley beyond, giving them a good view of the mountains on the other side of the valley, as well as Timberline Pass where the stage road ran.

"Look at the way those cliffs jut up," Ace said as he pointed them out to his brother. "They look a little like a stockade fence, don't they?"

"You think that's how come the town got the name Palisade?"

"It wouldn't surprise me."

"What are we going to do, Ace? I don't know about you, but I reckon it'd rub me the wrong way to just ride away from this whole mess."

"What would rub you the wrong way is to ride away from a couple good-looking girls in trouble," Ace said.

Chance grinned. "Well, there's that to consider, too. If we could give Bess and Emily a hand, there's a good chance they'd be grateful to us, don't you think?"

"And you wouldn't mind that."

"I wouldn't mind getting to know that blonde a mite better, that's for sure."

"Emily's got about much fondness for you as she would a rattlesnake."

"Yes, but I have a charming personality," Chance insisted. "I can win her over."

"I think I'd like to see you try," Ace said. "Might be pretty entertaining. I suppose that's as good a reason as any to hang around here for a while." He glanced at the sky. "It'll be dark before too much longer. Let's find a place to camp where that marshal won't find us if he comes looking. The stagecoach ought to be coming along here again by the middle of the morning tomorrow."

Chapter Seven

They found a spot well off the stage road to make camp and took turns standing guard during the night, after making a cold, scanty supper out of some biscuits left over from a couple days earlier. Coffee would have been good, even though they were running low on it, but they didn't want to risk a fire. The chances of Kaiser leading a posse into the valley to search for them during the night were so small as to be almost nonexistent, but there was no point in being careless.

Just as both brothers expected, the night passed peacefully.

In the morning, they risked a fire to boil some coffee. They could buy more when they got to Palisade.

As they got ready to break camp, Ace said, "I think I'll ride back into the gap and make sure Tanner—or whoever it was—doesn't try to ambush the stagecoach again."

"I was thinking the same thing," Chance agreed. "Let's go."

They spent an hour combing through the gap, checking every boulder and clump of trees for hidden gunmen, but the place was deserted. By the time they had assured themselves that Bess and Emily wouldn't be driving into a trap, they could see a column of dust rising from the stage road in the distance.

"Here they come," Chance said. "I'm looking forward to seeing those gals again."

"I'm not so sure how happy they'll be to see us. We're probably wanted fugitives. Even if we didn't ambush Tanner, we assaulted a town marshal."

Chance laughed. "*You're* the one who punched that law dog, brother, not me."

"I was trying to get both of us out of that mess."

"Yeah, but I'm innocent of that much, anyway."

"You haven't been innocent since the day you were born," Ace muttered as they sat their horses at the entrance to Shoshone Gap, waiting for the stagecoach to arrive.

When it did, Bess began slowing the horses as soon as she saw the Jensen brothers. Dust swirled around the coach as she brought it to a stop.

"What are you two doing here?" Emily asked. "I figured you'd be headed back where you came from, or at least putting some miles between you and Bleak Creek."

Chance frowned. "Why, we want to make sure that you ladies get back home safely. What sort of gentlemen would we be if we didn't?"

"I wasn't aware that gentlemen went around punching peace officers," Emily said with a pointed look at Ace.

"That so-called peace officer was going to lock us up for something we didn't do." Ace wondered when people were going to start getting that through their heads. "Why'd he take Tanner's word over ours? Is Tanner some sort of important man around here?"

"He got the railroad to build that spur," Bess said. "Bleak Creek was barely a wide place in the trail before that."

Ace nodded. "I thought it must be something like that. Everybody in town wants to stay on his good side, even the marshal. But here's another question. Why would Tanner lie about us trying to kill him? We've never even met the man, unless you want to count seeing him on the back of his horse trying to get away after his ambush failed."

Emily said, "We can't just sit here hashing all this out. We have to get back to Palisade. It'll take most of the day."

"Do you want to come with us?" Bess asked.

"That's the idea," Chance answered. "Eagleton might send his men to make another try for you."

Bess slapped the lines against the backs of the team, and the horses leaned into their harness and got the stagecoach rolling again.

As Ace and Chance fell in alongside it, Ace glanced into the coach. "No passengers again today, eh?"

"We don't carry a lot of passengers," Bess said.

"Sometimes some miners going to work in the Golden Dome. That's Mr. Eagleton's mine. Or some drummers who sell merchandise to the stores. But that's about all."

"That's why the mail contract is so important to us," Emily elaborated. "The line probably couldn't survive just on carrying passengers. The mail keeps us afloat."

Ace thought for a few seconds, then asked, "How does Eagleton get the ore from his mine out? Does he ship it on the stage?"

Emily laughed. "Ha. He wouldn't do business with us, except for sending and receiving mail, and he doesn't have any choice about that."

"He has his own wagons to carry the gold," Bess explained. "And they're heavily guarded."

"Any problems with outlaws trying to hold up those gold wagons?" Chance asked.

Emily shook her head. "Not that I've ever heard of. The men who work for him are pretty tough. That's how come he can use them for things like harassing honest business owners who don't want to be gobbled up by his little tinpot empire."

Ace looked over at his brother and knew that Chance was trying to figure it out, too. Maybe there was no connection between Eagleton, Tanner, and the ambush in Shoshone Gap . . . but that seemed like too much of a coincidence to the Jensens.

As they rode west across the valley, the talk

turned to other things. Chance wanted to know more about the Corcoran sisters, and while Emily was taciturn, Bess was willing to fill in some of their background.

"Pa worked for the Butterfield line and for Wells Fargo for a long time. He started out as a hostler and worked his way up to managing stage stations. Emily and I were born at stage stations, different ones because Pa had been transferred in the time between. Emily was born in Julesburg, and I was born in Silver City, both down in New Mexico."

"We've been to both places," Chance said. "The fella who raised us moved around a lot, too."

"Pa said he wanted to settle down in one place, but I'm not sure he really did. Our ma would have liked it, though."

Emily said, "Too bad she died before she ever got to."

"Yes, that seemed to change Pa," Bess said with a sigh. "He regretted that he never gave Ma what she wanted, but he knew she thought Emily and I should have a real home, so he decided he wanted to start his own stage line, someplace with a fairly short route so he could run it and still have time for us. He saved his money, and when he heard about the boom in Palisade he moved us there right after it started and established his business. Mr. Eagleton probably would have started his own stage line when he got around to it, but Pa beat him to it."

"That's one more reason Eagleton's so damn determined to take us over," Emily put in. "The man can't stand losing out on anything, even if it's something that really doesn't matter that much to him."

"What about you two?" Bess asked. "You said you never knew your real folks, and you were raised by a gambler, but surely there's more to your lives than that."

"Not much," Ace said with a shrug. "Doc Monday brought us up the best he could. I'm not sure he was really cut out to be raising kids, but he tried hard, I'll give him that. We always had plenty to eat, decent clothes, and a roof over our heads. He made sure we got an education, too."

"That's right," Chance said. "By the time I was four years old, I could shuffle a deck of cards better than most. You should've seen the way I handled those pasteboards!"

"I was thinking more of the way he always made sure we went to school, wherever we were. He said our mother had been a schoolteacher at one time, so he figured it would be important to her for us to learn as much as we could. We both like to read, so I reckon we probably got that from her."

"Your father might have liked to read, too," Bess suggested.

Ace shrugged. "Maybe. We don't know a thing about him. I'm not sure Doc ever knew anything about him, except that his name was Jensen."

"Like Smoke Jensen," Emily said. "The gunfighter. I've heard of him."

Chance groaned. "Don't get Ace started on Smoke Jensen. As it happens, we actually met that hombre not that long ago, and he has been wondering ever since then if we might be related."

"You met Smoke Jensen?" It was the first time in the relatively short time they had known Emily that she actually seemed impressed by something about the brothers.

"Yeah, just briefly," Ace said. "We got in a little scrape in a town back down the trail a ways, and he stepped in to give us a hand. I think he was just passing through and happened to be in the same saloon we were."

Emily leaned forward on the driver's seat as she asked, "Did he shoot anybody?"

"You don't have to sound so bloodthirsty," Bess told her.

"There wasn't any shooting," Ace replied with a shake of his head. "Just a little ruckus. He did draw his gun once, though. He just didn't have to shoot."

"Was he as fast as everybody says?"

"Hard to tell. We were slapping leather at the same time, so we weren't really watching him. At least I wasn't."

Chance said, "To tell you the truth, I think I shaded him just a hair."

"You did not!" Emily cried in disbelief. "You did not outdraw Smoke Jensen."

Chance shrugged casually. "You weren't there. I'm just tellin' you what it looked like to me."

"How gullible do you think I am?" Emily said with a snort. "Some saddle tramp outdrawing Smoke Jensen . . . that'll be the day!"

It was after noon by the time the stagecoach reached the foot of the long climb to Timberline Pass. Making the ascent would take most of the rest of the day, Bess explained as she stopped to rest the team. Going up was a lot slower job than coming down had been.

"Of course, the last time we had to come down faster than we usually do, since Mr. Eagleton's men were chasing us and shooting to spook the horses," she added.

"I've been thinking about that," Ace said. "They shot over your heads deliberately, didn't they? That way, if the stagecoach went off the trail and crashed, your bodies would be found in the wreckage but wouldn't have any bullet holes in them. Nothing to tie back to Eagleton what happened. That's pretty cunning."

"Nobody ever said Eagleton wasn't smart," Emily put in. "Just that he's a lowdown skunk."

"Yes, but if he'd go to that much trouble to cover his tracks, why have somebody ambush you in Shoshone Gap? If you were gunned down, everybody would know you'd been murdered."

Emily shrugged. "Don't ask me how a varmint like Eagleton thinks."

"One way or another," Chance said, "he wanted you two girls to wind up dead . . . and that's something he can't get away with."

"We can talk about that later," Bess said. "We usually stop here and have something to eat. By the way, we picked up those supplies you boys left at the general store in Bleak Creek."

"We appreciate that," Ace said. "We'll pay you back for them."

"Darn right you will," Emily said. "We're not made out of money."

They ate in the shade of some aspens, making do with bacon, coffee, and some biscuits the Corcoran sisters had brought from the café in Bleak Creek. It was actually a pretty pleasant meal, as even Emily relaxed and wasn't as prickly as she had been most of the time.

However, the shadow of the trouble that had been plaguing the stage line still hung over them, and none of them could quite manage to completely forget about it.

When the meal was finished and the team was rested, they started the climb to the pass. As Bess had said, it was slow going as the big draft horses strained against the harness and the stagecoach creaked and wobbled. Ace and Chance followed it on horseback, since the road wasn't wide enough for them to ride alongside.

Both brothers constantly scanned the slope above them for any sign of another ambush or any other sort of trouble. By the time the coach reached the halfway point of the climb, nothing unusual had happened.

Bess brought the vehicle to a halt on a wider, level spot where the trail doubled back on itself in one of those hairpin turns. "We always stop here for a half hour or so to let the horses blow again. Then we'll tackle the last stretch to the top."

Ace and Chance dismounted so their horses could rest, too. From where they were, they could look out across the valley and easily see all the way to Shoshone Gap ten miles away.

"From up here it looks like the stage road runs straight as a string," Ace commented.

"Well, not quite," Bess said. "There are a few turns. But yes, it's almost straight. It's an easy route."

He nodded. "That makes it good for a stage-coach. This part we're on now is the roughest part of the whole run, I reckon."

Emily said, "That's the truth."

"Ever have a coach go off the road on the way up or down?"

"Not yet. Hopefully not ever."

Chance said, "If one ever did, anybody unlucky enough to be on it wouldn't survive the fall."

"Let's not talk about that," Bess suggested. "We know what the risks are, and we're willing to run them." She started to pick up the reins. "The horses are probably rested enough by now—"

Before she could go on, a loud scraping noise came from somewhere above them, followed by an ominous rumble. Ace jerked his head back, looked up toward the pass, and saw dust starting to rise. That could only mean one thing.

"Avalanche!" he yelled.

Chapter Eight

The boulders bouncing and crashing down the slope were headed straight for where the stagecoach was parked. Bess had already turned it to head up the next stretch of trail, so at least it was pointed in the right direction as she slashed and yelled at the team. The horses leaped forward and jolted the coach into motion. Getting out of the way of the rockslide was the only chance.

It was no good, Ace saw almost immediately. The stagecoach wouldn't have time to get clear, but the road was a little wider, wide enough for one man on horseback to get past if he was careful.

Unfortunately, there wasn't time to be careful, either. Ace jabbed his boot heels into the chestnut's flanks and galloped up next to the coach. The sheer drop down to the next lowest section of trail was only inches away from the horse's pounding hooves. Chance followed close behind.

"Bess!" Ace shouted over the growing thunder of the avalanche. "Come on!"

She glanced frantically over her shoulder at him and cried, "I can't abandon the coach!"

"You have to! Jump while you can!"

It was a matter of moments before the falling rocks would sweep over them. Bess saw how desperate the situation was and let out a cry of despair. She dropped the reins and launched herself off the driver's box, landing on the chestnut's back behind Ace and clutching at him.

He reached back with his free hand to grab her as the horse stumbled and Bess started to slip. His fingers closed tightly on her vest and hung on. The chestnut recovered and surged ahead of the valiantly struggling team.

Chance moved up and shouted, "Emily! Come on!"

Her face, shadowed by the broad-brimmed brown hat and framed by curly blond hair, was pale and drawn with fear. Only seconds remained, but Emily didn't budge. Chance leaned over in the saddle, held out his free hand to her, and shouted again, "Emily!"

Finally, she broke the grip of terror that paralyzed her and slid over on the seat. She stood up and launched herself into space as she reached for Chance's hand. He locked his fingers around her wrist and pulled her toward him.

She landed in front of him and wrapped her arms around his neck as he embraced her waist and held her tightly. The horse lunged ahead.

A heartbeat later, the first boulder struck the coach and crashed through its roof. The impact made the vehicle lean far out over the brink. The horses screamed in pain as the leading edge of the avalanche swept over them and pushed them off the trail. The coach went, too, vanishing along with the team in the deadly wave of rocks and dust.

Chance and Emily cleared the avalanche's path by a few feet but Chance didn't slow down. The onslaught of falling rocks could still spread out and threaten them. He didn't haul back on the reins until they reached the next turn in the road, where Ace and Bess waited.

All four of them were covered in dust and quite shaken by the close call. As Chance brought his horse to a stop, Emily and Bess slipped down and ran to each other, hugging fiercely.

Bess said, "Are . . . are you all right?"

"Barely." Emily was breathless as she went on, "I . . . I wouldn't be . . . if it wasn't for . . . Chance."

"Ace saved me." Bess turned to look at the brothers. "You saved our lives."

"I'm sorry we couldn't save the stagecoach and the team," Ace told her. His face was grim and angry.

"Those poor horses," Bess said. "Losing the coach hurts, but we have another one. And we have more horses, of course, but—"

"We damn near lost a lot more than that." Emily had caught her breath. "We were almost killed!"

"That rockslide didn't start by accident." Ace said.

"How do you know that?" Bess asked. "Did you see something?"

Ace shook his head. "I heard a scraping sound, like somebody was prying a boulder loose somewhere above us. I can't prove that's what happened, but I'm confident I'm right."

Carefully, Bess leaned over the edge to look down at the wreckage of the coach and the broken bodies of the horses visible at the base of the slope. "The road looks like it was damaged in places, but I think we can still get down there. We need to try to recover the mail we picked up in Bleak Creek."

"That's right," Emily said. "Failing to deliver it could cost us the mail contract with the government. Eagleton could still beat us that way, even if his men didn't manage to kill us!"

With Ace and Chance leading their horses, the four of them started back down the trail, picking their way around the debris left behind by the avalanche. Bess was right about the road being damaged—chunks of it had been knocked out—but there was room for them to make their way to the bottom where the rocks had spread out, only partially covering the destruction.

Bess cried over the dead horses. Emily was more stoic, but tears glittered a little in her eyes, too. They concentrated on digging through the wreckage of the stagecoach with help from Ace and Chance until they found the box that contained the mail pouch. The lid was broken but hadn't come off. Ace wrenched it loose, took out the pouch, and handed it to Bess.

"I'll hang on to this," she said. "We can still take it to Palisade."

"We won't get there before nightfall, though," Emily pointed. "The mail will still be late."

Ace frowned. "Late's not as bad as not getting there at all. Under the circumstances, I don't see how the government could be upset with you for the delay."

Emily continued. "That depends on how much pressure Eagleton brings to bear. He's rich enough to have some friends in high places."

"We'll worry about that later," Bess said. "For now we still have a long climb ahead of us."

That was true. Still on foot, they started up toward the pass once more.

When Bess and Emily began to wear out, Ace and Chance insisted that they ride the horses. Both sisters argued but in the end, they went along with it.

"Emily and I could ride double on one of the horses and the two of you could take the other one," Bess suggested.

"Or Ace and I could ride our own horses and one of you girls could double up with each of us," Chance responded without hesitation.

Ace said, "The horses don't need to be carrying double going up this slope. Chance and I can walk." He ignored the glare that his brother directed toward him, took hold of the chestnut's reins, and began leading the horse up the trail while Bess rocked along in the saddle.

They reached the summit and Timberline Pass just as the sun was setting. Enough light remained in the sky for Ace to look across the broad bench that stretched for several miles before the mountains rose again.

Emily pointed. "Palisade is at the base of that sawtooth peak. The entrance to the Golden Dome is about halfway up the mountain above it."

After letting the horses rest for a while, they mounted up again. Ace and Bess were on the chestnut.

Emily was reluctant to accept riding behind Chance, but he pointed out, "You were happy enough to ride with me after I pulled you off that stagecoach."

"That was different. That was a matter of life and death."

Chance just sat there in the saddle smiling as he extended a hand to her.

Emily shook her head, blew out her breath disgustedly, and gripped his hand to swing up behind him. "I'm riding back here. You got a little too free with your hands when I was in front of you."

"Purely accidental, I assure you." Chance looked over at Ace and Bess and dropped a wink where Emily couldn't see him. Even under the circumstances, Bess had to laugh.

"What?" Emily demanded.

"Let's just go," Ace said. "It's going to be well after dark before we get there."

The sky turned a deeper blue and then faded to black as the stars began to come out. Twinkling lights appeared in the distance to mark the location of the settlement. Those yellow glows came in handy, giving Ace and Chance something to steer by as they guided their mounts through the darkness.

Even before they reached Palisade, they heard raucous music coming from the town. "It sounds like your saloons are pretty lively places," Chance commented.

"What do you expect in a mining town?" Emily asked. "Men who work underground all day like to blow off a little steam at night."

"What's the law like?" Ace said.

"There's a town marshal," Bess said. "Claude

Wheeler. But he doesn't really work for the town. He's an employee of the Golden Dome Mining Company, and so are his deputies."

"So Eagleton's got the law in his pocket, is what you're saying."

"I'm afraid that's right. It won't do any good to report what happened to us. Marshal Wheeler will say that he'll look into it, and that'll be the end of it."

"Wheeler's just another of Eagleton's gun-wolves," Emily said bitterly. "He keeps the peace in the saloons, but that's all he's really good for. That and intimidating anybody Eagleton sics him on."

"He's not going to intimidate Ace and me," Chance boasted.

"We'll see." Emily's tone made it clear she didn't think much of the Jensen boys' chances if they crossed Palisade's star-packer.

"There's no telegraph line between here and Bleak Creek, is there?" Ace asked.

Bess said, "No, although there's been talk about stringing one eventually. It wouldn't be easy bringing a telegraph line up the mountain, though."

"Having to go up and down that trail to the pass makes everything more difficult, doesn't it?"

"Yes, it does."

They'd reached the outskirts of town. The music from the saloons was pretty loud, the different songs blending together to form a discordant melody. Light from half a dozen different drinking and gambling establishments spilled brightly into the main street of Palisade, which Emily explained was named Eagleton Avenue.

"As if you'd expect it to be called anything else," she added. "The man's got such a high opinion of himself you'd think the air would be too thin to breathe up where he is."

Most of the businesses up and down the street were still open, even though the hour was late.

"They don't roll up the boardwalks at dark around here, do they?" Chance said as they rode past several stores that were still brightly lit up.

"Like I said, the men work all day," Emily replied. "Actually, some of them work all night, too. The mine never stops operating. The crews have three different shifts."

"You said Eagleton owns just about everything in town," Ace said, "but the saloons all have different names and so do the other businesses."

"Since when do names matter?" Emily wanted to know. "Anyway, the deeds may be in someone else's name, but it's Eagleton's money behind them. For all practical purposes that makes them his, doesn't it?"

She was right about that, Ace thought. Samuel Eagleton might not be sitting on a throne, but from everything Ace had heard, the mine owner was the uncrowned king of Palisade and the surrounding area.

"There's the stage line office," Bess said, indicating a neat frame building on the left side of the street with a large barn and corral beside it.

Ace and Chance turned the horses toward it. As they came up to the hitch rack in front of the building, Ace looked through the large window. A burly, barrel-chested man paced back and forth in the brightly lit room as if in a worried frenzy.

He caught sight of them and stopped short in his pacing. He rushed to the door, flung it open, and charged out onto the porch. "Bess! Emily!" he cried. "Thank God! Are you all right?"

The sisters slid down from the horses and quickly stepped up onto the porch, where the man threw an arm around each of them and hugged them at the same time.

"We're fine, Pa," Bess assured him.

"But the coach isn't, and neither is the team," Emily said. "They're wrecked at the bottom of the mountain."

"Good Lord!" Corcoran exclaimed. "What happened?"

"An avalanche almost got us when we were climbing up to Timberline Pass." Emily paused. "An avalanche started by Eagleton's men."

"We don't know that for sure," Bess said. "It seems pretty likely, though."

Corcoran stepped back and regarded his daughters solemnly, with a hand on the shoulder of each of them. His face, which sported a close-cropped salt-and-pepper beard, was flushed with anger. "Tell me what happened."

Bess did most of the talking and Emily added curt comments, until Bess finally turned to the Jensens. "If it wasn't for the help these men gave us, we wouldn't be here. Pa, this is Ace and Chance Jensen."

Corcoran barely glanced at them and didn't acknowledge the introductions. "Eagleton is behind this, damn him."

"That's the way it looks to us, too," Emily agreed.

Corcoran jerked his head in a nod, then surprised them by turning and stepping back into the office. He was only there for a second, though. When he came out again, he held a coach gun like the one Emily had carried. "I'll teach him to come after my daughters." He started along the street with a determined stride. "I'll blow his damn head off!"

Chapter Nine

"Pa!" Bess called after him. "Pa, no!"

"Damn it," Emily muttered. "We've got to stop him. He's the one who'll get his head blown off if he tries to get past Eagleton's hired guns."

The two young women hurried after their father. Ace and Chance looked at each other, and Chance said, "We'd better give them a hand."

"I think you're right," Ace agreed. "Mr. Corcoran didn't look like he was in any mood to listen to reason."

The brothers went after Bess and Emily, their longer strides allowing them to catch up fairly quickly. Ahead of them, Corcoran had angled across the street and reached the steps leading up to the front gallery of what appeared to be the best hotel in town, Palisade House.

Ace figured that Samuel Eagleton owned it and might even live there.

Corcoran bounded up the steps and threw the double doors open. Bess and Emily were right behind him as he went in, and Ace and Chance were a step behind them. Bess grabbed hold of her father's left arm, and Emily took his right. They stopped him a few feet inside the door.

The sight of him carrying the shotgun was enough to set off a commotion in the hotel lobby.

Ace and Chance stepped into the room in time to see several well-dressed men—probably guests—moving quickly through an arched entrance into a dining room. A couple others were headed up the stairs, obviously wanting to get out of the line of fire in case any gunplay broke out.

That looked like a distinct possibility. Three men had gotten up from chairs across the room and stood tensely, their hands hovering over the butts of holstered pistols. Cigars smoldered in an ashtray on a table between two of the chairs.

One of the men was something of a dude and wore the same sort of suit, vest, boiled shirt, and cravat that a whiskey drummer might wear, along with a bowler hat. The reddish tinge to his sun-bronzed, pockmarked features testified that he had some Indian blood. The well-worn grips of the Colt jutting up on his hip showed that the gun had seen plenty of use.

The two men flanking him wore range clothes but looked equally tough and hard-bitten. The threat of danger seemed to ooze from all three men.

"What do you want, Corcoran?" asked the man in the bowler hat. "You know you can't come in here and start waving a scattergun around."

"Where's Eagleton?" Corcoran demanded. He tried to shake off his daughters, but they clung to him stubbornly so he couldn't use the shotgun. "He tried to kill my girls!"

Bowler Hat's thin lips curved in a cold, humorless smile. "The boss didn't try to kill anybody, old man. You're plumb loco. He's been right here in town all day. Plenty of folks have seen him."

"What in blazes does that mean?" Corcoran asked. Immediately, he answered his own question. "I'll tell you what it means. Nothing! He gives the orders and sits back like . . . like a fat old spider in his web, just licking his chops and waiting to see what's going to happen!"

"Spiders don't lick their chops," Bowler Hat said, still with that ugly smile on his face. "Maybe you better study up before you start making accusations again."

Ace and Chance had been behind the three Corcorans where they couldn't be seen very well. They moved out into the open, Ace to the right and Chance to the left.

The sight of them caused the smile to disappear from Bowler Hat's face. His spine stiffened, and so did those of the other two gunmen. Clearly, they regarded the Jensen brothers as more of a threat than Bess, Emily, and their father.

"Who are your friends, Corcoran?" Bowler Hat asked harshly as he hooked his thumbs in the gun belt slanted across his hips.

"Never mind them, Buckhorn," Corcoran snapped. "Where's Eagleton? I want him to look me straight in the eye and tell me he didn't have anything to do with my girls almost dying not once but twice!"

"The boss is up in his suite. He's already turned in for the night, and I'm not going to disturb him to make him listen to the rantings of a crazy man. Go on back to your little stagecoach office. You may have lost a coach, but your girls are fine. They're standing right there."

Ace frowned and cocked his head a little to the side. "How did you know the stage line lost a coach, mister? We just rode into town and haven't told anybody except Mr. Corcoran what happened."

Buckhorn's face darkened. He snapped, "Are you accusin' me of something, kid?"

"We're curious, that's all." Chance's pose was casual, but his hand was close to his lapel where it could dart under his coat and, in the blink of an eye, pull the Lightning from the shoulder holster. "How do you know something you shouldn't know?"

Buckhorn's face twisted in a sneer. "I was on the boardwalk a few minutes ago and saw the four of you ride in on a couple horses. I knew Bess and Emily left town yesterday on the stagecoach, and they were comin' back riding double with a pair of strangers. How smart do I have to be to figure out something happened to the damn coach?"

That was a quick-witted answer, Ace thought. Buckhorn might not look very smart, but obviously there was a brain behind that brutal exterior. Ace didn't believe for a second, though, that Buckhorn's reply was sincere. The gunman knew about the wrecked coach because he worked for Samuel Eagleton and Eagleton's men had been behind the attacks on the Corcoran sisters.

Buckhorn went on. "Now do like I told you. Turn around and go home, Corcoran. We don't want any trouble with you, but by God, that's what you'll get if you don't back off."

A footstep sounded in the doorway, and a new voice said, "I'm telling you the same thing, Brian. You won't accomplish anything by storming in here except to get somebody hurt, probably you or one of your girls."

Ace glanced behind him and saw a thick-bodied, hatless man with wispy fair hair. The tin badge he wore pinned to his vest was much like the one Marshal Kaiser had sported back in Bleak Creek.

Corcoran said hotly, "If you'd do your job, Wheeler, citizens wouldn't have to take up arms—"

"I do my job," the marshal broke in sharply. "I keep the peace in Palisade, and I'm asking you, for the sake of that peace, to settle down and go back to your place."

Corcoran breathed heavily for a few seconds, then said brokenly, "Damn it, I lost a coach and a team. Even worse, I . . . I almost lost Bess and Emily. I . . . I can't go on like this."

Marshal Wheeler looked at the two young women and said gently, "Why don't you take him on home, girls?"

"We will," Bess said as she and Emily finally succeeded in turning their father away from the confrontation with Eagleton's gunmen and toward the hotel's front door.

"But he's right, Marshal," Emily snapped. "Most lawmen would want to get to the bottom of somebody trying to kill us twice in the past two days."

Wheeler's fleshy features hardened. "You come to my office tomorrow, Miss Corcoran, and make an official report. I'll listen to whatever you have to say."

Emily's disdainful sniff made it clear just how much she thought that offer was worth.

Wheeler stepped aside to let the Corcorans leave. When Ace and Chance tried to follow, he put out a hand and moved to block their path. "I don't recall seeing you fellas in town before. Who might you be?"

"Law-abiding citizens, Marshal," Chance said. "You've got no call to stop us from going with our friends."

Buckhorn and the other two gunnies came

across the lobby and moved up closer behind Ace and Chance.

Buckhorn said, "You didn't answer the marshal's question, mister. You got something to hide?"

"We don't have anything to hide," Ace said, which wasn't exactly true. He wasn't going to volunteer any information about the ambush in Shoshone Gap the day before or the run-in with Marshal Kaiser in Bleak Creek. "Our name's Jensen. I'm Ace, and this is my brother Chance. We ran into the Corcoran sisters out on the trail yesterday and since they were having trouble, we decided they needed somebody to give them a hand, that's all."

"And it's a good thing we did," Chance added, "because somebody's got it in for those girls. Yesterday some no-good polecats tried to spook the stagecoach team into stampeding right off the side of the mountain, and today they used an avalanche to wreck the coach and nearly kill Bess and Emily, not to mention my brother and me."

"This is the first I've heard about it," Wheeler insisted. "I can't do anything about a problem if nobody reports it."

"Consider it reported." Ace was uncomfortably aware of Buckhorn and the other two men crowding them from behind. It was possible the gunmen were trying to goad him and Chance into a fight. That would be a good excuse for killing them and depriving the Corcorans of a couple potential allies. He hoped Chance would keep a cool head.

For once that seemed to be Chance's intention. "We're not looking for trouble, Marshal." A cocky grin appeared on his face. "Shoot, we just ran into a couple really good-looking fillies and wanted to help 'em out. Get on their good side, you know what I mean?"

Buckhorn chuckled. "I sure do. The Corcoran sisters are mighty easy on the eyes, even if they *are* a mite proddy, especially that Emily."

Wheeler grunted. "Yeah, I suppose so. But listen, you two are strangers here, and you might not know what you're getting into. That whole family tends to be troublemakers, always upset about something and trying to stir up a ruckus. So, pretty or not, you might want to give some thought to steering clear of those girls."

"We'll think about it, Marshal," Chance promised. "Anyway, I suppose there are plenty of other good-looking gals here in Palisade."

Wheeler finally seemed to relax. He smiled slightly. "You're right about that, my young friend. Go on over to the Three Deuces Saloon and you'll find some of the prettiest women in the whole territory."

Chance slapped his brother on the shoulder. "We'll take you up on that suggestion, Marshal. Won't we, Ace?"

"Sounds good to me," Ace agreed, playing along with what Chance was doing. "I could use a drink, too."

Buckhorn said, "Tell the head bartender over there, fella named Carlsby, that the first drink's on me. I'd like to sort of pay you back for our little misunderstanding earlier."

"Yeah, we were about to get off on the wrong foot, weren't we? We're much obliged to you, Mr. Buckhorn."

The gunman waved that off. "Forget about it. Glad to do it."

Wheeler got out of their way as Ace and Chance moved to leave the hotel. The marshal nodded to them. "You fellas have a good night."

"Thanks, Marshal," Ace said.

He and Chance stepped down from the hotel porch. The Three Deuces was easy to spot on the other side of the street in the next block. It appeared to take up almost the entire block, and its batwinged entrance was on the corner.

As the brothers angled toward it, Ace said quietly, "You think they bought that whole act?"

"Well, they pretended to, anyway," Chance said. "That gave Wheeler and Buckhorn the opportunity to let us go without it looking like they were backing down. That would be important to a couple hardcases like them."

"It looks like the odds are really stacked against Bess and Emily and their pa."

"Yeah, but things are different now that you and I are here."

"You really think we can take on Eagleton's whole gun-crew, plus his tame lawman?"

"Why not?" Chance said. "We're Jensens, aren't we?"

"Yeah, but right now, I wouldn't mind if old Smoke was here, too, relative or no relative!"

Chapter Ten

Figuring that Wheeler and Buckhorn were keeping an eye on them from the hotel as they crossed the street, Ace and Chance went into the saloon and had a beer, although they didn't hunt up the head bartender and tell him about Buckhorn's offer to buy the first round. Once they were finished, they sauntered over to a side door and let themselves out.

"Let's get back to the stagecoach office," Ace said. "I want to talk to the girls and their pa and make sure they're all right."

"And that Mr. Corcoran isn't about to do something loco again," Chance added.

Even though they had never been in Palisade before, the town wasn't so big that they couldn't find their way through the back alleys to the rear of the stagecoach office. Ace knocked on the building's back door, and a moment later, Emily swung it open, standing with the coach gun her father had taken to the hotel. She looked like she was primed to blow a hole through somebody.

When she saw the Jensen brothers, she lowered the weapon. "Oh, it's you two."

"And we're mighty glad to see you, too," Chance said with a grin.

Emily stepped back and motioned with her head for them to come in.

"There you are." Bess stood beside a desk. "We wondered what had happened to you, but it seemed like we needed to get Pa back here. . . ."

Her father sat in a chair, his shoulders slumped and his head hanging down. An uncorked bottle and an empty glass sat on the desk next to his elbow.

"Marshal Wheeler and that fella Buckhorn just wanted to give us a little trouble before they let us go," Ace explained. "They wanted to spook us and convince us we shouldn't try to help you."

"Joe Buckhorn is enough to spook anybody," Bess said with a little shiver. "He's a cold-blooded killer."

Emily said, "It looks like they didn't manage to scare you off."

"We're pretty stubborn," Chance said. "We don't give up easy"—he smiled again at the blonde—"no matter what we're trying to do."

She rolled her eyes, turned away, and placed the coach gun back in a rack on the wall with a couple other double-barreled shotguns.

At the desk, Corcoran drew in a deep breath and then lifted his head with an obvious effort. He looked at Ace and Chance. "I'm sorry. I was rude to you boys earlier. I . . . I appreciate everything you've done to help my daughters. They told me all about it." He forced himself to his feet and held out his hand. "I'm Brian Corcoran."

"Ace Jensen." He shook hands with the older man.

"And I'm Chance Jensen." He gripped Corcoran's hand, too.

Corcoran nodded toward the empty bottle. "I'd offer you a drink, but we seem to be out."

"There was only a little in it," Bess said quickly. "Just enough for a bracer. Pa needed it."

"No, what I need is for the Good Lord to strike Samuel Eagleton dead, him and all his hired guns." Corcoran sighed. "But I don't think that's going to happen. God doesn't seem to take much of an interest in what happens in a hellhole like Palisade."

"The town doesn't look that bad to me," Ace said. "Maybe the people who live here just need to be more like you, Mr. Corcoran, and stand up to Eagleton."

"And get themselves killed? That's happened

before, you know. There were several smaller mines around here, starting out. They came in right after Eagleton made his strike. One by one their owners got scared off . . . except for the ones who died in cave-ins and so-called accidental explosions and the like."

"That sounds like murder to me. Something the law ought to take an interest in."

"No way to prove it," Corcoran said glumly. "And when you're talking about crooked lawmen like Claude Wheeler or incompetent ones like Jed Kaiser over in Bleak Creek . . . well, it doesn't take long to realize you can't count on the law for much of anything around here."

Emily said, "Maybe not, but we can't just give up, Pa. This stage line is your dream. We have to keep fighting for it."

Corcoran's head jerked up and his eyes blazed with anger. "We Corcorans have never given up," he snapped. "We've always been fighters, ever since we came over from the ould sod. But now—" The momentary anger seemed to go out of him, leaving him deflated again. "Now that it may cost you girls your lives, it's just not worth it anymore."

"You can't think of it like that, Pa," Bess said. "Emily and I know what the risks are. You know we've always been willing to help. That's why we volunteered to take the run to Bleak Creek."

"It's not a matter of whether or not you're

willing," Corcoran insisted. "I won't stand by and watch the two of you get hurt." He nodded slowly but decisively as if his mind were made up. "Sam Eagleton gets what he wants. I'll go see him tomorrow and find out if he's still willing to buy the line. Chances are he won't pay as much as he offered before, but I don't care about that anymore."

Bess and Emily stared at him as if they couldn't believe what they were hearing. Bess looked like she was about to cry, and Emily seemed to be on the verge of exploding in anger.

Ace and Chance looked at each other. Chance nodded, and Ace said, "Hold on a minute, Mr. Corcoran. I know you don't want your daughters risking their lives taking the stagecoach through anymore . . . but how do you feel about Chance and me giving it a try?"

The two young women looked at him in surprise, but Corcoran frowned and asked, "Are you saying you and your brother want to work for me, lad?"

"You need a driver and a guard," Chance said. "There are two of us."

"Have either of you ever actually *driven* a stagecoach?"

"Well, no," Ace admitted. "But if—" He stopped as Bess glared at him.

"But if what? If a *girl* can do it? Is that what you were about to say, Ace?"

To tell the truth, it was, but he wasn't going to confess that, not with Bess staring daggers at him. "No, what I was about to say was that if Bess could give me a few pointers, I'll bet I could do it."

"And I know how to use a shotgun just fine, so no problems there," Chance added.

Bess said, "Handling a team isn't easy, especially on a road like the one leading down from Timberline Pass."

The thought of taking a stagecoach down that zigzag road high above the valley was enough to make him nervous, but he said, "I'm willing to give it a try."

Corcoran scratched his bearded jaw. "Let me think it over. The next run isn't scheduled for a couple days. That gives us some time."

Emily said, "I think it's the craziest idea I've ever heard. You won't let us do it, your own daughters, but you'll trust the future of the line to a couple complete strangers?"

"Ah, but they're not strangers," Corcoran pointed out. "You and Bess know them. And there's one more advantage to hiring them."

"What's that?" Bess asked.

"When Eagleton has them killed, I'll be mighty sorry . . . but it won't break my heart like it would if it was you two girls."

Joe Buckhorn had told Corcoran that the boss had turned in for the night. It was a convenient fiction. Rose Demarcus hadn't come down yet from Eagleton's second-floor suite. She always gave him a smile when she passed through the lobby on the way back to the house she ran.

Buckhorn knew Rose was just having a little sport with him—she was a lovely, middling-rich woman who had no real interest in an ugly half-breed gunfighter—but she was so blasted beautiful he always enjoyed their brief interaction anyway.

Knowing that she was still inside made him a little nervous as he approached the suite's door. He knew the boss wanted to be informed of what had happened, but he wouldn't like being disturbed while he was with Rose.

Of course, there was a good chance they were already finished with whatever they were doing in the suite's bedroom and were in the sitting room, enjoying a glass of brandy. Eagleton could even be smoking one of his expensive cigars.

Buckhorn came to a stop at the door and raised his left hand. He hesitated just a second longer, then rapped softly on the panel. The summons was quiet enough that if Eagleton and Rose were still in the bedroom, they wouldn't hear it, yet Buckhorn could honestly say he had tried to let the boss know what was going on.

The response from inside the suite was instant. Eagleton said in a loud, annoyed voice, "What is it? Who's out there?"

"Joe Buckhorn, boss," the gunfighter replied.

Eagleton knew Buckhorn wouldn't disturb him if it wasn't important. His tone was slightly mollified as he said, "Come on in."

Buckhorn opened the door and stepped into the opulently furnished sitting room. Eagleton stood next to a beautiful cherrywood sideboard pouring amber liquid from a crystal decanter into a snifter. He was a short man, mostly bald and almost as wide as he was tall, or at least that was the way he looked in the silk dressing gown he wore. He swirled the liquor around and then took a sip before he asked, "What is it, Joe?"

Buckhorn couldn't help but notice that Rose wasn't in the sitting room. The door to the bedroom was closed, so he supposed she was in there. Getting dressed, maybe. Or still lounging in the big four-poster bed . . .

Buckhorn shoved those images out of his head. "The Corcoran girls got back into town a little while ago."

Eagleton took another sip of the brandy. "I thought they were going to have trouble on their way back from Bleak Creek."

"They did . . . but they had help from a couple kids who like to stick their noses in other people's business."

Eagleton scowled. "What the hell are you talking about?"

"Two young fellas named Jensen. The coach

was wrecked, but thanks to them, Bess and Emily got out alive."

As Buckhorn spoke, something nagged at his brain. It took him a second to realize that it was relief. As odd as it sounded, considering that Sam Eagleton paid his wages, he was glad the Corcoran girls hadn't been killed. He had gunned down plenty of men . . . hell, he had shot a few unlucky ones in the back . . . but something inside him didn't like the idea of killing women. Especially young, pretty women.

He would never say anything about that to Eagleton. And if the boss ever gave him a direct order to handle something like that personally . . .

Well, Buckhorn hoped it never came to that. So far, his job had been to see to it that Samuel Eagleton remained alive, and he'd been good at it. Some of the other men had been given the job of handling the Corcoran problem, and that was just fine with him.

Eagleton was too upset to continue sipping the brandy. He tossed back what was left in the snifter and set it down on the sideboard. "You say Corcoran lost the coach, anyway?"

"That's what I was told," Buckhorn replied. "And the team, too, of course."

"Well, that's something, anyway."

"And when he left the hotel, he sounded like he was just about ready to give up."

Eagle stiffened. "Corcoran came here?"

"Yelling and waving a coach gun around," Buckhorn said with a nod.

Eagleton stared at him for a few seconds, then burst out, "You fool! You damn fool!"

Buckhorn was a little taken aback. "Boss, he never got anywhere near the suite—"

"That's not what I'm talking about! You had a chance to kill him, and you didn't. For God's sake, Buckhorn, what were you thinking? A man busts into my hotel and threatens me, and you don't gun him down? You even had Starkey and Byers with you. Corcoran wouldn't have stood a chance. It would have been self-defense, everything legal and aboveboard."

Especially with your own pet lawman in the marshal's office, thought Buckhorn. Claude Wheeler would never question anything Eagleton or any of Eagleton's men told him.

"I'm sorry, boss. I didn't think of it. Corcoran's daughters were with him—"

"And you didn't want to kill a man in front of his children? That never stopped you when you were working as a regulator up in Montana Territory."

Buckhorn struggled to keep a tight rein on his temper. He'd been tempted at times to tell Eagleton to go to hell, saddle his horse, and put Palisade behind him. The problem with that was that Eagleton paid so damn well. Unlike a lot of rich men, he wasn't miserly with his money . . . only with power.

Before either of them could say anything else, the bedroom door opened and Rose came out. She wore a simple blue dress that she managed to make look elegant and expensive and a lace-trimmed shawl around her shoulders. Due to the elevation, the evenings could get pretty chilly, even in the summer. Not a bit of the sleek, dark brown hair that curved around her face was out of place.

As she smiled at Buckhorn, he felt his heart slug harder in his chest. The small scar that just touched her upper lip on the right side of her mouth made her stunningly beautiful, a tiny bit of imperfection that made a man realize just how lovely the rest of her was.

Buckhorn was glad to know he wasn't the only man she affected that way. Dozens of men in Palisade would have cut off an arm if she'd asked them to. They had to content themselves with the girls who worked in the house she ran, though. The only man she went with was Samuel Eagleton.

"Hello, Joseph," she said in the husky voice that drove most gents half-crazy.

Buckhorn touched the brim of his bowler hat. "Miss Demarcus. It's good to see you, as always."

Rose pulled on a pair of soft leather gloves as

she turned to Eagleton. She wasn't a particularly tall woman, but she had an inch or two advantage in height over him. She leaned forward, kissed him on the cheek, and murmured, "Good night, Samuel."

"Good night," Eagleton said, sounding half-choked.

Her gloved left hand patted him lightly on the right cheek, then still smiling, she turned and walked out of the room.

Glided, thought Buckhorn. Or drifted, like some beautiful phantom, a spirit glimpsed only in a dream . . .

His jaw clenched hard enough to make his teeth grind together. One hell of a thought for a half-breed gunfighter to be having, he told himself. Next thing he knew he'd be writing a damn poem.

When Rose was gone, Eagleton pulled a hand-kerchief from the pocket of his dressing gown and mopped his forehead and his bald pate. Buckhorn could almost see him forcing Rose out of his thoughts and turning them back to the Corcoran problem.

"You said Corcoran acted like he was ready to give up. You'd better hope that's the case. If he comes to see me tomorrow and offers to sell out, we'll forget about your little lapse tonight."

"Are you gonna offer him the same amount you did before?" Buckhorn asked.

Eagleton let out a disgusted snort. "Good Lord, no. I'll offer him a third as much and go up to half if I have to."

"Some folks might say what you offered him before was highway robbery."

"Do you believe I honestly care what people think about me, Buckhorn?"

The gunfighter knew Eagleton didn't care. "No, sir, I reckon you don't."

"That's right. If Corcoran comes to the hotel in the morning, bring him on up. Unless he's armed. Then for God's sake, go ahead and kill him! Now get out of here. I'm tired."

Buckhorn nodded. "All right, boss. If he comes in here with a gun, he dies."

Chapter Eleven

Brian Corcoran told Ace and Chance they could put their horses in the stage line's barn, then added, "You can sleep in the loft, too, if you'd like. If you go to any of the hotels in town, you're just putting more money in Sam Eagleton's pockets, and he sure as hell doesn't need that."

"We'll take you up on that offer, sir, and we're obliged to you," Ace said quickly before Chance could turn it down. He was sure Chance would have preferred sleeping in an actual bed, even if it meant venturing into a hotel owned by a man who was turning out to be their enemy.

Bess said, "And you'll join us for breakfast in the morning. You might not think so to look at her waving a gun around, but Emily's an excellent cook."

Emily glared at her sister for a second, then switched the look to Ace and Chance. "We'll talk more about this crazy idea of you two handling the stage run, too."

They left the office and went out to get the horses. As they led the animals into the barn, Chance said, "I don't know, brother. You're always accusing me of acting without thinking and getting carried away because of a pretty girl, but it seems to me like you're the one who's doing that here."

"What do you mean by that?" Ace asked.

"You saw that road! Do you really think you can drive that stagecoach down it without killing us both?"

"Well, I'm sure going to try. I've driven wagons before. It can't be that much different."

"How about this? Where does that stage route go?"

"You know that," Ace said. "Across the valley, through Shoshone Gap, and then on to . . ."

"Exactly." Chance nodded as his brother's voice trailed off. "It goes to Bleak Creek. Where you punched the marshal in the face, stole his gun, and we rode out with people shooting at us!"

Ace groaned, closed his eyes, and scrubbed a hand over his face. His brother was right. The two of them going back to Bleak Creek was just asking for trouble with the law. Marshal Kaiser hadn't struck him as the sort to forget or forgive.

"Maybe we can get in and out of town without anyone noticing us," Ace said. "We won't spend the night there like the girls do. We'll just drop off the mail at the depot, pick up the mail pouch for Palisade, and start back right away. We can spend the night on the trail somewhere."

"That *might* work," Chance allowed. "If the marshal happens to be busy elsewhere or taking a nap in his office. Assuming nobody who sees us remembers what happened and recognizes us and runs to tell him about it."

"By the time we get there, four or five days will have passed. People will have forgotten about it by then."

Chance frowned. "Sure they will." He didn't sound convinced.

Another stagecoach was parked inside the barn, so as soon as they'd put their horses in stalls, unsaddled them, and made sure they had water and grain, they studied the vehicle by the light of a lantern that Ace took from the nail where it hung. He was especially concerned with knowing where the brake was located and how it worked.

119

That was going to be important going down the road from Timberline Pass.

Chance leaned over to take a closer look at the brake assembly. "You'll have to be careful going down the mountain or you'll wear that block down to a nub. Either that or overheat it so much it catches on fire."

"Well, I didn't intend to drive hell-bent for leather all the way down," Ace said.

"Neither did Bess on the last run, I'll bet, but you saw how that worked out."

His brother had a point, Ace thought. Once word got around Palisade, as it was bound to, that he and Chance were working for the Corcoran Stage Line and would be making the next run to Bleak Creek, there was a high probability that Samuel Eagleton would have his gunmen waiting for them.

"Doc would say that we're playing against a stacked deck, wouldn't he?" Ace asked with a sigh.

"And he'd be right." Chance slapped Ace on the shoulder. "But buck up, brother! Sometimes you win, even against long odds."

Early the next morning, before dawn, they woke to hear a man singing a hymn in a cracked, elderly voice. The brothers had spread blankets in the hayloft—although not without some complaining on Chance's part—and slept fairly well. Groggy from being woken up, they crawled over to the edge of the loft to look down into the stalls.

A dozen draft horses were in the barn, along with their two saddle mounts, and a wizened little old man was forking fresh straw to them.

He felt Ace and Chance looking at him and looked up, giving them a gap-toothed grin. "Don't just stand there gawkin', you two," he called to them. "Get on inside. Coffee's on. Take a sniff, and you can smell it."

"I can't smell anything except manure," Chance said.

"You best rattle your hocks," the old-timer went on, " 'fore Miss Em'ly throws it out. You don't want to get that little gal mad at you."

"Yeah, we figured that out already." Ace waved at the old man and went back to pull on his boots and gather up his gear.

When they climbed down the ladder from the loft a couple minutes later, the old-timer was waiting for them. "They call me Nate. I'm the hostler around here. I take care of all these stagecoach horses."

"We figured as much," Ace told him. "We're Ace and Chance Jensen—"

"I know who you are," Nate said. "Miss Bess told me all about you fellas and how you helped 'em when Eagleton's gunnies came after 'em. I sure am mighty obliged to you boys for that.

Them little gals mean the world to me. I been workin' for their pa since they was little bitty. Seen 'em both grow up into fine young ladies, I have."

"You probably don't care for them risking their lives on those stagecoach runs, then," Ace said.

The old-timer grimaced. "I done my damnedest to talk 'em out of it. I told their pa I'd take the stage through. I used to be a jehu, years ago 'fore I got so stove up. We had it all figured out. I'd handle the team, and Brian 'd ride shotgun. But them two . . ." Nate sighed and shook his head. "They come out here, hitched up the team, and drove off 'fore either of us knew what was goin' on. That was a few weeks back. Nothin' happened durin' the run to Bleak Creek and back, so Brian let 'em keep on with it. Reckon we both knew, though, it was only a matter of time 'fore all hell broke loose."

"Well, we'll be handling the run from now on," Ace said.

"Until things settle down," Chance added. "We're not staying here permanently."

Nate scratched his grizzled jaw. "Yeah, you two boys don't look like the sort of fellas who let much grass grow under your feet."

"Can't," Chance said with a grin. "There's too much to see and do in this world. We don't want to miss any of it."

They left the old-timer tending to the stock and

went into the stage line office. The door between the office and the living quarters in the back was open, and as Nate had said, they could smell the coffee brewing. The aroma was mixed with the smell of bacon frying, and that blend was one of the most appealing scents in the world.

Bess heard Ace and Chance come in and called through the open door, "Back here. We're just sitting down to breakfast."

The Jensen brothers went through and found themselves in a spacious kitchen with a heavy table in the center. Bess and her father were already seated at the table while Emily, wearing a somewhat incongruous apron over her denim trousers and buckskin shirt, set platters of bacon and flapjacks in front of them.

"Sit," she said to Ace and Chance. "I'll get your food and pour some coffee for you."

Chance smiled as he sat down. "I could get used to being waited on like this."

"Don't," Emily snapped. "You probably won't be around here long enough for that."

The boys dug in, and the food was as good as Bess had promised it would be, as good as it smelled. When they were finished, they lingered over a second cup of coffee.

Corcoran leaned back in his chair. "Now that you've had a night to sleep on it, are you still determined to take over that run to Bleak Creek?"

Ace glanced at his brother, who gave him a tiny shrug, leaving it up to Ace.

"We are," Ace told Corcoran. "I'm sure we can handle it."

"I'm not sure of anything anymore," the older man said. "But if you want to give it a shot, I won't stop you. And you'll have my gratitude, as well."

Ace looked at Bess. "Maybe we can take the coach out today and I can get some practice handling the team."

"Fine," she said, although it was obvious she was still reluctant to accept the idea.

Emily asked Chance, "What do you need help with?"

"Not a thing," he told her. "I'm perfect just the way I am."

That drew a disgusted snort from the blonde. "That'll be the day."

A short time later, Bess, Ace, and Chance went out to the barn where Nate was still working. Bess told the old hostler, "We need to show the boys how to hitch up a team, and how to change teams, for that matter. They'll need to do that in Bleak Creek."

They spent half the morning working on that, hitching and unhitching teams while Bess and Nate showed them what to do and supervised the task until Ace and Chance were confident they could handle the job on their own.

With that done, Bess said, "All right, hitch up a team again, and we'll let you try your hand at driving, Ace." She paused, then added, "Emily can pack a lunch for us."

"All right," Ace said. "That sounds like a good idea."

"I'll go ask her." Bess left the barn and went into the office.

Chance grinned at Ace. "So, you and Bess are gonna have a little picnic."

"No, I'm going to practice driving the stage-coach," Ace replied solemnly.

"And have lunch out on the trail somewhere—which is a picnic."

"Yeah, but you're making it sound like more than it really is. There's nothing romantic about it."

Chance grinned. "You never know until you try."

Ace scoffed at that. "Come on. Let's get those horses hitched up like she told us."

As they worked at the task, Chance asked the old hostler, "What do you think, Nate? You've known Bess a lot longer than we have. Is she interested in Ace?"

"That there is the most level-headed gal I've ever knowed in my life," Nate replied. "She ain't never gonna do nothin' without thinkin' it through six ways from Sunday. Howsomever, once she makes her mind up about somethin', she

125

ain't gonna budge from it. So if she *is* smitten with you, young fella—and I ain't sayin' whether she is or she ain't—you might as well just accept it, 'cause it ain't gonna change."

Ace shook his head. "I'm sorry. I just don't think Bess is interested in anything right now except keeping this stage line going and stopping Eagleton from ruining her father's business."

"Then you don't mind if I suggest that Emily and I come along for this practice run of yours," Chance said.

"Not at all," Ace said, although to tell the truth he was a little disappointed. He hadn't minded the idea of spending a little time alone with Bess. He would never admit that to his brother, though. Chance could already be insufferable enough at times without telling him he was right about anything.

"Well, I'll just go do that while you finish hitching up the team," Chance declared, and before Ace could stop him, he walked toward the stage line office, whistling a tune as he stuck his hands in his pockets.

Ace muttered to himself, shook his head, and got busy backing the draft horses into position in front of the stagecoach.

From where he sat on a three-legged stool, the hostler said, "I'll bet that brother o' yours is a handful."

"He can be," Ace agreed.

By the time he finished getting the team ready, Chance came back out to the barn and announced, "The girls will be ready in a few minutes." He carried one of the coach guns. "Might take a few potshots with this while we're out on the trail. I haven't fired a shotgun in a while."

Emily carried a wicker basket when she and Bess joined them. She opened one of the coach doors and placed it inside, then motioned for Chance to climb in.

"You should go first," he told her. "You're the lady."

Emily tugged her flat-crowned hat down tighter on her hair. "Just get in there."

Ace and Bess climbed to the driver's seat. The coach was turned so that he could drive straight out through the barn's open double doors.

"You said you've driven a wagon, so you know how to get a team to go and stop and turn," she told Ace. "The main thing you have to think about with a stagecoach is that it's built differently from a wagon. It's not as stable on the road and will turn over easier if you're going too fast. Just take it easy and you should be all right."

Ace gripped the reins, licked his lips, and nodded. "Are we ready?"

Bess leaned over and called through the coach's windows, "Everybody all right in there?"

"We're fine," Emily replied. "Ready to go."

Bess straightened and nodded to Ace. "All right. Take the coach out."

He made sure the brake lever wasn't engaged, lifted the reins, and slapped them lightly against the backs of the team as he called out, "Hyaaahh!"

The horses were experienced and knew what to do. They moved ahead at a walk, leaning against their harness, and the coach lurched into motion.

Bess rocked back and forth on the driver's seat but steadied herself by gripping the brass rail at the side of it. "A little tighter on the reins next time, but that wasn't a bad start. Now turn left and take us out of town. We'll head out on the mine road. It's nice and flat and straight."

"The flatter and straighter the better," Ace muttered under his breath as he hauled the team around and sent them trotting out of Palisade.

Chapter Twelve

From the town to the base of the mountain where Samuel Eagleton's Golden Dome Mine was located was only about a mile. The road was fairly wide and very hard packed from the hundreds of ore wagons that had rolled over it.

Ace had always had the knack of picking up new skills pretty quickly, so he didn't have much trouble guiding the stagecoach team along the route. He started feeling comfortable within half a mile.

"You're a good driver," Bess told him. "The horses respond well to you."

"Thanks."

"Watch the reins, though. You're still a little loose with them. Not too tight, though, or the horses will start to fight you."

Ace modified his grip on the reins as the coach continued rolling toward the mountain. It swayed some, but it was designed to do that. The leather thoroughbraces had to have some give to them to absorb the bumps from the rough places in the road.

"What about the damage that avalanche did to the trail below the pass?" Ace asked. "Will the coach be able to get through?"

"I think so," Bess replied. "It'll be a narrow squeeze in a few places but it won't be like that for long. Mr. Eagleton will have his men out repairing it. They may already be doing that. It wouldn't surprise me a bit. He has to be able to get his gold wagons out."

"The way you've talked about him, the fella must be as rich as old King Midas."

"He's rich, all right. No telling how many tons of ore he's taken out of the Golden Dome, and it's pretty high-grade, too, from what I've heard."

"And yet he wants to ruin your father and take over the stagecoach line."

"It doesn't make a lot of sense," Bess agreed. "But I guess when you're used to having that much money and power, you don't like it when people say no to you."

Ace chuckled. "I wouldn't know. I've never been rich *or* powerful. So I never really had to worry about it. Give me a good horse and somewhere to go, and I'm happy."

"In other words, you're a saddle tramp."

"Chance and I have been called that," Ace admitted. "I like to think we just have restless natures."

"Emily's more restless than I am," Bess said. "I think she'd like to drift around like you and your brother do. Women aren't really allowed to do that, though. We're expected to stay in one place and make a home."

"Well, not many of 'em drive stagecoaches or ride shotgun, either," Ace pointed out. "There ought to be room for all kinds of folks in the world."

"It's a nice thought." Bess pointed ahead of them. "See that wide place in the road? You're going to turn around there. Think you're up to it?"

"I'll give it my best try," Ace promised.

Inside the coach, Chance rode in the seat facing backward while Emily sat on the forward-facing seat with the picnic basket beside her. He would have preferred sitting side by side with her, but she'd told him to sit across from her and he didn't think it was a good idea to argue with her.

It was always better to make a gal think what he was doing was her idea, not his.

He patted the smooth wooden stock of the coach gun across his knees and asked, "Have you ever had to use one of these?"

"What do you mean? I've fired a shotgun plenty of times."

"At somebody who was trying to shoot you?"

"Well . . . no," she said, glaring at him. "But you don't exactly look like Wild Bill Hickok to me. How many shoot-outs have *you* been in?"

"Ace and I shot at those fellas who were trying to run you off the road a couple of days ago," he pointed out.

"Yes, but they were shooting at us, not you."

"They fired back at us. Didn't come close, but still, they were shooting."

"You know what I mean. Just how many showdowns have you been in, anyway?"

"A few," Chance said. "More than I like to think about. And more than I like to talk about."

That was true, and for once he was serious. He and Ace had been in some shooting scrapes. They had come through all right every time—so far— but Chance hadn't forgotten the heart-pounding experiences. It hadn't been fear, really, that made his heart race, although he didn't believe anybody could face up to being shot at without experiencing even a trace of fear. Nor was it excitement. Mainly, he thought, it was the fact that everything went so damn *fast*. Usually, there wasn't time to be too scared or too excited. He just had to act on instinct. See the threat, react, the crash of guns going off, tighten muscles in anticipation of the smash of a bullet—and then it was over. Gun smoke drifted in the air and bodies lay sprawled on the ground and pumped out blood. Struggle to grasp the concept that *he was still alive . . .*

"What's wrong with you?" Emily asked, breaking into Chance's thoughts. "You looked like you just wandered off into the wilderness."

"Sorry." He put his usual smile back on his face. "I was just thinking about what's in that picnic basket. What have you brought for us to eat?"

"Fried chicken and rolls and a jug of buttermilk. Nothing fancy like what I'm sure you're used to."

"Don't be so certain of that. I like to dress well, but Ace and I are a far cry from having a lot of money. It's hard to earn much when we're always on the drift like we are."

Emily leaned back against the seat. "I think I'd like to do that. Ride around and see some new places. Pa moved our family a lot when Bess and I were growing up, but that's different. When you're a kid you don't have any choice where you go. Your parents decide that for you. You're lucky that—" She stopped short. "Oh, hell."

"Lucky we never knew our parents and were raised by a shiftless gambler?"

"That's not what I meant. Well, not exactly that way. But you have to admit, your lives have been a lot more carefree than ours."

Chance shrugged. "I reckon so." *And more lonely, too.*

Before they could continue the conversation, the coach slowed.

Chance looked out the window. "Now what are we doing?"

"Turning around, I'd guess. Bess must be confident that your brother can handle the team all right. It's time for him to try something else."

"Like what?"

"Timberline Pass," Emily said.

"You want me to what?" Ace asked.

"Drive through the pass and down the mountain into the valley," Bess said.

Ace stared at her as he sat on the driver's box next to her. He had swung the coach around without any trouble in the wide spot in the road she had indicated, then brought it to a stop.

"This is the first time I've ever driven a stagecoach, and you want me to take it down that road with all those hairpin turns."

"We need to check out the damage from the avalanche, like you mentioned earlier. And do you really think driving back and forth a few more times between here and town would prepare you better? The next run to Bleak Creek is the day after tomorrow. We need to find out now if you'll be ready."

What Bess said made sense, Ace supposed, although he still thought the idea of driving down the mountainside over that twisting road was pretty daunting. It would certainly be easier, though, with her sitting right beside him to show him the ropes.

He sighed. "All right." Then he got the team moving again.

It didn't take long to reach Palisade and drive through the settlement. As they approached Timberline Pass, Ace looked out through the gap and saw the valley spread before them. The mountains on the other side of the valley, ten miles away, were easily visible in the clear air. And the distance down to the valley floor was a little breathtaking.

Chance stuck his head out one of the coach windows and raised his voice. "Wait a minute. Are we really going down there?"

"We are," Bess told him.

"Then maybe Emily and I should, uh, get out first . . . Oof!"

Emily took hold of the back of his coat and pulled him away from the window. "Quit being such a baby. We'll be fine."

Up on the box, Ace said, "Chance is just a little nervous. So am I, to be honest."

"Just take it slow and easy and you'll be all right."

Ace drove through the gap between two of the giant slabs of rock that resembled palisades and gave the nearby settlement its name. The ground slanted down under the stagecoach's wheels. His instinct was to reach for the brake lever, but he knew the slope wasn't steep enough to need it yet so he resisted the impulse.

The road followed a gentle curve that brought it around a shoulder of the mountain and into the route that zigged and zagged back and forth down to the valley.

"It's not as bad as I thought it would be," he said after a few minutes.

"It'll get worse," Bess told him. "Feel the way the weight of the coach is making it move a little faster?"

"Yeah, I think so."

"Pull the brake lever back and slow us down a little . . . Now release it. Use it when you have to keep us about this same speed."

As they neared the first of the hairpin turns, Ace asked, "Now what do I do?"

"Use the brake and slow down a little more. You can see that there's plenty of room for the team and the coach to turn."

Ace supposed she was right about that, but with

so much empty air looming only a few feet away, the space available to make the turn probably seemed a lot smaller than it really was. To Ace's inexperienced eyes, it looked like he had no room for error at all.

"All right, start turning the team," Bess told him.

Carefully, he pulled on the reins and brought the horses' heads around enough that they began to turn. With the thoroughbraces creaking, the coach followed. Ace held his breath as he felt the vehicle's momentum shift, but it stayed solidly where it was supposed to be on the trail and as the team straightened out again, he relaxed slightly.

"Good job," Bess said. "A little brake now. It's all a matter of getting the feel for it."

As he drove, Ace mostly kept his eyes on the road in front of him, rather than looking out at the valley falling away so dramatically, but he couldn't keep himself from glancing in that direction occasionally. He thought about how Bess had taken the coach down the same road at such a breakneck pace a few days earlier.

"You must have been really scared when those fellas ambushed you and the team ran away," he said.

She shook her head. "Wasn't time to be scared. I was more concerned with keeping the wheels on the road. I knew the horses would do what I told them. As long as the brake didn't burn up or

bust, I figured we could make it. And we did."
She smiled. "Emily probably wouldn't admit it,
but I think she was pretty scared. But that's
because all she had to do was hang on. I was too
busy to worry much."

"I guess that's the secret to a lot of things. Just
stay busy."

Ace made the next turn with no trouble. The
road got a little steeper, so he had to use the brake
more often, but as Bess had said, he began to
develop a feel for it. He glanced over at her, and
she nodded in approval.

From time to time as they descended, he looked
up at the slope looming above them. Today
wasn't a regularly scheduled stagecoach run, so
he thought it wasn't very likely Eagleton's hired
killers would be up there trying to start another
avalanche. They would have had to spot the
coach going back through the settlement, figured
out where it was headed, and followed them.
That certainly wasn't impossible, but Ace
thought the risk was small.

"How many turns are there?" he asked. "I never
thought to count them the other day."

"Ten," Bess replied. "You're almost halfway
there."

The thoroughbraces, the wheels, and the
horses' hooves made a surprising amount of
noise, so it was hard to hear much over them.
After the next turn, however, Ace heard what he

thought sounded like men's voices somewhere below them.

Bess heard them, too, and frowned slightly. "That might be a work crew Mr. Eagleton sent down to repair the road."

"Will we be able to get past them?" Ace asked.

"There are a few places where the road is wide enough for a vehicle to get over and let another one past, but not many. I suppose a coach and a wagon might be able to scrape past each other on a turn, but that would be pretty nerve-wracking for whoever was on the outside."

It made Ace feel a little cold and clammy just to think about it. He hoped the situation wouldn't come to that and mused that maybe Bess hadn't quite thought through all the things that could go wrong with this practice run. . . .

He saw a large work wagon make the next turn down and start up toward them.

"Oh, shoot," Bess muttered beside him.

Ace reached for the brake lever without being told. Careful not to haul too hard on it, he brought the stagecoach to a halt. About fifty yards ahead, the burly driver of the work wagon had stopped, too, looking up at them in anger and surprise.

The two vehicles faced each other, headed in opposite directions with no place to go.

Chapter Thirteen

After glaring at them for a moment, the man on the wagon seat bellowed, "Get that damn stagecoach out of the way!" He was tall and broadshouldered, built like a tree, with a bullet-shaped bald head that looked like it had been blistered by the sun numerous times in the past.

"That's Horace Wygant, the foreman at Mr. Eagleton's mine," Bess said quietly to Ace. "I guess Mr. Eagleton put him in charge of repairing the road."

"Did you hear me?" Wygant demanded harshly. He waved an arm. "Get out of the way!"

"I'm sorry, Mr. Wygant," Bess called to him. "There's nowhere for us to go. I think you can back down to the turn without much trouble. We can get by you there."

"I thought you said that would be pretty risky," Ace murmured.

"It will be, but I'll take the reins. You and Chance and Emily can get off the stage so you won't be in any danger. I can make it."

Ace didn't like that idea, but he wasn't fond of the notion of trying to drive past the work wagon on that turn, either. Bess had a lot more experience handling the stagecoach than he did, so it made sense for her to take over the reins. It still rubbed him the wrong way, despite the logic of it.

The question might be moot, though, as Wygant sneered at them. "I'm not backing up. Once I start somewhere, I keep going."

From inside the coach, Emily called, "What's the problem out there? Why are we stopped?"

"I'm taking care of it," Bess told her sister.

Ace wasn't sure that was the case. Wygant struck him as the sort of man who wouldn't be easy to budge but figured he would give it a try. "Look, mister, be reasonable. We can't turn around or back up. You can."

"I can get some men up here to shove that damn stagecoach off the road, too," Wygant snapped. "I told you to get out of my way, and I meant it."

One of the coach doors opened and the vehicle shifted as Chance stepped out with the short-barreled shotgun tucked under his arm. "I reckon anybody who wants to wreck this stage will have a hard time making it up the trail."

Ace bit back a groan. He didn't blame Chance for being angry, but the show of defiance would just make Wygant dig in his heels, most likely.

That was exactly the reaction Wygant displayed. He twisted on the wagon seat and shouted down to the lower section of trail. "Hey! Some of you men get up here! We've got a problem!"

Bess said nervously, "This isn't good. Everybody who works for Mr. Eagleton knows about the problems we've had with him. They can curry favor with him by causing trouble for the stagecoach line."

"We'll just have to put a stop to that," Ace said, sounding more confident than he felt. He and Chance could hold their own in a brawl, but if they were outnumbered by burly mine workers, the outcome wouldn't be in much doubt, and it wouldn't favor them.

On the other hand, they had that coach gun in Chance's hands to help even the odds. The problem with that was the law considered gunning down unarmed men to be murder, no matter what the odds. That was especially true when the law in Palisade was firmly in Samuel Eagleton's pocket.

Half a dozen men almost as big and burly as Wygant stalked around the turn carrying shovels and pickaxes. They may have come out to repair the road, but they were well-equipped for causing trouble, too.

Ace handed the reins to Bess. "Stay on the coach." Before she could stop him, he vaulted down to the ground, landing lithely next to Chance.

Without leaving the wagon seat, Wygant gestured toward the coach and told his men, "Get that damn stagecoach off the road so I can go past."

The workers didn't hesitate. They strode past the wagon and started up the sloping trail toward the stagecoach.

"Should I fire a load of buckshot over their heads?" Chance asked.

As far as Ace could see, none of the men were armed with guns, but he spotted the barrel of a Winchester sticking up from the floorboard of the wagon next to Wygant. He figured if Chance fired the coach gun, the foreman would use it as an excuse to grab the rifle and blaze away at them. "Not yet. Don't fire unless you absolutely have to. Let's see how they like looking down the barrels of that scattergun."

Chance lifted the shotgun and snugged the butt against his shoulder as he pointed it at the workers. His face was cold and grim. Beside him, Ace rested his hand meaningfully on the butt of his holstered Colt.

The threat was enough to make the men stop, at least for the moment. It was difficult for any man to walk right up to the gaping muzzles of a double-barreled shotgun.

One of the workers looked back over his shoulder at the wagon. "Horace, I don't know about this."

"For God's sake. They're not going to shoot you!" Wygant raged. "That'd be cold-blooded murder."

"Looks more like self-defense to me," Ace said.

"When you start attacking people with picks and shovels, you can expect to get shot."

Wygant sneered at him. "I reckon you're right, kid." He paused as an ugly grin spread across his face. "Throw those tools down, boys. You can handle 'em with fists!"

Ace bit back a curse. Wygant was right. He and Chance would be outnumbered three to one, with their opponents being men who spent their days swinging sledgehammers in a mine. He and Chance were doomed to lose the battle. But if they cut loose with their guns, it would be murder.

Eagleton's men knew that, and grinning like their foreman, they tossed the picks and shovels to the ground and charged up the slope toward the stagecoach.

"Chance!" Emily called from the driver's seat where she had climbed to join Bess. "Throw me the gun!"

Chance turned and tossed the coach gun up to her. Emily caught it, turned it so the barrels were facing the charging workmen, and told Ace and Chance, "Get down!"

"Look out!" one of the men exclaimed as they suddenly slowed. "That crazy Corcoran girl's got the gun now!"

"Crazy is right," Emily snapped. She fired over the heads of the horses as Ace and Chance dived to the ground.

The load of buckshot tore into the ground right

in front of the workmen, making them stumble and run into each other as they tried to throw the brakes on their charge. Ace came up on one knee and saw Wygant standing up on the wagon's box, raising the Winchester.

Ace was at a bad angle, but he drew and fired anyway, the Colt leaping into his hand with blinding speed. The bullet angled up and struck Wygant in the left shoulder, twisting him around as he pulled the trigger. The two shots came so close together they almost sounded like one, but Ace had gotten his bullet in first, forcing Wygant's shot to go wild. The rifle slug plowed harmlessly into the mountainside.

Wygant dropped the Winchester, clutched his shoulder, and collapsed on the wagon seat. The workers milled around in front of the wagon, the momentum of their charge blunted by the coach gun blast.

"You men know me!" Emily told them. Her voice was shrill with anger. "You force my hand and I'll blow you all to hell!"

"You'll hang if you do!" one of the men shouted back at her. A few of them started to edge forward.

"You really think a jury would hang a woman who defended herself against six men, even in Eagleton's town? I'll take my chances." She laughed coldly. "Anyway, even if I swing, you'll be too dead to see it!"

From the wagon seat, Wygant growled weakly, "Damn it, you idiots. I'm hurt! I need to get to the doc before I bleed to death."

"Then back down to the turn so we can get by," Ace hollered, "and you can be on your way." He gestured with the Colt in his hand to emphasize the point.

The pain Wygant was in trumped his natural belligerence. "One of you come take the reins and move this wagon."

"But Horace—"

"Now, damn it!"

One of the men went to the wagon and climbed up onto the seat. Wygant grimaced as he slid over to make room. The workman reached down to pick up the reins as the others retrieved the tools they had thrown down.

While they filed past the wagon on foot, their comrade carefully backed the vehicle toward the turn. The wagon team was composed of mules, and they weren't very cooperative. After a lot of cussing, the man finally got the wagon to the turn and then back around it.

"That's far enough," Bess called. "Stay right where you are. I can get the coach past." She turned to Emily. "You climb down, just in case."

"The hell I will," Emily replied. "I'm staying right here where I've got a good vantage point to use this gun if I need to. Let the boys walk. It'll be safer for them."

Chance frowned. "Hey, nobody asked for any favors from you."

"Good, because I'm not the sort of person who grants them most of the time," the blonde said.

"I'm starting to get that idea."

"We'll cover your back," Ace said, to end the bickering between Chance and Emily as much as anything.

Chance had drawn the Lightning from his shoulder holster, and Ace didn't think the workers would challenge the two revolvers, especially as long as Emily held the coach gun. The brief flurry of gunplay seemed to have knocked the fight out of Eagleton's men.

Bess flapped the reins, called out to the team, and got the coach moving again. She drove past Ace and Chance, who fell in behind but had no trouble keeping up because Bess had to take it slow and cautious as she drove down the slope toward the turn.

Horace Wygant's cursing was a monotonous drone that floated up from the lower stretch of road.

When Bess reached the turn, she eased the coach around it. Emily sat tensely beside her, shotgun still raised. She hadn't replaced the shell she'd fired earlier, but she still had a lethal load of buckshot in the weapon. She kept it pointed in the general direction of Eagleton's men.

The wagon hugged the mountainside just

beyond the turn, leaving just enough room for the coach to scrape past on the outside. The wagon's sideboards and the coach literally scraped. The coach's outer wheels were no more than four inches from the edge of the trail. With the brink that close, Ace held his breath until the coach was past the wagon and Bess was able to swing it away from the edge a couple feet.

She brought the coach to a halt and turned on the seat. "How does the road look down below, Mr. Wygant? Did the avalanche do much damage?"

"You're asking me that?" Wygant said through clenched teeth. "You can fall off the damn mountain for all I care!" He fixed his angry glare on Ace. "You shot me, kid. I'm not going to forget that."

"Don't make me sorry I tried not to kill you," Ace said.

From the box, Emily said, "You two get on here. We've wasted enough time."

She kept the shotgun trained on Wygant and the other men while Ace and Chance climbed into the coach. The idea of Ace taking the coach down from the pass into the valley was forgotten for the moment. Bess got the team moving again and they left Wygant and the others behind.

As they reached the lower sections of road they saw that Wygant's crew had cleared away the dirt and rocks left behind by the avalanche.

Here and there, a boulder had knocked a chunk out of the edge of the road, but the path was still wide enough for the coach to get by. Bess kept the team moving, working the reins and the brake with an expert's touch until the coach finally rolled onto the level ground at the base of the slope.

Bess brought it to a stop. Ace and Chance climbed out to find Emily holding her sister and patting her on the back while Bess shuddered.

Emily glanced down at the brothers. "She's not really as icy-nerved as she acts sometimes."

"But you are," Chance said. "I really believed you were willing to blow holes in all those varmints."

"That's because I was. Anybody who threatens me or my sister deserves whatever they get, including a load of buckshot."

Bess straightened up and took a deep breath. "I'm all right now."

"You sure?" Emily asked.

"Yes. I just had to let my nerves settle down for a minute."

"All right." Emily broke open the shotgun, replaced the spent shell with a fresh one from her pocket, and snapped the weapon closed. "Now, how about we find a good place for that picnic?"

Chapter Fourteen

Joe Buckhorn's room was on the same floor of the hotel as his employer's suite, right across the hall, in fact. He was always at Eagleton's beck and call, twenty-four hours a day, and was never far from the mining magnate.

Eagleton had a bellpull in the suite that alerted the hotel cook down in the kitchen whenever he was ready for breakfast, which was usually in the early afternoon. The boss had a habit of sleeping late, especially when the lovely Rose Demarcus had visited him the night before.

Until that summons came, Buckhorn was free to sit in the hotel lobby or drink coffee in the dining room or have Rose send over one of her girls, but he always went up with the waiter who carried Eagleton's breakfast tray and got his orders for the day.

He was in the lobby, reading a two-week-old Denver newspaper. He had learned to read at the reservation school before he was old enough to understand just how much his people despised him because of his white blood. Once that realization sunk in, he had left to make his way in the white man's world, only to discover that he was equally hated there because of the Indian blood in his veins. It didn't help in either place that he was big and ugly and mean.

If everybody was going to hate him anyway, he could stop worrying about it, he'd decided, and just got tougher and meaner and good with a gun. The people who valued those skills—like Samuel Eagleton—didn't give a damn about his ancestry. All they cared about was how good he was at killing people they wanted dead.

A bit of commotion in the street made Buckhorn glance up from the newspaper and look out through the hotel's big front windows. A wagon rolled past in the street carrying two men. One of them was Horace Wygant, the mine foreman. His bald, bullet-shaped head was unmistakable. He was also the only hombre in these parts who was almost as big and mean as Buckhorn himself.

Wygant didn't look tough at the moment, though. He huddled on the wagon seat while the other man handled the team of mules. Wygant clutched his left shoulder where his shirt displayed a large, dark bloodstain.

That looked like a gunshot wound to Buckhorn. He had seen plenty of them, so he ought to know.

He frowned. Before going to bed last night the boss had left orders for Wygant to take a crew out to Timberline Pass and check the road down to the valley for damage from the avalanche—an avalanche, Buckhorn had thought wryly at the time, that some of Eagleton's own hired guns had caused in an attempt to wreck the stagecoach.

Sometimes he wondered just how much the boss thought things through. He would never express that thought to anyone, of course.

It baffled him who could have shot Wygant, so he put the paper aside, stood up, and went outside. The wagon had drawn to a stop in front of the office of Dr. Josiah Truax, and the workman was helping the injured Wygant down from the vehicle.

"Wygant, what the hell happened to you?" Buckhorn asked.

"What the hell does it look like?" the foreman snapped. He and Buckhorn had never gotten along well.

"It looks like you've been shot, but you were out working on the road. Who'd want to take a shot at you for doing that?"

"It's none of your damn business, 'breed," Wygant snarled, "but it was one of those Jensen boys. You know, the ones who've been sniffing around Corcoran's girls and taking their side."

Buckhorn nodded. He recalled the Jensen brothers from the confrontation in the hotel the previous night. Their names were Ace and Chance, he remembered. Stupid names.

"Which one?" he asked.

"How the hell should I know?" Wygant

groaned. "Help me inside, damn it. This blasted shoulder is killin' me!"

Buckhorn lifted a hand "Wait a minute. Why would one of the Jensens shoot you?"

"They were going down the mountain road in Corcoran's other stagecoach. Don't ask me why. I started up in the wagon and met them just past one of the turns. They wanted me to back up so they could get past."

"And you didn't want to do that."

"Hell, no! I know how the boss feels about that bunch. He wouldn't want any of us backing down from them."

"So what happened?"

Wygant was a little pale, probably from loss of blood along with the pain he was in, but he said, "That crazy blond girl Emily Corcoran took a shot at us with a coach gun. Then the Jensen kid winged me. We didn't have any choice but to back off. They would have killed somebody if we hadn't."

Buckhorn nodded slowly. He understood. Wygant and his crews, for all their toughness, were miners and construction men. They weren't killers. They weren't skilled in gunplay.

That took a special sort of man.

Evidently the Jensen brothers fell into that category. That didn't surprise Buckhorn. He'd been able to tell by looking at them that they were young but not green. They would be dangerous enemies if he ever had to face off against them.

He would remember that.

Buckhorn gestured toward the door of the doctor's office and told the other man, "All right. Take him on in there and get Doc Truax to patch him up. And tell the doc to send the bill to the boss."

"Damn right he will," Wygant muttered as he made his unsteady way into the doctor's office with the other man helping him.

Buckhorn turned around to head back to the hotel. Eagleton would be getting up soon, and he would want a report on what had happened out on the road. He didn't like to be kept in the dark about anything.

Buckhorn hadn't taken more than a step when he spotted Rose Demarcus coming along the boardwalk toward him. He stopped short, and his left hand lifted to pinch the brim of his bowler hat respectfully.

"Why, hello, Joseph." She was dressed in an expensive dark blue suit with the jacket cinched tight around her slender waist.

Buckhorn didn't doubt that her waist was so trim because she was laced into a whalebone corset, and the image that thought planted in his head made his heart thump a little harder.

Rose's hair was piled up on her head in an elaborate arrangement of curls, and a hat that matched the suit was perched on it. A little feather stuck up from the hat. She looked elegant and lovely and any man who looked at her was going to have a hard time taking his eyes off her.

Joe Buckhorn was no exception to that.

He found his tongue and said, "Good afternoon, Miss Demarcus. You weren't looking for the boss, were you? I don't know if he's awake yet."

"No, I'm just out doing a little shopping." With a little frown, she asked, "Was that Horace Wygant I saw being helped into the doctor's office just now?"

"Yes, ma'am."

"Is he all right?"

Buckhorn hesitated. He wasn't sure he ought to mention the incident on the mountain road to anyone else before he reported it to the boss . . . but it was Rose asking. What man could fail to tell her whatever it was she wanted to know?

"He was wounded in a little shooting scrape out on the road from Timberline Pass down into the valley." Although there was no real justification for it, he added, "I reckon he'll probably be all right."

"Well, I'm glad to hear that, I suppose. I'm not all that fond of Mr. Wygant—he's gotten upset and caused trouble a time or two in my house— but I don't like to see harm come to any of Samuel's employees. To be honest, I'd be much more troubled if you were hurt."

"I, uh, appreciate that, ma'am."

"You can call me Rose, you know. At least when it's just the two of us like this."

He wasn't sure if she was teasing and flirting with him or if she was sincere. Either way, he knew he had to tread carefully. He didn't want to do anything improper that would get back to the boss. Rose Demarcus was Eagleton's woman, and he wouldn't stand for anyone messing with her, certainly not his own bodyguard. His *half-breed* bodyguard.

"I appreciate that, too, ma'am, but—"

"I mean, we're friends, aren't we?" she interrupted.

"Sure. I guess. The boss might not care for it, though. He won't put up with anybody not showing you the proper respect."

The smile that curved her red lips held a touch of cynical bitterness in it. "I run a brothel in a mining town, Joseph. As long as I get paid, that's all the respect I'm entitled to."

"Now, I wouldn't say that—"

"Samuel would. But the last thing I want to do is cause a problem between the two of you, so you can go on calling me ma'am or Miss Demarcus or whatever you want. Just don't forget that I consider you a friend." With that she moved past him and went on down the boardwalk toward the general store.

Buckhorn turned to watch her go. Most of the

155

men she passed tipped their hats to her from a combination of her own beauty and the common knowledge that she was Samuel Eagleton's kept woman. Nobody wanted to offend the man who owned pretty much the whole town.

The women Rose passed didn't acknowledge her presence. To them, her relationship with Eagleton didn't matter as much. She was still a lady of the night.

Seeing that made Buckhorn feel a pang of sympathy. Both of them were outsiders, he thought. With Rose, it was a matter of choice rather than birth, but the end result was pretty much the same.

Folks were willing to pay them for the things they were good at—but that didn't mean they would ever be anything except gutter trash to most people.

Buckhorn sighed, tried to put that thought out of his mind, and went to see if the boss was awake yet.

Bess parked the stagecoach under some aspens that grew along the creek bank, and Emily took a blanket from the basket to spread on the ground so she could set out the food.

As the four of them sat on the blanket and ate and talked, Ace couldn't deny that it was mighty pleasant. The fact that not even an hour earlier they had been shooting guns and nearly fighting for their lives seemed far away in the idyllic surroundings.

"I almost feel guilty for relaxing and enjoying myself," Bess said. "There's been so much trouble lately. . . ."

"That's the best time to forget about it," Chance told her. "You can't do anything about it right now, can you?"

"Well . . . no more than what I'm already doing, helping the two of you get ready to take over the Bleak Creek run."

"There you go," he said with a grin. "You're doing what you can. Don't worry about the rest of it."

Emily said, "Telling Bess not to worry is like telling a dog not to bark. It just comes naturally to her."

"Don't you ever worry about anything?" Ace asked her.

"Sure I do," Emily replied with a shrug. "But if it's not something I can fix, I try not to think about it. That just seems like a waste of time and energy to me."

Bess said, "You can't fix everything with a load of buckshot from a coach gun."

"Maybe not, but it's a good start."

Ace and Chance laughed. Bess frowned at them for a second, then chuckled as well.

"What's funny about that?" Emily demanded. "I believe in simple solutions. Solutions don't come much more simple than buckshot."

"I don't reckon anybody could argue with that," Ace said.

"Not unless he wanted his rear end dusted," Chance added with a grin.

Emily rolled her eyes, shook her head, and reached for the jug of buttermilk, which she had kept cool on the trip out by wrapping it in several layers of wet cloth.

When they had finished the meal, Ace dug a hole with his knife and buried the chicken bones while Emily packed up everything else in the basket. She and Chance got back inside the coach and Ace and Bess resumed their places on the driver's seat.

Bess handed the reins to Ace. "All right. Take us back to Palisade."

He looked at the mountains looming above them and the road leading to Timberline Pass and felt a little trepidation but didn't let that show. He flicked the reins against the team's rumps and got the horses moving.

Going back up the road was slower but much easier in a way because he didn't have to worry about using the brake. The coach's own weight made the going difficult enough. The slower pace meant that the turns were easier, too.

"You're doing fine," Bess assured him.

"I didn't get to finish driving all the way down," Ace reminded her.

"No, but you did well enough that I'm confident you can handle the team and the coach . . . as long as nothing unusual happens."

"And if it does, I'll do the best I can."

"Just don't wreck this coach. It's the only one we have left. If anything happened to it, that really would be the end. Pa would just have to give up."

"He couldn't afford to buy another coach?"

Bess shook her head. "Not even a chance."

From inside the coach came a question. "Did I hear my name?"

"No, just go back to whatever you were doing," Ace told him. To Bess, he said, "Does anybody keep an eye on the coach while it's parked in the barn?"

"Well, Nate does. But we haven't really been guarding it—" She paused. "We should, shouldn't we?"

"You'd be out of business without it. If Eagleton had somebody burn down the barn with the stagecoach in it, that would take care of his problem."

"He'd never do that," Bess declared. "It would be too dangerous, not just to our operation but to the whole town. A fire like that could spread and burn Palisade to the ground."

Ace nodded. "I reckon you're right about that. But he could try something else to disable the coach. For that matter, he could have his men steal your horses. You can't have a stage line without horses."

"I'll talk to Pa when we get back. I think the world of Nate, but I'm not sure he could stop anybody who got in there and tried to do mischief."

"Well, you've got Chance and me sleeping up in the hayloft now," Ace pointed out. "That'll make it a lot harder for anybody to try anything funny. We can take turns staying awake and standing guard."

"Emily and I can help, too."

"What are you volunteering me to do?" Emily called from inside the coach.

"I'll tell you when we get back," Bess replied.

It wouldn't be long now, Ace saw. They had just reached Timberline Pass. He was glad to have the steep road and the hairpin turns behind them, urged the team to a slightly faster pace, and headed for Palisade.

Chapter Fifteen

Buckhorn waited for the boss to get some coffee down, then explained about seeing Horace Wygant being helped into the doctor's office. Eagleton's face got redder than usual as he listened to the story.

When Buckhorn was finished, Eagleton asked, "How badly was Wygant hurt?"

"I don't really know, boss," the gunfighter replied. "He was shot through the shoulder and it looked like he'd lost a considerable amount of blood. I don't reckon he'll die unless he comes down with blood poisoning or some such, but he's bound to be laid up for quite a while."

Eagleton was as angry as Buckhorn had expected him to be. He slammed his fist down on the table hard enough to make the china and silverware on his breakfast tray jump and rattle. "Damn it! I need him out at the mine. I can't afford to have him hurt like this." His eyes narrowed. "You say one of the Jensens shot him?"

"That's what he told me. I didn't see it happen."

"Which one?"

"He doesn't know their names."

Eagleton waved a meaty hand in a slashing, dismissive motion. "It doesn't matter, does it? They're both troublemakers. I know that, and I haven't even laid eyes on them."

Buckhorn nodded. "I reckon you're right about that, boss."

Eagleton slurped down some more coffee and frowned in thought for a moment. "What in blazes was the stagecoach doing out there, anyway? The next run to Bleak Creek isn't until tomorrow."

Buckhorn had given that very question some thought while he'd waited for Eagleton to wake

161

up, and he believed that he had arrived at the answer. "I think those Jensen boys have gone to work for Corcoran. They're going to take over the stagecoach runs. They took the coach out today so Bess and Emily could show them the ropes. That's the only thing that makes any sense to me."

"We can't have that." Eagleton was still angry, but he wasn't as flushed and furious as he'd been. A cold and calculating look appeared on the mining magnate's beefy face. "Brian Corcoran is ready to give up. I don't want him to have any reason to hope. If the Jensens took the stagecoach out for a practice run, they'll be coming back to town." He picked up a roll and began buttering it. Without looking up from what he was doing, he went on, "Go out to the pass, wait until they come back, and kill them."

Buckhorn stood there for a long moment, breathing evenly as he digested that order. Then he said, "I thought my job was keeping you safe, boss."

"Your job is doing whatever the hell it is I tell you to do," Eagleton snapped. He took a bite of the butter-slathered roll and started chewing.

Buckhorn drew in a breath and blew it out through his nose. "What about the Corcoran girls?"

"What about them?"

"If they're with the stagecoach, do I kill them, too?"

Eagleton considered the question for a moment, then shook his head.

"Those two dying in an accident is one thing. Gunning them down is another. I still have to live here and do business here. Murdering women could make that more difficult, especially if any evidence led back to me. So, no, don't shoot them. Just the Jensen brothers. Nobody's going to give a damn about a couple dead saddle tramps."

The boss was probably right about that, Buckhorn mused. Eagleton had a good sense of what he could get away with and what he couldn't.

The gunman nodded. "All right. You want me to send one of the boys up here before I leave?"

Eagleton shook his head. "No, just make sure a couple of them are down in the lobby. I'm not expecting any trouble, but there's no point in not being careful."

Buckhorn nodded and swung around to leave.

"Joe," Eagleton said to his back, "don't mess this up. I'm close to getting what I want, and those damn Jensens aren't going to ruin my plans."

"Sure, boss," Buckhorn agreed automatically, but he didn't actually know exactly what Eagleton's plans were or why it was so important for him to take over Corcoran's stagecoach line.

But that didn't matter. The money Eagleton paid him did.

• • •

The added speed made the coach lurch a little as it hit a bump emerging from the pass, and Ace swayed back and forth on the seat. He felt something whip through the air next to his ear and knew instinctively that it was a bullet.

He reacted instantly as he realized someone was shooting at him. Knowing a target was harder to hit the faster it moved, he slashed the horses with the reins and shouted at them. It caused them to break into a gallop, which threw Bess back against the top of the coach.

She grabbed the seat to steady herself and exclaimed, "What are you doing? What's wrong?" She didn't know about the shot and thought he'd gone crazy.

"Ambush!" he told her. "Keep your head down!"

A bullet spanged off the brass rail at the side of the driver's seat, inches away from him. The rifleman was good, whoever he was. Ace knew he'd be dead if luck—and a bump in the road—hadn't made him sway to the side just when he did.

Chance and Emily both shouted questions from inside the coach. Ace ignored them. He had to concentrate on his driving. He hadn't had the team going anywhere near as fast. He hauled on the reins to force them to one side of the road, then veered back the other way, to make it more difficult for the rifleman to draw a bead on them.

The wind plucked his hat off his head and it dangled at the back of his neck, hanging by its chin strap.

He spotted a muzzle flash in a clump of pine trees just to the right of the road about fifty yards ahead. "Chance!" he yelled. "Bushwhacker in the trees to the right up ahead!"

"I'll get him!" Chance called back.

Ace felt the coach shift as his brother leaned out the window.

Chance's Lightning barked as he peppered the trees with bullets.

It would be pure luck if one of those slugs found the bushwhacker, but Ace was more interested in forcing the hidden gunman to keep his head down. He had no way of knowing whether Chance's shots were accomplishing that, other than the fact that he was still alive.

As the coach flashed past the pines, Emily's coach gun boomed from inside the vehicle. She was at the other window on the same side, joining in the fight.

That came as no surprise to Ace, but he was a little taken aback when Bess hauled the old revolver from the holster at her waist, twisted around on the seat so she could aim behind his back, and opened fire on the trees as well.

With that much lead coming his way, the bushwhacker must have hunted some cover as Ace didn't hear any more shots come from the pines, although it was hard to be sure. The horses' hooves were thundering loudly on the hard-packed road.

The hammer of Bess's gun fell on an empty chamber. She said, "Do you think we got him?"

"I don't know, but the important thing is that he didn't get us!" Ace hoped that was true. "Better check on Emily and Chance!"

Bess twisted the other way on the seat and leaned over to call through the windows on the coach's left side, "Are you two all right in there?"

"We're fine!" Emily shouted in reply. "Were either of you hit?"

"No, we're all right." Bess looked at the road ahead of them and asked Ace, "Do you think there are any more?"

"I don't know. I'm going to keep the coach moving pretty fast until we get back to town, though, if that's all right."

She nodded. "The team can handle the pace. I'll keep an eye out for any more bushwhackers." She reloaded the revolver.

As fast as they were going, it didn't take long to reach the outskirts of Palisade. Ace slowed the stagecoach as they entered the settlement. Quite a few people were standing on the boardwalks, looking curiously in the coach's direction. They had either heard the shots or seen the big cloud of dust boiling up from the stagecoach's wheels and knew that something was wrong.

Ace headed straight for the stage line's barn. As he drew to a halt in front of it, Brian Corcoran and the old hostler Nate emerged from the barn.

"You been runnin' these horses," Nate said in an accusatory tone. He frowned at the sight of the foamy sweat flecking the animals' flanks.

"It's all right, Nate," Bess said. "Ace didn't have any choice. Somebody was shooting at us."

"Shooting!" her father echoed. "Good Lord! Are you and your sister all right?"

"We're fine, Pa," Emily said as she swung one of the coach doors open and stepped down to the ground. "The varmint took a few potshots at us, but he missed."

Emily didn't know how close that first bullet had come, Ace thought as he climbed down from the driver's box. He had a hollow feeling in the pit of his stomach from being aware of just how near death he had come.

"I don't want either of you girls leaving town until this is over," Corcoran said. "It's just too dangerous."

"How is it going to be over?" Emily wanted to know. "Do you really think Eagleton will give up? This won't stop until he gets what he wants—or he's dead."

"Don't talk like that," Corcoran snapped. "The answer isn't killing."

Eagleton obviously believed it was, Ace thought. He had no doubt that the mine owner

167

was behind this latest ambush attempt. Despite Corcoran hoping for a peaceful solution, Ace knew sometimes that just wasn't possible.

Sometimes there was just one answer to hot lead, and that was bullets of your own.

Buckhorn didn't stop cursing to himself until he got back to Palisade later that afternoon. He had ridden a long way around because he hadn't wanted to show up in town right after the failed ambush attempt on the stagecoach.

That Jensen boy who'd been driving the coach was the luckiest son of a gun Buckhorn had ever seen. He had drawn a good, steady bead on the kid's head with his Winchester and squeezed off the shot so smoothly that a miss was virtually impossible.

At least it would have been if the blasted coach hadn't rocked just then.

Even at that, Buckhorn knew he hadn't missed by more than a couple inches. Unfortunately, those inches were as good as a yard.

He cursed as he rode. The bullet burn on his cheek stung like blazes. The slug hadn't broken the skin, just scraped along his cheek and left a welt, but it was irritating. Not just from the pain, but also from the knowledge that one of the shots fired at him from the coach had come even closer to killing him than he had to killing Jensen!

It was an insult to his professionalism.

He came to the livery stable where he kept his horse, dismounted, and turned the animal over to the kid who worked there.

"What happened to your face, Mr. Buckhorn?" the youngster asked.

Buckhorn thought about telling him it was none of his damn business, but then he growled, "Ran into a low-hanging branch while I was riding."

The kid nodded in acceptance of that explanation. "That's too bad."

Buckhorn just grunted and stalked out of the barn.

Reaching the hotel, he went into the lobby. The pair of gunmen he'd left there stood up from their chairs.

Buckhorn asked, "Any trouble while I was gone?"

"Not a bit, Joe," one of them answered. "Well, there was some commotion in town earlier when the stage came in, but I don't really know what it was about."

"Doesn't matter," Buckhorn commented curtly. He went upstairs and knocked on the door of Eagleton's suite.

Eagleton called to him to come in. He was standing in front of a mirror tying a string tie around his thick neck. Looking in the glass at his gunman, he asked, "Is it taken care of?"

"No," Buckhorn answered bluntly. He was a

plainspoken man when he was angry, even when it was at his own expense. "I missed."

Eagleton turned slowly to look at him and raised one eyebrow. "I don't pay you to miss," he said coldly.

"I know that, boss. That's why it won't happen again."

It wasn't just about his job anymore, Buckhorn thought. Now he had a personal reason for wanting those Jensen boys dead.

And he wasn't going to stop until they were.

Chapter Sixteen

"I still wish I was going with you," Bess said worriedly the next morning as Ace and Chance hitched up the team under the watchful eye of old Nate.

"We'll be fine," Ace assured her.

"Unless somebody ambushes us again," Chance added, ignoring Ace's frown. "The way things have been going, you can't rule it out."

"One way or another, that mail pouch has to get to the railroad station in Bleak Creek today," Ace said. "So there's no point in worrying about it."

"That's one way of looking at it," Emily said. "I think you should take your rifle as well as the shotgun, Chance. If you see anything that looks the least bit suspicious, blaze away at it."

Chance grinned. "No wonder you're a girl after my own heart."

"You can keep your heart," Emily said with a snort. "I'm more interested in your shooting eye."

"Let's just hope nobody has to do any shooting," Ace suggested, but he was going to be very surprised if the run turned out that way.

Brian Corcoran entered the barn, carrying the mail pouch he had collected from the post office inside the general store. He placed the pouch in the box mounted underneath the driver's seat. "You wouldn't know from the weight of it how important that pouch is to the line's survival, boys. Take good care of it between here and Bleak Creek."

"We will," Ace promised. "The team's ready, and so are we." He looked at his brother. "Right, Chance?"

He nodded. "Right." He took his Winchester from their gear and slid it onto the floorboard where it would be handy but not in the way.

The brothers climbed onto the stagecoach and Ace took up the reins. He gave the three members of the Corcoran family a smile and slapped the lines against the horses to get them moving. The coach rolled out of the barn and into Palisade's main street.

Chance took off his hat and waved farewell to Bess, Emily, Corcoran, and Nate. He kept waving to the people on the boardwalks. Quite a few of the citizens were watching the stagecoach pull out. Some waved back, and a few even gave discreet cheers.

Most folks in Palisade didn't openly support Brian Corcoran against Samuel Eagleton because the mine owner wielded too much power, but the stage line was important to them, too. The mail carried by the coach was their only line of communication with the rest of the world.

As Ace drove past the hotel, he glanced up and thought he saw a curtain flick back over one of the windows. He wondered if that was Eagleton watching them leave. He had no way of knowing which windows went with the mine owner's suite, but somehow his gut told him he was right.

"We're going to run into trouble on the way, aren't we?" Chance asked as they left the settlement behind and rolled toward Timberline Pass. "Either there or in Bleak Creek."

"I wouldn't be surprised," Ace agreed. "But we'll be ready for it."

"You hope."

"I'm counting on it. And so are the Corcorans."

Eagleton growled a curse as he turned away from the window after watching the stagecoach pass.

Buckhorn knew his boss didn't like being

awake so early, but for some reason had wanted to watch the stagecoach leave town. "You're sure you don't want me to go after them?"

"You had your chance yesterday," Eagleton snapped. "I sent a rider to Bleak Creek last night. Those damn Jensens will have a warm welcome waiting for them when they get there."

Buckhorn shrugged. "Whatever you want, boss." Anger bubbled inside him. He didn't like being talked to that way . . . but Eagleton paid his wages, so he could talk any way he wanted to.

"I'm going back to bed," Eagleton said as he started to untie the belt of his dressing gown. "I won't need you for a while."

Buckhorn nodded and left the suite. When he reached the lobby, he thought about getting his horse and going after the stagecoach on his own. If he caught up to it, killed the Jensen brothers, and wrecked the coach, the boss wouldn't have any choice but to admit he was still the best. Buckhorn knew that shouldn't matter to him, but it did.

He looked through the window, saw Rose Demarcus on the opposite boardwalk, and forgot about the blasted stagecoach and Eagleton's troubles. He stepped out and crossed the street with long-legged strides, angling so that his path would intersect Rose's. He didn't look directly at her. Watched her out of the corner of his eye, instead. He wanted it to appear as if their meeting was accidental.

That seemed to work. As he stepped up onto the boardwalk, Rose said from his left, "Good morning, Joseph."

Buckhorn stopped and turned his head toward her. "Morning, ma'am." He touched a finger to the brim of his bowler hat and smiled, even though he knew that didn't make his craggy face any less ugly. It was impossible to look at Rose Demarcus and *not* smile, he thought.

"Oh, my goodness." She reached up to touch a fingertip to the bullet burn on his cheek. "What happened?"

Just that mere touch sent a jolt through him. He didn't want to talk about what had happened the day before—he certainly didn't want to admit to her that he had failed in a task given to him by his boss—so he fell back on the same fiction he had used when he was talking to the stable boy. "Nothing important. Just got scraped by a low-hanging branch while I was riding." Then he changed the subject by adding, "You're out and about sort of early today."

Rose smiled. "Or very late, if I haven't been to bed yet."

"Yeah, I reckon that's true."

"But as a matter of fact, I am up early. I take a morning constitutional like this now and then. I enjoy destroying people's illusions of me as strictly a nocturnal creature, like an owl."

"I don't figure anybody would ever mistake you for an owl, Miss Demarcus."

"Rose," she insisted.

"Well . . . all right, Rose." He fell in beside her and they strolled along the boardwalk.

"I don't suppose you've seen Samuel this morning." Rose asked.

"Actually, he was up early, too, but he's gone back to bed, I think."

"Really? What made him stir from the sheets before the crack of noon?"

Buckhorn had to laugh but grew serious again. "He wanted to watch the stagecoach pull out. Those Jensen boys have taken over the Bleak Creek run from the Corcoran sisters."

"I've heard some gossip around town about that. Samuel still wants to take over Mr. Corcoran's stagecoach line, doesn't he?"

Buckhorn had no idea how much Rose knew about Eagleton's plans and schemes. Generally, the boss was a closemouthed man, but when it came to pillow talk, plenty of fellas had spilled more than they intended to, more than they would have in any other circumstance.

It seemed safe enough to nod and say, "Yeah, I reckon he's still got his eye on it."

"He won't be satisfied until he owns every-thing in Palisade, will he?"

"I wouldn't know about that," Buckhorn replied cautiously.

Rose stopped, so he did, too. She looked over at him. "You know, Samuel doesn't own my house or my business."

Buckhorn figured he must have looked surprised because she went on.

"You didn't know that, did you?"

"No, ma'am, I didn't," he admitted. "I just thought—"

"And he doesn't own *me,* either," Rose said sharply. "Sometimes I think he's forgotten that. But you should remember it, Joseph."

"Yes, ma'am." Buckhorn had no idea what she meant by the sudden, vehement declaration.

She relaxed and smiled again. "I should be getting back now, I suppose. There's always work to do when you own a business."

"Yes, ma'am."

"See, you've already forgotten that you're supposed to call me Rose, not ma'am."

"I'm sorry, Rose. I can walk you back to your place . . ."

"That's not necessary. I'm sure I'll see you later, Joseph."

"I'll be around," he promised.

"Yes, you will. I've grown to count on that."

An uneasy feeling stirred inside him as he watched her walk away. It was like standing on a cliff and looking down into a deep mountain lake

176

and wondering what might be waiting under the surface . . . and just how deep a man might go if he ever dared to dive into it.

Ace was tense as the stagecoach started down the road from the pass. He concentrated, remembering everything Bess had told him the day before as well as the experience he had gained from handling the coach then. He had no trouble with the first turn.

Beside him, riding easily with a foot propped on the front of the box, Chance said, "Well, I'll admit, I was a mite worried, but you seem to know what you're doing."

"You just keep an eye out for bushwhackers and I'll handle the driving."

Chance chuckled. "Gladly. You're the sober, serious one, after all."

As they rounded each of the turns, Ace's confidence grew. He became more comfortable using the brake. After a while he said, "You know, I'll bet we could get jobs working on another stagecoach line if we needed to. Temporarily, I mean."

"We never take any other kind of jobs, do we?" Chance asked. "A permanent job would mean settling down, and I don't reckon either of us are cut out for that." He glanced over at his brother. "Unless you're thinking that maybe you and Bess might want to get hitched one of these days."

"I never said that! Shoot, we barely know each other. She's mighty nice and all, but I don't think either of us are ready to get married—"

Chance laughed again. "Take it easy, brother. I'm just joshing you."

"Fine," Ace groused. "I'd say you're more likely to marry Emily than I am to marry Bess."

"That'll be the day!"

They reached the valley without incident and started across it toward Shoshone Gap, which was already visible in the distance. Both brothers were alert, their gazes constantly roving over the landscape around them as they searched for any potential dangers. From the looks of things, though, the trip was going to be a peaceful one.

"Who do you reckon put in this stage road?" Ace asked at one point.

"What? I don't know. I suppose Mr. Corcoran built it. Or else Eagleton put it in so he could get his ore wagons out to the spur line in Bleak Creek. What does it matter?"

"I don't know that it does," Ace said, but stray thoughts kept roaming around in his mind. He hadn't made any sense out of them yet, but he was starting to get the feeling that they might come together and form an interesting picture if he kept prodding at them.

At midday, they stopped to rest the horses and eat the biscuit and bacon sandwiches Emily had packed for them, washing the food down with water from canteens. Chance stretched out on the grass under some trees, slanted his hat brim down over his face, and dozed off while Ace hunkered on his heels and used a stick to draw lines in the softer dirt at the edge of the road. Every so often, he nodded as if some bit of understanding had come to him.

When the horses were sufficiently rested, they pushed on and drove through Shoshone Gap about four o'clock in the afternoon. They would have plenty of time to drop off the mail pouch at the train station, pick up the pouch going to Palisade, and get back out of town before dark.

Of course, that all depended on getting in and out of Bleak Creek without anyone—like Marshal Kaiser—trying to stop them.

Both brothers had their hats pulled low as Ace drove into the settlement. He didn't look to the right or left as he headed straight for the depot at the far end of town. It was like running a gauntlet, he thought, though no one seemed to be paying much attention to the stagecoach.

He brought the team to a halt in front of the station and Chance hopped down to the ground without wasting any time. He got the mail pouch from the box while Ace dropped off the coach on the other side and stood next to the horses, using the big draft animals to obscure the view of anyone looking at him. Chance carried the pouch inside.

A moment later, he surprised his brother by calling, "Hey, Ace. You'd better come in here."

Ace turned to look and stiffened as he saw Chance standing in the depot's entrance, his hands in the air and men holding guns on either side of him.

Chapter Seventeen

Before Ace could react, he heard a soft footstep behind him and then hard metal poked into his back. He stiffened, his muscles tensing for action.

"Don't move, Jensen," a stern voice ordered. "After what you pulled last time, I'm not taking any chances. Give me any trouble and I'll shoot."

Ace bit back a groan of despair as he recognized Marshal Jed Kaiser's voice and knew that was a gun the lawman had pressing painfully into his spine.

Kaiser raised his voice. "Bring the other one out here, boys. I want these two locked up where they can't cause any more trouble."

The men holding six-guns on Chance prodded him out of the depot. Each of them wore a deputy's badge.

Ace had known they were running a risk by coming back to Bleak Creek, but he never expected everything to go to hell quite so rapidly and disastrously. It was almost like Marshal

Kaiser had known they were coming and had set up this trap for them at the train station. . . .

As that thought flashed through Ace's mind, suspicion blossomed. If Kaiser *had* known they were taking over the stagecoach run and would be in Bleak Creek today, then someone in Palisade must have gotten word either to the marshal or to a confederate in the larger settlement who could pass the tip along. It was no secret in Palisade that the Jensen brothers were working for Brian Corcoran. Plenty of people could have sent such a message to Bleak Creek.

Ace would have bet a brand-new hat that Samuel Eagleton was the culprit.

Kaiser lifted Ace's Colt from its holster as the deputies marched Chance out of the train station.

Ace didn't see any way out of the predicament, but if he and his brother were locked up, they'd never get the mail pouch back to Palisade. That would probably mean ruin for the Corcoran Stage Line.

Somewhere down the street, a shotgun suddenly boomed like thunder, and people screamed and shouted.

The gun moved away from Ace's back as Marshal Kaiser jerked around instinctively toward the disturbance.

Ace seized the opportunity to pivot and lash out at the lawman. He was going to wind up in more trouble for hitting Kaiser again, but there was nothing else he could do. He and Chance had to get away.

Even if they did, they couldn't complete their task and fulfill the requirements of the government mail contract.

Kaiser reacted swiftly, darting aside so that Ace's fist just grazed the side of his head. It was enough to make the lawman stumble and nearly lose his balance. Ace made a grab for his Colt, vaguely aware that more shooting and yelling was going on in Bleak Creek. He hoped Chance hadn't been hurt.

His hand closed around the cylinder of his Colt, but before he could wrench the weapon out of Kaiser's grip, the marshal slashed at Ace's head with his gun. The blow didn't land cleanly, either, but it had the weight of a loaded revolver behind it.

Pain exploded through Ace's skull. Red starbursts ignited behind his eyes. He felt his knees fold up under him and knew he was falling. He made a grab for Kaiser, but the lawman walloped him again with the pistol.

The sun was still up, but a darkness deep as the fall of night swallowed Ace and wouldn't let go, dragging him down until it had swallowed him completely.

Chance was trying to figure out a way he could get away from the deputies without getting himself shot, when all hell broke loose down the street.

Ace started struggling with Marshal Kaiser, and Chance reacted just as quickly. He twisted to his right and swung his arm, knocking aside the gun held by the deputy on that side. Chance lowered his shoulder and bulled into the man, hoping that the left-side deputy wouldn't shoot for fear of hitting his partner.

The right-side deputy tried to grab Chance in a bear hug, but he was off balance and when Chance lifted his left fist in a short but powerful uppercut, the man went over backwards. Chance bounded over him and stumbled a little, which probably saved his life as the left-side deputy triggered a shot at him just then. The bullet whipped through the air mere inches over Chance's head.

Righting himself, Chance sprinted for the corner of the building. His instincts told him to stay and fight, but common sense said otherwise. He still had his Lightning—the deputies thought he was unarmed when they got the drop on him in the depot and hadn't checked under his coat— but the idea of shooting it out with lawmen, even under the dire circumstances, didn't appeal to him. Too many fellas wound up dancing on air for doing things like that.

More shots blasted behind him as he darted around the corner. Bullets chewed hunks of brick from the depot wall and sent brick dust flying into the air. Chance looked around desperately for someplace he could hide.

Hoofbeats pounded the ground somewhere close by. A horse lunged around the rear corner of the building. Chance skidded to a halt, thinking that he might have to fight after all, when a shock of recognition went through him.

Long blond curls whipping in the wind, Emily Corcoran galloped toward him.

"Come on!" she cried as she stretched out her left hand.

Chance didn't stop to think about what he was doing. He was operating mostly on instinct. He reached up, grabbed Emily's wrist, and her hand locked around his wrist as he leaped up and swung his leg over the back of her horse.

She hauled him in and he landed hard behind her, jolting most of the air from his lungs. He gasped for breath as he slid his other arm around her waist and hung on. It was reminiscent of when she had leaped off the stagecoach onto his horse, but a little different. She was the one saving his hide instead of the other way around.

Emily veered her mount sharply to the right, away from the front corner of the building, as the two deputies charged into view. They jerked up their guns and fired, but the bullets screamed past Chance and Emily without hitting them.

The horse stretched its legs, running fast and

flashing past startled townspeople. Emily jerked the animal to the right again, into an alley. The horse faltered and almost went down, then recovered and lunged ahead.

"Ace is back there!" Chance shouted.

"I know, but we can't help him now!" Emily replied without looking around. "We have to get out of here before they catch us!"

Chance wanted to argue, but logically, he knew she was right. If they turned around and went back for Ace, they'd probably be gunned down by the trigger-happy deputies, not to mention the vengeance-seeking Marshal Kaiser. At best, he and Emily would be locked up, too.

He couldn't stand the thought of her behind bars.

They emerged from the alley and galloped behind several buildings before she rode into another narrow passage, slowed the horse, and then stopped. Her mount's sides heaved as it tried to catch its breath.

Chance listened and heard men shouting, but they sounded like they weren't very close. But Bleak Creek wasn't really a big town, and it was only a matter of time until the searchers found them.

Chance took advantage of the opportunity to ask her, "Where in blazes did you come from?"

"Don't you mean thanks for keeping me out of jail?" Emily responded tartly.

"Thanks. But we may wind up there anyway. I still want to know what you're doing here."

"I followed the stagecoach. I wanted to make sure you got here all right."

"What do you mean, you followed the stagecoach? I kept an eye on our back trail, and I never saw you!"

"Maybe you're not as observant as you think you are." Emily smirked. "I'm here, aren't I?"

Chance couldn't argue with that. "Does your pa know about this? I'm betting the answer is no, since the whole idea of me and Ace taking over the stagecoach run was to keep you and your sister out of danger!"

"That was your idea, not mine," she snapped. "And Pa went along with it because he worries about us. He didn't stop to think that it was just going to cause more trouble."

"How do you figure that?"

"The mail's not going to get through now, is it?"

Chance scowled. She was right. The stage line was going to be in breach of its contract if the mail pouch didn't get back to Palisade by the end of the next day.

When Chance didn't say anything, because there really wasn't anything he could say, Emily heeled the horse into motion again. She rode cautiously to the end of the alley, paused, and looked around. The shouting was nearer.

"We're going to make a run for the creek and try to get into the trees on the other side," she told Chance.

"I can't abandon my brother."

"You're not abandoning him. We'll try to figure out a way to come back later and get him. But if we let Kaiser catch us, there's nothing we can do for Ace, now or later."

She was right and Chance knew it. That didn't mean he had to like it. He said roughly, "Fine. But we're getting him loose. I won't let him stay in jail."

"Let's try to keep *us* out of jail first. Hang on." With that, she jabbed her boot heels into the horse's flanks and sent it leaping into the open.

The pursuers heard the pounding hoofbeats and a moment later, guns began to boom behind them as they raced toward the creek. Water splashed high in the air as the horse charged across the shallow stream and into the trees on the far side.

Chance looked back and saw men on horseback riding hard after them "Can you give them the slip?"

"Damn right," Emily said in a grim, determined voice.

Ace groaned as he regained consciousness. He was lying on something hard, but it didn't really feel like the ground. After a few moments, he realized it was a bunk with no mattress, only a folded blanket. He wasn't surprised when he forced his eyes open and saw that he was in a jail cell. Iron bars surrounded him on three sides, and on the fourth side was a stone wall with a high, small, barred window set in it.

He swung his legs off the bunk and sat up, making the world spin crazily around him for several seconds. When it settled down, he risked standing up and stepping over to the bars. He wrapped his hands around a couple iron cylinders and hung on in case another wave of dizziness hit him.

The other cells in the cell block were empty, and a feeling of relief washed through him. Chance had gotten away somehow.

That relief quickly disappeared and dread replaced it. Maybe Chance wasn't there because he was dead and laid out down at the local undertaker's parlor.

He looked to his right. The heavy wooden door probably opened into the marshal's office. Still clinging to the bars, he shouted, "Hey! Hey, is anybody out there?"

A moment later, a key scraped in the lock and the cell block door swung open. Marshal Kaiser walked into the aisle between the cells, a self-satisfied smirk on his weathered face. "Not such a desperado now, are you, Jensen?"

"I was never a desperado, Marshal. I'm sorry for the trouble, but all I was ever trying to do was keep you from arresting me for something I didn't do."

"Attacking an officer of the law is a crime. You've done it twice now."

"There were"—Ace searched his mind for a word he had read in a book—"extenuating circumstances. There were extenuating circumstances, Marshal."

Kaiser stopped smirking at him and glowered. "You save that fancy legal talk for the judge," he snapped. "He'll be here, week after next. In the meantime, you can just cool your heels in there."

"All right," Ace said. "The judge might find it interesting to hear that you interfered with delivering the mail, too. That's a federal crime, you know." Ace knew he shouldn't have made that comment, but the startled look on the marshal's face was worth it.

Kaiser glowered at him. "You better be careful, boy." He nodded as if to emphasize that, then added, "By the way, there's somebody out here who wants to have a look at you. I can't blame him for being curious."

Ace didn't know what to say to that, so he didn't say anything. He just stood there, gripping the bars while Kaiser went back into the office.

The marshal returned a minute later, followed by a well-dressed man in his thirties. In a dark suit and hat, sporting a narrow mustache, the man

189

looked like many of the gamblers Ace had seen over the years.

The visitor was no gambler, though.

Marshal Kaiser said, "This is one of the fellas who ambushed you the other day, Mr. Tanner."

"I'm not surprised," Jacob Tanner said. "He looks like an owlhoot."

So that was Jacob Tanner, thought Ace. He suspected the man of bushwhacking him and Chance in Shoshone Gap, then reporting just the opposite to the marshal. Tanner was a railroad surveyor, Ace recalled.

"I'm glad to see you've got him safely locked up," Tanner went on. "What about the other one?"

"My deputies have a posse out looking for him right now," Kaiser said. "I'd like to be on the trail myself, but this bad hip of mine won't let me sit a saddle for hours at a time like I used to."

"That's all right, Marshal. The people of Bleak Creek have every confidence in you and your men. I'm sure your posse will catch the other one and they'll get everything they deserve."

"You can count on it," Kaiser declared.

Tanner stepped closer to the bars, slipped a slender black cigarillo from his vest pocket, and put it in his mouth. He snapped a lucifer to life with his thumbnail, lit the stogie, and puffed on it for a second before he took it out of his mouth and looked directly at Ace. "I would like to know why you shot at me, son. I never did anything to you and your brother."

"Not for lack of trying," Ace said.

"Here now!" Kaiser said sharply. "Watch your mouth, Jensen."

Tanner turned and waved the hand holding the cigarillo. "That's all right, Marshal. The young man's bravado doesn't bother me." He looked back at Ace. "There's not a damn thing he can do to hurt me now."

Tanner was taunting him, Ace realized, with his words and with that stogie. Ace was more sure than ever that the surveyor was the one who had tried to kill him and Chance.

And he thought that he finally had a pretty good idea why.

Chapter Eighteen

True to her word, Emily left the pursuers from Bleak Creek far behind as she angled to the west, back into the foothills of the mountain range that divided the broad flats where the settlement was located from the valley beyond.

She was riding one of the draft horses, so it wasn't very fast, but the animal was strong enough to carry double without getting worn out. She seemed to know all the narrow, twisting trails, too, which certainly helped them elude the posse.

"How did you learn your way around this country?" Chance asked as they rode along the foot of a towering bluff.

"We came to Palisade right after Eagleton founded the town several years ago. Not much was there then, just a couple tent saloons and a little store that didn't have much in the way of supplies. If we wanted meat, somebody had to hunt it. I was always a good shot with a rifle and a decent rider, so I roamed all over this part of the country looking for game. Pa said it wasn't very ladylike for me to be doing that"—she snorted—"but hell, he'd given up on that a long time ago."

"So you never grew out of being a tomboy."

"I reckon not. Anything wrong with that?"

Chance shook his head. "Nope, not as far as I'm concerned. Who'd you shoot back there in Bleak Creek to start such a ruckus?"

"I didn't shoot anybody. Do you think I'm loco? I just fired in the air, and that was enough to start folks running around and yelling. That was all I wanted, just something to distract Kaiser and his deputies."

"You did a good job of that. How did you know they were going to arrest us?"

"I didn't. But when I rode into town the first thing I spotted was the marshal with his gun in Ace's back, and I knew things had gone to hell."

She turned her head to look back at Chance. "Did you at least deliver the mail pouch from Palisade before the deputies threw down on you?"

"As a matter of fact, I did. I had just given it to the stationmaster when those star-packers moved up on either side of me and stuck guns in my ribs. So half the job was finished." His eyes narrowed. "You wouldn't happen to be thinking the same thing I'm thinking, would you?"

"The pouch going to Palisade must still be in the train station," Emily said. "If we could get our hands on it and take it back with us . . ."

"I'm more interested in getting Ace out of jail," Chance said sharply.

"Maybe we can do both."

"Maybe," he allowed but thought that if it came down to choosing, he was going free his brother before he worried about delivering the mail pouch to Palisade.

Of course, if they went back to Bleak Creek for either of those things, there was a good likelihood he and Emily would wind up behind bars, too.

That was a risk they would just have to run.

Ace sat on the bunk in the cell, hands clasped between his knees, and listened as the afternoon waned. Through the window in the door between the cell block and the marshal's office, he could hear at least some of what was being said in there.

He listened as Marshal Kaiser talked to the

editor of the local newspaper, bragging about how he and his deputies had captured the notorious bushwhacker Ace Jensen and would soon have the other Jensen brother behind bars, too.

It was the first time he had heard himself described as *notorious* and didn't care for it. He and Chance had always tried to be law-abiding. They didn't quite make it all the time, but they came close. The few scrapes they'd had in the past had been minor, usually the result of some overambitious lawman trying to lock them up for something they hadn't done.

The trouble in Bleak Creek was one more example of that, but it was more serious. He really had punched Marshal Kaiser a couple times. The judge would likely send him to prison for that.

Ace didn't know if he could stand that. He was certain Chance couldn't.

Confident that his brother would come back for him, Ace clenched his hands into fists as he listened to the marshal's boasting. Kaiser was mighty pleased with himself, but it might not stay that way.

As evening settled down, Ace heard a lot of horses come into town. A few minutes later, the door of the marshal's office opened, and heavy, booted footsteps entered, spurs chinging.

"Well?" Kaiser demanded. "Where is he?"

Ace figured the marshal was talking about

Chance. The newcomers had to be the deputies, returning to Bleak Creek with the posse.

"He got away, Marshal," one of them reported.

Relief flooded through Ace as he heard that confirmation of what he had hoped.

Kaiser didn't take the news so well. He roared, "Got away? Damn it! A dozen of you can't catch one man?"

"Jensen had help, Marshal, and we saw who it was—one of those Corcoran girls from Palisade. The blond one."

Emily, Ace thought. He was surprised to hear that she'd been in Bleak Creek, but he was glad that she had helped Chance get away.

"Hell, I know that," Kaiser snapped. "I got descriptions of her from witnesses who saw her riding around shooting that shotgun of hers. That's what caused all the commotion when we were trying to arrest those two. She's gonna be mighty sorry she stuck her pretty little nose in our business."

"Anyway," the deputy said with a sigh, "they gave us the slip up in the foothills. We lost and found the trail half a dozen times, then finally lost it for good. When it started gettin' dark, we figured we might as well turn around and come back in. Even if we hadn't lost the trail, we couldn't track at night."

Kaiser let out a few more bitter curses, then said disgustedly, "All right. But you'll be out again at first light in the morning trying to find them, you hear?"

"Sure, Marshal." The deputy's resigned tone made it clear that he didn't think the effort would do much good.

A few minutes later, Kaiser opened the door, stalked into the cell block, and glared at Ace through the bars. "Looks like your brother has deserted you, boy. If you were hoping he'd come back to bust you out of here, you can forget it. He's long gone."

"I hope you're right, Marshal. This is my problem, not Chance's."

"Not anymore. He walloped one of my deputies. He's just as guilty of resisting arrest as you are. Maybe the warden will put you in the same cell at the territorial prison, but I wouldn't count on it." Kaiser paused, then continued, "You know, the judge might go a little easier on you if you'd confess the reason you and your brother tried to kill Mr. Tanner."

Ace didn't answer the question directly. "Folks around here think pretty highly of Tanner, don't they?"

"Well, why wouldn't they?" Kaiser barked. "He's responsible for bringing the railroad here. Bleak Creek wouldn't amount to much without it."

"I reckon he must be in charge of all the spur lines in this part of the territory."

"That's right." The marshal's eyes narrowed with suspicion. "Now I understand! You and your brother have something against the railroad, don't you? You're outlaws, like that Jesse James. Damn train robbers!"

Ace didn't say anything, just smiled as he sat on the bunk. Let the marshal think whatever he wanted.

Kaiser pointed at him through the bars. "I'm gonna go through all my wanted posters again. I'll bet there's a reward out for you boys!"

Ace chuckled as the marshal hurried out of the cell block and slammed the door behind him. Kaiser was going to be disappointed if he thought he was going to cash in on his prisoner. As far as Ace knew, there was no paper out on him or his brother.

Of course, that would probably change if Chance succeeded in breaking him out of the jail. . . .

Chance and Emily waited until well after dark before approaching Bleak Creek again. They followed the town's namesake creek, keeping to the deep shadows under the aspens and cotton-woods that lined the stream's banks. The moon wasn't up yet, and the thick darkness helped conceal them.

"We're going to have to steal at least one horse," Chance said quietly as they neared the

197

settlement. "I don't cotton to the idea of horse thievery, but even this big fella of yours can't carry all three of us."

"He won't have to, and we won't have to steal any horses. The stage line has half a dozen in one of the stables. I'll get a couple for you and Ace. I reckon you can ride bareback?"

"If we have to. I didn't think about the fact that you'd keep an extra team here."

"Then it's a good thing you've got me along to do the thinking, isn't it?"

He didn't answer that. She really was an exceptionally good ally, but he wasn't going to give her a swelled head by admitting it.

Still, there was no denying that Emily Corcoran was smart, beautiful, and plenty tough. He had no interest in getting hitched and settling down, as he had gibed at Ace about doing, but if he ever decided to attempt such a far-fetched thing, it would have to be with a woman like Emily. . . .

She reined in. "All right. We'll go the rest of the way on foot."

Chance slid off the horse's back and Emily swung down from the saddle, bringing the coach gun with her. They were in the trees across the creek from the settlement.

She pointed and whispered, "There's the jail. Take the horse with you. I'll head for the depot and get that mail pouch, then I'll go to the stable and pick out a couple horses. When I make a commotion, you be ready for Kaiser to rush out of the marshal's office. You can jump him and get the key to let Ace out of jail."

"Sounds pretty risky for both of us," Chance commented.

"What? You don't want to live up to your name?"

"I never said that. I reckon what I'm trying to say is . . . be careful, Emily. I don't want anything to happen to you just because my brother and I can't stay out of trouble."

"The two of you wouldn't *be* in trouble if you hadn't been trying to help my family," she pointed out. "The Corcorans owe you this, Chance."

"Well, if there's a debt to collect—"

Before she realized what he was doing, he put his right hand behind her neck, sliding his fingers under the thick blond curls, and brought his mouth to hers in an eager kiss. She stiffened in surprise, then he felt her lips soften in response.

It lasted only a moment before she jabbed the shotgun's twin barrels into his midriff hard enough to make him gasp as he broke the kiss.

"Damn you," Emily whispered. "What'd you have to go and do that for?"

"There's a chance . . . something might happen . . . to one or both of us," Chance said as he tried to catch his breath. "I didn't want to spend the rest of my life . . . wondering what kissing you would be like."

"And now that you know?"

"All the more good reason to stay alive"—he grinned in the darkness—"on the remote possibility I might get to do it again someday."

"Maybe not all that remote . . ." she muttered. Her tone grew more brisk and businesslike as she went on. "But there's no time for such foolishness now, understand? You'd better have your brother loose by the time I get there with the horses, or I'll just have to leave you. That mail pouch has got to make it back to Palisade."

"I understand. We'll be ready."

"All right. Good luck."

He hoped for a second that her wishing him luck might mean she would kiss him again, but that didn't happen. She vanished soundlessly into the shadows.

Chance led the horse and headed for the back of the building she had pointed out as the jail.

Chapter Nineteen

Night had fallen and the cell block was dimly lit by a single lantern before one of the deputies brought Ace any supper. The man carried in a tray with a plate and cup on it and handed it to Ace through the slot in the bars designed for that. The plate held a steak that more resembled a chunk of charred leather, a half-raw potato, and a piece of stale bread. The coffee in the cup was bitter and watery.

"The town doesn't believe in feeding prisoners very well, I see," Ace commented.

The deputy glared at him. The man had a bruise on his jaw where Chance had punched him. "As far as I'm concerned, you're lucky to get anything at all, mister. The marshal says you and your brother are train robbers. You'll probably be in prison before too much longer."

"He didn't find any reward posters on us, though, did he?"

"That don't matter," the deputy said sullenly. "You're still guilty as hell." He stalked out and left Ace to enjoy the dubious pleasures of the meal.

The food was better than nothing, Ace decided . . . but not by much.

He had just downed the last of the coffee when he heard a voice at the window, hissing his name.

Ace set the tray aside and stood up on the bunk. He still wasn't high enough to see out the barred window, but he was able to whisper through it, "Chance? Is that you?"

"Yeah. Are you all right, Ace?"

"I'm fine," Ace answered honestly. The headache he'd had when he first regained consciousness had faded to nothing. "How about you?"

"Same here," Chance replied. "We've come to get you out of here."

"We?" Ace repeated. "Who else is out there?"

"Well, she's not here right now, but Emily's the one who helped me get away this afternoon. She's gone to the railroad station to fetch the mail pouch bound for Palisade."

The knowledge that Emily was in Bleak Creek came as a surprise to Ace, but not much of one. She was just as reckless and impulsive as his brother was, he thought.

Of course, he was a fine one to talk, he reminded himself. He was the one behind bars at the moment.

"I'll tell you all about it later," Chance went on. "The important thing right now is we gotta get you out of there. Just sit tight. Is the marshal in his office?"

"I don't think so. I believe he went home or went to eat supper and left one of the deputies on duty."

"Just one?"

"As far as I know. I haven't heard him talking to anybody, and it sounds like there's only one man moving around in there."

"That'll do," Chance said. "Be ready to go. I'll see you in a few minutes."

Ace heard soft footsteps receding outside the

jail. He had no idea what Chance's plan was, but as he stepped down from the bunk and picked up his hat—the only thing he had in here—he hoped this rescue wouldn't backfire and leave both of them in jail . . . or worse, dead.

Chance led the horse along the alley next to the squat stone building that housed the marshal's office and jail. It was black as sin in there, which was fine with him. Anybody passing by in the street wasn't likely to spot him lurking there.

He left the horse's reins dangling and hoped the animal was smart enough to stay ground-hitched. Keeping close to the wall, he edged along it until he reached the front corner. He wasn't sure what Emily planned to do to raise a ruckus that would draw the deputy out of the office—but whatever it was, he figured it would be spectacular.

At least fifteen minutes had passed since they'd split up on the other side of the creek and his mind was turning. Had she gotten the mail pouch from the railroad station yet? Would the station-master, if he was still there, just hand it over to her? She had a right to it, since her family held the mail contract from the government and she was a Corcoran.

If she'd been recognized during the ruckus that afternoon, the marshal might have already filed charges against her. The stationmaster might refuse to turn over the mail.

In that case, Chance had no doubt that she would take it at gunpoint if she had to.

He stood still, breathing shallowly and listening. So far, he hadn't heard anything except the normal noises of a town at night—some rinky-dink player piano music from one of the saloons, men and women talking and laughing, wagon wheels squeaking as a buckboard rolled slowly down the street, the clip-clop of hoof-beats as a few riders came and went. Bleak Creek seemed to be a mighty peaceful place at the moment.

That peace was abruptly shattered by a loud, strident clanging. Chance stiffened as he recognized the racket as the ringing of a fire bell. Frontier towns lived in terror of any uncontrolled blaze. The flames could spread and burn the whole settlement to the ground in less time than it took to talk about it.

Swift, heavy footsteps slapped the floorboards in the marshal's office.

Chance darted onto the boardwalk, sliding his hand under his coat. It emerged with the Lightning from the shoulder holster. He reversed the .38 as he neared the door, which was flung open violently. The deputy, hatless and fumbling to buckle on a gun belt, charged out of the office.

Chance struck with the speed of a rattlesnake, smacking the gun butt into the deputy's balding head just behind his right ear. He hit the man hard enough to knock him out for a few minutes, without busting his skull and killing him.

He'd judged the blow correctly. The deputy pitched forward on his face, out cold. Chance flipped the Lightning around again in case he needed to use it, then knelt to check the deputy's pockets for the keys to the cell block and the cells.

Nothing. Chance grimaced as he realized the man wasn't carrying the keys. It was going to be a real problem if Marshal Kaiser had taken them with him when he left the office. Chance left the unconscious deputy sprawled where he was and dashed into the building.

Relief flooded through him as he spotted a ring of keys hanging on a nail in the wall behind the desk. He snatched them off the nail and began trying keys in the lock on the cell block door. From the corner of his eye, he darted glances toward the deputy, who he could see lying on the boardwalk.

The third key he tried turned the lock. He swung the door back and charged into the cell block.

Ace stood at the door of the first cell on the left, his hat on, ready to go. "What's going on out there? Is that the fire bell I hear?"

"Yeah," Chance replied as he tried one after another of the keys in the lock. "But I'm pretty sure there's not really a fire. It's just Emily's way of creating a diversion."

"It worked," Ace said. "The whole town's going to be in an uproar."

"That means they won't be paying attention to us." Chance grunted in satisfaction as the key in his hand clicked over in the lock. "That's it! Come on!" He yanked the door open and Ace hurried out.

"I don't suppose you saw my gun belt anywhere in the office?"

"Nope, but maybe you can check Kaiser's desk," Chance suggested. "Just don't take too long about it. If we're not out there when Emily gets here with the other horses, she's liable to ride off and leave us. Especially if she's got that mail pouch. Delivering that mail on time is more important to her than we are, I'm afraid." He moved to the left of the door, keeping watch outside while Ace searched for his gun.

"I don't blame her for feeling that way." Ace started opening the drawers in Kaiser's battered old desk. He reached into the bottom one on the right side and brought out his coiled shell belt and holstered Colt.

Marshal Kaiser suddenly charged up to the door carrying a shotgun. "Jensen!" Kaiser yelled as he swung the weapon toward Ace. "I'll blow you to hell!"

The marshal hadn't noticed Chance, who

lowered his head and launched himself through the door in a diving tackle. He caught Kaiser around the waist and drove him backward. The lawman whooped in surprise and jerked both of the Greener's triggers as he toppled off the boardwalk. The shotgun went off with a thunderous roar and spewed both loads of buckshot toward the heavens as flame spouted from its twin barrels.

Chance had managed to hang on to his revolver during the collision, lifted it, and brought it down in a slashing blow to Kaiser's head. The marshal went limp and dropped the empty shotgun.

Rapid hoofbeats thudded close by in the street. Chance looked up, ready to use the Lightning, and saw Emily reining one horse to a stop. She was leading another mount. Both horses wore simple hackamores with reins attached to them but no saddles.

"Well?" Emily demanded as she looked down at Chance. "Are we getting out of here or do you plan on wallowing around in the street all night like a hog?"

He scrambled to his feet, biting back the angry retort that wanted to spring to his lips. Ace was out of the marshal's office and had paused on the boardwalk to buckle the gun belt around his hips.

People were shouting and running around all over town, panicking because of the alarm bell, which had gone silent. They were all looking for the fire and not paying attention to what was going on in front of the marshal's office. Not even the shotgun's blast had been enough to distract them from their fear of a devastating conflagration.

"The other horse is in the alley," Chance said.

"You'd better ride it," Emily snapped. "I figure a dude like you needs a saddle more than Ace or I do."

Under other circumstances he might have defended himself and argued with her, but there wasn't time for that. As he ran toward the alley, he wondered why the hell she seemed so irritated with him. As far as he could tell, the plan was working just fine. He had even spotted the mail pouch hanging by its strap over her shoulder.

There was only one explanation, he realized. Her prickly attitude had to be because of that kiss he had stolen earlier.

He would ponder that later. He grabbed the horse's reins, led it into the street, and swung up onto its back. Ace was already mounted on the third horse.

Emily called, "Follow me!" and kicked her horse into a run.

The Jensen brothers were right behind her as she galloped out of Bleak Creek. Chance wasn't sure, but he thought he heard a few gunshots popping behind them. Maybe some of the towns-people had realized there wasn't a fire and figured out that a jailbreak was going on.

If anybody was shooting at them, none of the bullets came anywhere close. The three riders raced on into the night and soon left the settlement behind.

Emily didn't slow down until they had passed through Shoshone Gap and ridden a mile or so into the valley beyond. When they stopped, Ace listened intently but didn't hear any hoofbeats pursuing them.

The horses' sweat-flecked sides heaved from the hard run.

As the animals rested and tried to catch their breath, Chance asked Emily, "Did you have any trouble getting the mail pouch?"

"No. No one was on duty in the station except one ticket clerk named Jeff Ramsey. I've known him for a while. He unlocked the cabinet the pouch was in and gave it to me."

"Just like that?" Chance asked in astonishment.

"Well," Emily said matter-of-factly, "Jeff's been smitten with me ever since we moved to this part of the country. He was glad to do me a favor."

"Even though it's probably going to cost him his job?" Chance asked. "Did the poor varmint at least steal a kiss in return for that favor?"

"No," Emily replied coldly. "Although maybe I wouldn't have minded if he had."

Ace sensed some tension between them and wondered what had happened. He had a hunch that Chance had given in to an impulse and done something to offend her. Actually, Ace was a little surprised something like that hadn't already happened.

At the moment, he didn't really care. "You've got a right to have that mail pouch in your possession, since your father's company has the government contract, so nobody can claim there's anything wrong about that. Marshal Kaiser will be pretty upset about you ringing that fire bell and helping us escape, though."

Emily laughed. "I don't think anybody saw me do it, so he can't prove anything. And I didn't steal these horses, either. They belong to the Corcoran Stage Line."

"So you're in the clear," Chance said. "That's good. Ace and I may have to hide out, though. I wouldn't put it past Kaiser to bring a posse over to Palisade and try to arrest us."

"Neither would I," Ace agreed. "I figure Eagleton's pet marshal would be inclined to help him do it, too."

"You're right about that," Emily said. "You can't expect any help from Claude Wheeler."

"And your stagecoach is still in Bleak Creek," Ace said.

Emily shrugged. "That's not a problem. Bess and I can ride over and claim it tomorrow."

"That puts you right back at risk from Eagleton's men," Chance pointed out. "He still wants to put your father's operation out of business."

"You're not telling me anything I don't already know." She hefted the mail pouch. "But tonight we won. We've got this, and that means we beat Eagleton again. I don't know how, but I'm convinced he had something to do with causing this whole damn mess."

Ace was convinced of that, as well. He could have explained his suspicions to Emily but decided he would keep them to himself for the time being . . . until he figured out what to do with them.

She was right. They had won this round, and as the three of them rode toward the mountain road, Timberline Pass, and Palisade beyond that, Ace told himself to just enjoy the feeling of not being behind bars anymore.

Chapter Twenty

It was close to midnight when Emily, Ace, and Chance rode into Palisade. Since the Golden Dome ran three shifts of workers per day, some of the miners had finished their shift not long before and were still blowing off steam in the saloons. The other businesses were dark, closed for the night, but the music and the hilarity in the saloons went on.

"It's like this twenty-four hours a day," Emily commented. "And it will be until that mother lode inside the mountain plays out."

"When that happens there won't be a reason for the town to be here anymore," Ace commented. "Especially all the way up here at the top of that hellish road to Timberline Pass."

"You're right about that."

"Folks might be able to make something out of that valley, though," Ace said in a musing tone. "There's not enough graze up here for cattle, but the valley has water and pretty of good grass. If somebody wanted to run some stock on it, it would be pretty good ranching country."

"I suppose, but I'm not a rancher," Emily said.

"Neither am I. Just thinking out loud is all."

Chance said, "I'm thinking about a good night's sleep. This may be the last one we get for a while if we have to go on the run from the law." He sighed. "Doc would be ashamed of us, turning out to be common owlhoots."

"We're not fugitives yet," Ace pointed out. "We're not wanted anywhere except Bleak Creek, and all we did there was try to defend ourselves from unjust charges."

"You know good and well Kaiser's gonna come

after us. The man's got a real burr under his saddle where we're concerned."

Ace couldn't argue with that. He fully expected Marshal Kaiser to bring a posse to Palisade and try to arrest them.

He and Chance just needed to dodge that fate a little while longer, so he'd have time to finish figuring things out—including what to do about it.

Lamps burned inside the stage line office. Bess and her father had been up pacing and worrying about Emily's disappearance. As the three riders came to a stop in front of the office, the door burst open and Bess charged out onto the porch, crying, "Emily!"

Brian Corcoran followed his younger daughter as Emily slid down from her horse and hugged Bess, who threw her arms around her.

Corcoran leaned on the porch railing, his voice a mixture of relief and anger. "Saints be praised that you're all right, girl. Now, where the hell *were* you?" He frowned as he switched his gaze to Ace and Chance, who were still mounted. "What are you boys doing coming in in the middle of the night like this? And where the hell is my stagecoach?"

The Jensen brothers dismounted.

Ace said, "Your coach is all right, Mr. Corcoran. It's just, well, stuck in Bleak Creek, that's all."

"Stuck? You mean broken down?"

"No, we had to leave it there," Chance said. "We, uh, sort of got arrested."

"Arrested!"

"Well, Ace did," Chance said hurriedly. "I never was, actually—"

"Only because I rescued you before Marshal Kaiser could throw you in the hoosegow," Emily broke in.

Bess said, "What in the world are you talking about? Did you go to Bleak Creek?"

"Yes, and it's a good thing I did, or else both of these boys would be behind bars now, and we'd be losing that mail contract." Emily took the pouch off her shoulder and handed it to her startled father. "But the mail got through and Ace and Chance are free—for now, anyway."

Corcoran shook his head slowly. "I'll be damned if I understand any of this."

"Let's all go inside, and I'll explain everything," Emily said.

It would be a good trick, Ace thought, if she could explain what they were going to do next.

As for him, he had no idea.

Buckhorn was lounging on the hotel porch when he saw the three riders come into town. It was late, but it wasn't that unusual to see people coming and going at this hour. Something about them caught his interest, though. He moved into a patch of shadow so he could watch them ride past without being seen.

It was impossible to miss the Corcoran girl, of course. That mass of fair hair stood out like a beacon in the night. As the riders went through a ray of light slanting from a saloon window, he realized the two men with her were Ace and Chance Jensen.

Well, that was a surprise, the gunfighter thought —but not too much of one. Those two seemed to have as much luck and as many lives as a pair of cats. The boss had been confident he had things set up to take care of them and deprive Corcoran of his last allies. Clearly, that plan hadn't worked out.

Something had sure as hell happened, though. The Jensen boys had left Palisade on the stagecoach, and they were coming back in the middle of the night without it. Not only that, but one of them, as well as the girl, were riding unsaddled draft horses, probably from the stage line's barn in Bleak Creek. A faint smile tugged at Buckhorn's mouth. Whatever the story was, he figured it might be pretty interesting.

He watched Emily and the Jensens ride along the street to the stage line office, where Bess Corcoran and her father came out to meet them. They stood around talking for a few minutes, then went into the building.

The question was whether Buckhorn waited

until morning to inform the boss of the development or went up to the suite and told him right away.

Rose was still up there, Buckhorn thought. Something twisted in his guts.

Earlier, when she'd arrived, Eagleton had told him to go down to the lobby and wait there. That was their usual practice. Eagleton felt safe in the hotel, for the most part, but he wanted Buckhorn on the premises most of the time, even if he wasn't right in the suite. He had sat in the lobby for a while, reading old newspapers and smoking cigars, but he'd grown bored of that and stepped outside for a breath of fresh air. He'd still been there when Emily, Ace, and Chance had ridden into town.

Rose ought to be down pretty soon, he thought. He would wait until then to decide what to do.

He didn't have long to wait. The hotel door opened and she stepped out onto the porch, pausing to say, "Oh, there you are, Joseph. I didn't see you at your usual post in the lobby."

"Seemed a little close in there to me tonight," he explained.

She laughed as she closed the door and walked closer to him. "Goodness, I know what you mean. It's good to get out in the fresh air, isn't it? Have you ever ridden up higher on the mountain, past where the mine entrance is?"

"Can't say as I have."

216

"I did, once. I couldn't take my buggy, of course. I had to ride horseback, and then I went even higher on a path where the horse couldn't go. The place where I finally stopped, I was up so high I could look back to the east and see for what seemed like forever. It must have been fifty or sixty miles, at least. Far past Shoshone Gap and Bleak Creek, certainly. And the air! It was so cold and clear, it was like . . . like breathing wine. It was beautiful."

"Sounds like it," Buckhorn said. What was really beautiful was her face in the golden light coming through the hotel's front window as she described the place.

"We'll have to go up there together sometime, you and I," she said. "I'm sure I could find it again."

"That would be mighty nice," Buckhorn agreed, "but I figure the boss wouldn't like it."

"Well . . . I didn't say we'd ask Samuel, did I? Surely you have some time to yourself now and then, time when you don't have to account for your whereabouts."

"I could probably arrange that," Buckhorn said cautiously.

"And I told you before, Samuel doesn't own me or my business. If I want to take a ride up onto the mountain with a friend, he can't stop me."

Buckhorn wondered if she was really that naïve. Palisade was Eagleton's town, Eagleton's mine, Eagleton's mountain. The man could stop any damn thing he pleased. And Buckhorn was fairly confident Eagleton wouldn't like the idea of his own private woman spending that much time alone with his half-breed bodyguard.

Rose was just having some sport with him, Buckhorn suddenly told himself. That had to be it. A chill went through him. Even if she wasn't Eagleton's property, she could have just about any man she wanted. All she had to do was smile and crook one of her pretty little fingers. She couldn't really be interested in somebody as poor and common and ugly as him.

Rose came close enough to reach out and rest her fingers on his arm. He seemed to feel the warmth of her touch through his clothes. He smelled the delicious scent of her.

"What do you say?" she asked quietly. "Shall we do it?"

"I can't." He had to force a note of harshness into his voice. If he showed any weakness, she would keep at him until she wore him down—and then she would laugh in his face because he had fallen for it. "I've got to stay closer to the boss than that."

For a moment she didn't say anything. Then her hand fell away from his arm and she said, "All right." Her voice was cool and reserved. "It's a shame you feel that way. I think you would have enjoyed seeing the place."

"Maybe. But I'm meant to be down here, not up there."

She gathered her shawl closer around her shoulders. "Good night, then, Joseph."

"Good night, Miss Demarcus."

She didn't correct him, didn't remind him that he was supposed to call her Rose.

As she started to turn away, he remembered what her flirting had driven clear out of his thoughts for a few minutes. He called her back. "Miss Demarcus?"

She looked over her shoulder at him and said coolly, "Yes?"

"How did the boss seem when you left him?"

"Quite satisfied." There was an edge to her voice.

"No, I mean, did he say whether he was tired, was he going to be awake for a while, anything like that?"

"As a matter of fact, he mentioned that he was rather weary. I imagine he went straight to bed and is probably sound asleep by now."

"All right," Buckhorn nodded. "Thanks."

"Why do you ask?"

"Oh, I, uh, have some news for him. I reckon it'll wait until tomorrow, though. It's not important enough to wake him up." Buckhorn hoped he was making the right decision. Short of going over to the stage line office and killing

219

the Jensen brothers, he didn't see what could be done immediately about the problem.

"Very well," Rose said. "Good night again."

Buckhorn touched the brim of his hat. "Ma'am."

Even after everything that had just happened, he watched her all the way back to her house, keeping a close eye on her to make sure she got home safely.

He wondered if she felt his eyes on her, all the way down the street.

Marshal Jed Kaiser sat at his desk and held a wet rag to his head where that damn Jensen boy had pistol-whipped him. It didn't help much with the pain. It didn't do a thing to ease the fury that threatened to consume the lawman, either.

On the other side of the marshal's office, Deputy Andy Belmont sat on the old sofa with bad springs and groaned as he held his head in both hands. "I swear, Jed, it feels like I've been hit with an ax handle! He about busted my head wide open."

"Oh, shut up," Kaiser said sourly. "He knocked me out, too, you know. You don't hear me whining."

Belmont glared down at the floor and settled for muttering something under his breath. Kaiser didn't catch the words, but he didn't ask his deputy to repeat them. He knew they were probably curses directed at him, as well as at the Jensen brothers.

After a moment, Belmont asked, "When we catch those two, can't we just go ahead and string 'em up right then and there?"

"That wouldn't be legal," Kaiser snapped. "They'll get a trial. I'm not sure what they've done would be considered a hanging offense, though, no matter how much I'd like to see them dancing on air." He looked up as the door opened.

Jacob Tanner came into the room with a concerned expression on his handsome face. "I heard there was some trouble here, Marshal. Your prisoner got away?"

"Yeah, Jensen's brother busted him out of here," Kaiser answered.

"So they're both on the loose again," Tanner commented in a taut voice.

Kaiser could tell that Tanner was worried and figured he knew the reason why. "You don't have to worry. We'll round them up again. They'll be behind bars before you know it. They won't get a chance to come after you." He paused. "You still don't have any idea why they tried to bushwhack you the other day?"

Tanner had taken one of his customary cigarillos from his vest pocket and put it in his mouth. His teeth clenched on it as he said, "Sorry, Marshal. It's as much a mystery to me as it ever was. I never saw those two until they tried to kill me."

"Well, we'll get to the bottom of it sooner or later," Kaiser promised. "They left here with one of those Corcoran girls whose pa owns the stage line, so they probably went back to Palisade with her. I'm taking a posse over there first thing in the morning. I know Marshal Wheeler. He's a good man. He'll cooperate."

"Are you going to arrest the girl?" Tanner asked.

"I damn well might," Kaiser blustered. "She helped a prisoner escape from my jail. That's a crime right there."

Tanner nodded. "It certainly is."

"Not to mention the way she rang that fire bell and made all hell break loose around here. It took an hour for everything to settle down."

"I'm going with you."

Tanner's declaration made the marshal frown in surprise. "With the posse, you mean? I don't know if that's necessary, Mr. Tanner. I've got my deputies, and I can get plenty of volunteers. An important man like you shouldn't be mixed up in something as messy and dangerous as this."

"You forget, Marshal, I was the intended first victim of these desperados. I want to make sure they get what's coming to them."

"Well . . . all right. I don't reckon I can stop you. But you need to be mighty careful. The whole area is depending on you to help it grow."

Tanner smiled and said around the cigarillo in his mouth, "And I have plenty of plans, Marshal. You can count on that."

Chapter Twenty-One

As happy as Brian Corcoran was that Emily had been able to retrieve the mail pouch from the railroad station in Bleak Creek, he was despondent over the stage line's chances in the long run. As they all gathered in the kitchen of the living quarters behind the office the next morning, he said gloomily, "Without a stagecoach, I just don't see how we can carry on."

Emily set a big plate of biscuits in the center of the table. "Bess and I will ride over there and get the stagecoach. We can tie the saddle mounts behind it when we come back."

Chance said, "Plenty of people are bound to have seen you yesterday afternoon and last night. Marshal Kaiser knows you had a hand in both of those ruckuses. You'd never get in and out of town without him arresting you."

"I won't have that," Corcoran said. "I forbid it. I'll sell the damn stage line to Eagleton before I see one of my daughters in jail!"

Ace said, "That's exactly what he wants. He's been pulling the strings on this affair the whole time. We've managed to stop his plans, but he keeps getting closer to his goal anyway."

"That's true," Corcoran admitted. "Sam Eagleton's nothing if not a diabolical schemer. Everywhere I turn, there he is, ready to take away everything I hold dear."

Chance frowned. "It's almost like he has a personal grudge against you."

Corcoran shook his head. "No, there's nothing personal about it for him, and that makes it even worse. He does these things simply because he's power mad and thinks that whatever he wants is his by right. Maybe he wasn't that way before he made that Golden Dome strike and got filthy rich so fast. I reckon maybe money changes a man."

"I don't think so," Ace mused. "Money just allows a man to let out what was inside him all along."

On that dour note, they fell silent and concentrated on their breakfast, although no one had enough of an appetite to appreciate Emily's excellent cooking.

When the meal was finished, Corcoran sighed. "I suppose I'll take that mail pouch over to the post office. It'll actually be getting there earlier than it would have if you two fellas had brought the stagecoach back today."

"You know, I was just thinking the same thing," Ace said. "Does your contract with the government specify *how* the mail has to be delivered?"

Corcoran frowned and shook his head. "No, only that it be delivered twice a week from here to Bleak Creek and from Bleak Creek to here."

Bess exclaimed, "The Pony Express!"

"That's just what I was thinking," Ace said with a grin.

"Wait a minute," Chance said. "You're talking about carrying the mail on horseback?"

"It worked twenty-five years ago when Russell, Majors, and Waddell did it."

"But that was a cross-country route."

"Going from Palisade to Bleak Creek and back would be a lot easier." Excitement visibly gripped Bess. "We could do it. We have plenty of horses."

"But . . . but this is a stage line!" her father protested.

Emily was caught up by the idea, too. "You just admitted, Pa, that there's nothing in the contract saying we *have* to use a stagecoach. As long as the mail gets delivered, that's the only thing that matters."

"Well . . ." Corcoran rubbed his bearded jaw as he frowned in thought. "What about the passengers?"

"We're lucky if we have half a dozen in a month, and you know it."

Corcoran sighed. "Aye, the passenger business hasn't been nearly what I'd hoped it would be, no doubt about that."

"It would work," Ace said. "Bess would have to be the one who rode the route."

Emily frowned. "Bess? Why her? Why not me?"

"Because you'll probably be arrested if you set foot in Bleak Creek," Chance said. "The same holds true for Ace and me, or we'd do it."

"I don't mind doing the riding," Bess said.

"But not by yourself," Ace said. "I think we should all go. That'll be safer. But Chance and Emily and I will stop and wait outside the settlement. Bess can handle the last little bit by herself."

She nodded. "Sure I can. Admit it, Pa. This is the best way for the company to keep going."

"I just don't know. It still seems wrong. And we can't just leave that stagecoach over there in Bleak Creek."

"It won't be forever," Ace said. "Just for the time being, until things settle down."

Corcoran grunted. "Things won't ever settle down until Eagleton gets what he wants. He'll find some other way to make things tough for us."

"And we'll find some other way to beat him," Emily declared. "We've done it so far, haven't we?"

For a long moment, Corcoran didn't say anything else. Finally he nodded. "We'll give it a try. We'll bring back the blasted Pony Express!"

• • •

Palisade's postmaster was the man who ran the mercantile. Even though in his job as postmaster he answered to the government, he had a silent partner in the general store—Samuel Eagleton.

Corcoran explained all this to Ace and Chance, then added, "So five minutes after I drop off that mail pouch, he'll be up in Eagleton's suite at the hotel tellin' him all about it."

"It's hard to do anything without Eagleton knowing about it, isn't it?" Ace asked.

"Aye. That's what makes it so hard fighting him. He's got most of the town on his side. It's not that folks in Palisade are evil—"

"They just know which side their bread is buttered on," Chance finished.

"Exactly." Corcoran picked up the mail pouch from the desk in the stage line office. "I'll be back after I've dropped this off."

Ace, Chance, Bess, and Emily spent the rest of the morning talking about the planned "Pony Express" route between the two settlements. Now that they were back in Palisade, the Jensen brothers would be able to use their own horses for the journey, and Bess and Emily would pick out the best saddle mounts from the stock owned by the stage line.

"Nate can help us with that," Bess said. "He's a better judge of horseflesh than anybody else I've ever seen."

"They'll need to be fast," Emily said. "We may have to outrun trouble, like the old-time Pony Express riders did. Except it won't be Indians chasing us. It'll be Eagleton's hired guns."

That wouldn't surprise him a bit, Ace thought.

Chance said, "You know, I keep hearing about this fella Eagleton all the time and we've gotten into these scrapes with the men working for him, but Ace and I have never even laid eyes on the man."

"He stays in the hotel most of the time," Bess explained. "He comes out now and then to pay a visit to his mine or to walk around town so the sight of him will remind people who really runs things around here, but that's really the only time most folks see him."

Emily snorted disgustedly. "It's like Pa said. Eagleton just squats there in the hotel like a fat old spider in the center of a web. Nobody sees him much except Joe Buckhorn and Rose Demarcus."

"Who are they?" Ace asked.

"Buckhorn's his bodyguard. Spends most of his time in the hotel lobby or up in Eagleton's suite."

"Indian-looking hombre, wears a suit and a bowler hat?" Chance asked.

"That's right. He's fast with a gun and he doesn't mind using one, either. There's no telling how many men he's been hired to kill."

"I wonder if he's the fella who shot at us when

we were bringing in the stagecoach the other day," Ace mused.

"I wouldn't put it past him for a second," Emily declared.

Chance asked, "What about that Demarcus woman you mentioned?"

"She owns the brothel, but Eagleton is her own special customer. Her private customer, I reckon you could say." Emily grinned. "Just talking about it has little Bess blushing. Would you look at that?"

"I'm *not* blushing," Bess insisted, although it was obvious from the pink flush on her face that she was.

"She's had a sheltered life," Emily went on. "I'm not sure she even knows what goes on in such a place."

"Of course I do. I mean . . . well, I've heard things . . ."

Emily patted her sister's hand and said mockingly, "Don't worry. Nobody expects you to be anything other than an innocent."

Bess might have continued to insist, unconvincingly, that she was worldly, but at that moment the old hostler Nate hurried into the office. "A bunch of riders comin' into town, and that dang marshal from Bleak Creek is with 'em. I'd say it's a posse"—his gaze went from Emily to Ace to Chance—"and they're lookin' for the three o' you!"

• • •

Buckhorn was trying to enjoy a late breakfast in the hotel dining room, but he kept thinking about what had happened between him and Rose Demarcus late the previous evening. Doubts haunted him. What if the feelings Rose had hinted at were genuine, as unlikely as that seemed? If there was any truth to it, he might have thrown away a chance for the best thing that had ever happened to him . . . maybe the only really good thing that had ever happened to him.

Or maybe he had saved himself some heartache when he discovered that it was all a cruel joke.

Hell, he'd thought, snorting to himself, a gunfighter didn't have any business worrying about something like heartache.

The only thing that ought to pose any threat to a gunslinger's heart was a slug from a gun.

With all that whirling through his head, it was no wonder the food was pretty much tasteless to him, and the same was true of the coffee.

He glanced through the arched doorway between the dining room and the lobby and saw Palisade's postmaster, Hayes Clancey, hurry into the hotel and look around. It was a welcome distraction.

The postmaster saw him at the same time and started into the dining room toward him.

Buckhorn stood, picked up his bowler hat from

the table, and put it on as he moved to meet Clancey. He didn't have to worry about paying for the meal. Like almost every other amenity to be found in Palisade, it was free for him because of his association with Samuel Eagleton. "Morning, Hayes. You look like a man with something on your mind."

Clancey was a short, reedy man with thinning brown hair, a prominent Adam's apple, and spectacles. "Mr. Eagleton told me a while back that he wanted to be informed whenever the mail arrived."

"The stagecoach won't be back with the mail pouch until sometime this afternoon, will it?" Buckhorn asked, even though he knew perfectly well the stagecoach probably wouldn't be coming back at all. Something unusual had happened in Bleak Creek, as the late-night arrival of Emily Corcoran and the Jensen brothers proved. For the time being, Buckhorn was going to pretend ignorance.

Clancey frowned. "I don't know about the stagecoach, but Brian Corcoran just brought the mail pouch from Bleak Creek into the post office and turned it over to me. It beats me how he got it here so fast, but he did. I didn't even stop to sort the mail, just locked it up and came over here to tell Mr. Eagleton."

"The boss is still asleep. I'll pass along the news to him when he gets up."

Nervously, Clancey insisted, "He told me he wanted to be informed *right away*—"

"I said I'd tell him." Buckhorn put a menacing growl in his voice.

Clancey's Adam's apple jumped up and down in his throat as he swallowed hard and backed away a couple steps. "W-why, sure, Joe, I'm much obliged," he stammered. "I guess by g-giving you the information, I-I've done my duty here."

"Thought your duty was to the U.S. Post Office," Buckhorn drawled.

"Oh, it is, it is. You know what I mean—"

Buckhorn stopped him with a curt nod "Yeah. You better get on back. Folks will be wanting to pick up their mail, now that it's here."

"Sure, sure." Clancey turned around and all but ran out of the hotel, obviously eager to get away from the hard-faced gunfighter.

The man was right, Buckhorn thought with a weary sigh. Eagleton would want to know about it sooner rather than later, even if meant waking him up. He wouldn't be happy about being disturbed, but he would be even less happy to know that the mail from Bleak Creek had arrived after all, even earlier than it was supposed to. Buckhorn had no doubt that Emily and the Jensens had brought it with them, even though he hadn't spotted the mail pouch when he'd seen them ride in.

He was about to head upstairs, go into the suite,

and knock on the boss's bedroom door when he heard a commotion outside. Glad to have an excuse to postpone the conversation with Eagleton for a few minutes, he stepped out onto the hotel's porch to see what was going on.

A dozen men on horseback had just pulled up in front of Marshal Claude Wheeler's office. Buckhorn's eyes narrowed as he spotted the badge pinned to the coat of the sour-looking, middle-aged man leading the group.

That hombre was Jed Kaiser, the marshal from Bleak Creek. He had a couple deputies with him, also sporting tin stars, and the rest of the men had to be volunteers for a posse.

Buckhorn frowned. Why would Kaiser ride out of his bailiwick and bring a posse with him? It had to have something to do with the Jensen brothers and Emily Corcoran. Maybe he ought to just mosey over there and try to get some answers. He started in that direction.

His eyes narrowed as he got a good look at one of the posse men, a handsome, well-dressed gent with a thin mustache. Buckhorn recognized him—Jacob Tanner, the railroad surveyor.

The last time Buckhorn had seen Tanner was when the man was leaving Eagleton's hotel suite a couple weeks earlier. Could be a mighty interesting development.

Chapter Twenty-Two

Claude Wheeler emerged from his office before Kaiser could even dismount. The chunky, fair-haired marshal of Palisade looked up at his counterpart from Bleak Creek. "Why, howdy, Jed. What brings you all the way over here?"

"I'm looking for three fugitives from justice," Kaiser snapped as he settled back in his saddle.

"I don't doubt that you could find some lawbreakers here. You don't really have any jurisdiction outside the town limits of Bleak Creek, though, do you?"

"Don't get high and mighty about the law with me," Kaiser said, unable to control the anger that had been simmering inside him during the ride all the way to Palisade. "You wear a star, Claude, but you're not even an employee of the town. You draw your wages from the Golden Dome Mining Corporation."

The casual set of Wheeler's shoulders stiffened. "The Golden Dome Mining Corporation *is* the town. What's your point, Marshal?"

"I came to ask for your assistance as a fellow lawman, and I'm entitled to get it. I could have just ridden in and taken the fugitives I wanted, but I'm trying to show you some respect."

"Then quit muddying up the waters with a

bunch of talk about who pays my wages," Wheeler suggested as he hooked his thumbs in his gun belt. "Who are you looking for?"

"Emily Corcoran and those two ne'er-do-well saddle tramps named Jensen."

A surprised frown creased Wheeler's forehead as he repeated, "Emily Corcoran? She can be a little on the feisty side, Marshal, but she never struck me as being an owlhoot."

"She never helped bust a prisoner out of my jail before, either," Kaiser said. "But that's exactly what she did last night. And that was *after* she shot up my town yesterday afternoon and helped the other Jensen boy escape before I could even take him into custody."

"Well, that's pretty wild, even for Emily," Wheeler admitted. "I can see why you'd want to at least question her."

"Question, hell," Kaiser barked. "I'm taking her back and throwing her in jail like the common outlaw she is."

Wheeler stiffened again. "Now hold on. I don't care what you do to the Jensens, but the Corcoran family has friends here in Palisade."

"Enemies, too," Kaiser sniffed.

"That's as may be, but I still won't stand for any young woman being mistreated and man-handled, no matter who she is. I'm coming with you over to the stage line office, and we'll get to the bottom of this."

"That's all I asked for in the first place," Kaiser pointed out.

Wheeler stepped down from the porch in front of his office and pointed the way. "Come on."

Kaiser reined his horse around, and the other members of the posse followed suit. Wheeler remained on foot, striding diagonally along the street toward the headquarters of the Corcoran Stage Line.

When they reached the office, Kaiser hipped around in his saddle and told his deputies and the members of the posse, "Spread out and surround the place. The barn and the corral, too. If the Jensens and the Corcoran girl see us coming, they'll probably try to hide. Don't let them get away."

Deputy Andy Belmont asked, "If they give us trouble, Marshal, do we shoot 'em?"

Kaiser glanced at Claude Wheeler. "Well . . . be careful of the girl, of course. But do whatever you have to do to take the Jensen brothers into custody." He had just declared open season on Ace and Chance Jensen. He knew it and didn't care.

Whatever happened to those two, they had it coming.

Kaiser dismounted and started for the door, but Wheeler beat him to it.

He held up a hand. "I'm cooperating with you, Jed, but this is still my town. Let me talk to whoever is in here."

Anger welled up inside Kaiser again, but he tamped it down and jerked his head in a curt nod. "Very well. You know what you need to do."

"That'll depend on what we find," Wheeler said mildly. He opened the door and strode into the stage line office with Kaiser close at his heels.

Bess Corcoran sat at one of the desks in the office with what looked like a stagecoach schedule spread out in front of her. She looked up, appeared to be surprised to see the two lawmen crowding each other a little as they came into the room, and put a smile on her face. "Marshal Wheeler. And Marshal Kaiser. Well, this is something you don't see every day. What can I do for you gentlemen? Do you need to book seats on one of our trips to Bleak Creek?"

"Why would I need to do that?" Kaiser burst out. "I'm not even from here! I live in Bleak Creek!"

Wheeler gave his fellow lawman a reproving glance, then turned to Bess. "Sorry to bother you, Miss Corcoran, but we're looking for your sister Emily and for those two young fellas who've gone to work for your father."

"You mean Ace and Chance Jensen?"

"That's right."

Bess shook her head. "I haven't seen any of them for a while today. They might be out in the barn, though. Have you checked out there?"

"We have men looking there right now," Kaiser said.

"Is there some sort of problem?" Bess asked, looking confused.

Once again, Kaiser couldn't control himself. He took a step forward. "You know good and well there is, young woman! Those Jensens are outlaws! Fugitives! And so is your sister for helping them escape from the law!"

"Take it easy, Marshal. Yelling isn't going to help anything." Wheeler looked at Bess again. "You're sure you don't know where they are? This is the law asking, Bess. You don't want to lie to the law."

"I wouldn't. I give you my word, Marshal Wheeler. I really and truly don't have any idea where Emily, Ace, and Chance are right now."

The brothers followed Emily as she led the way up the steep, winding mountain trail.

It was a good thing Kaiser and Wheeler had stood around arguing for a few minutes, Ace thought as he climbed.

Nate had stood just inside the partially open barn door and kept an eye on the lawmen. As it was, the three of them had barely had time to throw saddles on their horses and lead the mounts out the back of the barn before it was too late.

Emily had taken them on a twisting path through the settlement's back alleys until they reached the outskirts of Palisade and started up the rocky slope.

Chance had said, "Wait a minute. Isn't this the way to Eagleton's mine?"

"Can you think of anywhere less likely for them to expect to find us?" Emily had asked.

She was right about that, but Ace was still worried. He looked around. Not much vegetation to use as cover. The nearby pass was called Timberline for a good reason. Some trees grew around the town, but they didn't have to go very far up the mountainside before the only growth consisted of small, scrubby bushes, which wouldn't offer any concealment if anybody happened to look up and see the three of them fleeing from the posse.

Emily didn't follow the main trail to the mine for very long. She veered off onto a smaller path that branched and grew still smaller as it weaved through giant slabs of rock that had tumbled down in ages past. When Ace looked down the slope behind them, he couldn't see the town anymore—which meant that anyone in Palisade couldn't see *them,* either.

Nor did he hear shouting or gunshots or any other sounds of pursuit, and noises like that would have carried in the thin, clear air. All he heard were the horses' hooves striking the rocky slope as he and his brother and Emily climbed higher.

Finally she called a halt at the base of a sheer bluff that jutted out from the side of the mountain. Some bushes grew there, watered by a tiny spring that bubbled out of the rock and formed a pool less than six feet across. It was enough for the horses to drink and for them to fill their canteens. When Ace hunkered on his heels and scooped up some of the water to taste, he found it to be so cold it seemed to numb his mouth.

"Rocky Mountain spring water," Emily said. "You won't find any better. I've camped here several times when I came up here to hunt."

"Does Bess know about this place?" Ace asked.

"She does."

"Kaiser and Wheeler may try to force her to talk," Chance said.

"Ha." Emily shook her head. "I like to josh with her, but nobody's tougher or more stubborn than my sister when she wants to be. Anyway, they can't get too rough with her. The townspeople wouldn't stand for it."

"I thought most of the townspeople were under Eagleton's thumb," Ace said.

"They are, but no matter how much money a person has, folks won't stand for a woman being mistreated."

Ace and Chance knew that was true. On the frontier, a decent woman was safe under almost any circumstances.

A man, on the other hand . . .

"They might try to force her to talk by going after your father," Ace said.

Emily looked like that suggestion worried her. "That's true," she admitted. "And Bess would cooperate with them if they threatened to hurt Pa, or even old Nate. She wouldn't be able to stand that."

"Kaiser's liable to bring his posse up here to search for us, even if Bess doesn't talk," Chance said.

"Let him. I can dodge a posse."

"You talk like Jesse James or Billy the Kid."

Emily tossed her head. "Maybe that's what I'll be—an outlaw. But if I am, they drove me to it. Men like Sam Eagleton who think they can run roughshod over everybody else. Somebody's got to stand up and fight them."

"You're doing a good job of it," Ace told her. "Is this where we're going to stay?"

"It's as good a place as any to wait and see what's going to happen," Emily said. "It'll get a little cold tonight, but I reckon we can stand that."

"Better than a jail cell," Chance said.

It didn't take long for word to get around town that the posse from Bleak Creek was looking for Emily Corcoran and the Jensen boys. Buckhorn lounged on the hotel porch and watched the

241

commotion with a sardonic smile tugging at his lips.

He had no use for Claude Wheeler, and from what he knew of Jed Kaiser, the Bleak Creek lawman was even worse. He wasn't cheerfully corrupt, like Wheeler was, but he was arrogant, stiff-necked, and full of himself . . . just the sort of star-packer who liked to make life miserable for a half-breed kid growing up. Buckhorn probably could have tracked down the Jensens himself if he'd wanted to, but he didn't give a damn if the lawmen succeeded in catching them.

He still had a grudge against young Ace and Chance, but he could bide his time and wait to settle it. Patience was a virtue in his line of work.

While the posse spread out to search everywhere in Palisade, Buckhorn lit a cigar and went into the hotel. He sauntered over to the desk and asked the slick-haired clerk, "The boss rung for his breakfast yet?"

"About ten minutes ago," the man said.

Buckhorn nodded in satisfaction. He hadn't had to disturb Eagleton's sleep after all, but it was time that his employer knew what was going on in town—including the fact that Jacob Tanner was in Palisade.

Buckhorn climbed the stairs to the second floor and went into the suite's sitting room without knocking.

The mining magnate glanced up from the table

where he was eating scrambled eggs and ham from fine china on a silver tray. "Did I hear something going on outside?"

"Marshal Kaiser from Bleak Creek is in town with a posse." Buckhorn tapped ash from his cigar into a fancy ashtray. "He and Marshal Wheeler are looking for Emily Corcoran and those Jensen boys."

Eagleton frowned. "Kaiser was supposed to arrest the Jensens when they showed up in Bleak Creek with the stagecoach yesterday. I had it all arranged."

"With your partner Tanner? He rode in with Kaiser and the others."

"Leave him out of this," Eagleton snapped. "My business arrangements are really none of your affair, Buckhorn."

"You're right, boss," Buckhorn said easily. "Unfortunately, those plans you had for the Jensens must not have worked out, because they rode back into town late last night along with Emily Corcoran. But no stagecoach."

"What happened to the stagecoach?"

"No idea," the gunfighter replied with a shrug. "I reckon it's still in Bleak Creek for some reason. The important thing is that they brought the mail pouch back with them, so the delivery was made on schedule. Ahead of time, actually."

Eagleton's fork rang against the tray as he threw it down. "Damn and blast!" he exclaimed.

"Those Jensens are turning out to be harder to get rid of than cockroaches. Brian Corcoran would have given up a week ago if it weren't for them."

"You could be right about that. I reckon he's just about run out of reprieves, though. With no stagecoach and the Jensens and one of his daughters on the run from the law, there's no way he'll be able to make the next run to Bleak Creek."

Eagleton scowled and drank some of his coffee, which Buckhorn happened to know was laced with brandy.

"You say there's a posse in town?"

"Yep. They're looking for Emily and the Jensens, but I've got a hunch they won't find 'em. That blond gal is crafty."

"Could *you* find them?" Eagleton asked bluntly.

Buckhorn didn't like the sound of that, but he answered honestly, "I probably could." He might not dress like a redskin, he thought, but he could track like one.

"Then that's your new job right now," Eagleton said. "Find those three and bring Emily Corcoran to me."

"What about Ace and Chance?"

"Do you even have to ask?" Eagleton said with a sneer. "Kill them, of course."

Chapter Twenty-Three

Ace lay stretched out on his belly atop one of the boulders that surrounded the place where he, Chance, and Emily had made camp. He had climbed up there to keep an eye on the trail, cuffing his hat to the back of his neck so it wouldn't stick up as far when he raised his head. He was careful to edge up just high enough to look back along the route they had taken.

Emily was convinced that neither Kaiser nor Wheeler knew the terrain as well as she did and that she, Chance, and Ace were relatively safe.

Ace hoped that was right. From where he was, he could see not only the trail but also across the bench where the settlement was located, over the giant rocks that had given Palisade its name, and across the valley to Shoshone Gap. As he studied the landscape stretching out before him for miles, he was more convinced than ever that the theory forming in his head was correct. He needed to find out the answer to one more question, and that would probably be the last thing he needed to confirm the idea.

A sound drifted to his ears, causing him to stiffen with alarm. It was the clink of a horseshoe against rock, just one, but enough to tell him that a rider was moving around somewhere up there and not too far away at that. His eyes intently searched every bit of the mountainside he could see, but he didn't spot any movement.

That didn't mean anything. If the rider was good enough to keep his mount that quiet, he was good enough not to be seen.

Ace turned and carefully slid down the boulder toward the spot where it dropped off into the camp. He had to warn Chance and Emily that they might have company soon.

Chance was glad his brother had volunteered to clamber up above the camp and keep watch. That gave him the opportunity to spend some time alone with Emily, which was always welcome. "I don't know if I thanked you for all your help," he said as she unsaddled her horse.

"Help with what?"

"Well, if not for you, I wouldn't have gotten away yesterday afternoon when Kaiser tried to spring that trap on us, and you deserve most of the credit for getting Ace out of jail. You came up with the plan, after all, and ran most of the real risk by causing that distraction."

"You thanked me." Emily set the saddle aside. "And you ran some risk, too, so don't go making it sound like I'm some sort of storybook heroine. I'm about as far from Joan of Arc as you'll find."

"I'm not so sure about that. Joan of Arc was supposed to be beautiful, wasn't she?"

246

"She was also a kid. I'm not."

Chance nodded. "I'm well aware of that."

Emily let out one of her customary exasperated snorts and picked up her rifle. "Maybe I'll climb up there and see if Ace needs a hand."

He put a hand on her arm. "Ace will be fine. He's got the best eyesight of anybody I've ever seen. If he spies anybody on our trail, he'll let us know right away."

"You sound mighty sure about that." She was tall enough that her eyes were almost on a level with Chance's.

"I am. I know my brother. We've been watching each other's back for years. We sort of raised each other. Doc tried, but he wasn't really cut out for the job."

"Is he still alive?"

"He is, or at least he was the last time we heard. He's in a sanitarium down in Colorado. His health took a turn for the worse, so he had to take a rest cure. Ace and I send money back there to pay for it and go visit him when we can." Chance shook his head. "That's probably not often enough, but . . ."

"But there's always something to see on the other side of the hill, isn't there? Believe me, I know the feeling."

The conversation had taken a turn he hadn't really expected, but he wasn't displeased with the way it was going. Emily seemed genuinely interested and sympathetic. He found that he enjoyed talking to her, and not just because she was so pretty. Although that certainly didn't hurt anything.

"If you wanted to see some of the rest of the world, I'm sure your sister could help your pa run the stage line," he suggested. "Well, once all this business with Eagleton is settled."

"Do you think it ever will be? Like we've said before, Eagleton's not going to give up. Not until he's dead. Maybe what I ought to do is march over to that hotel where he spends most of the time and ventilate his ugly hide." She looked utterly fierce as the words came out of her ruby-lipped mouth.

Chance couldn't help but admire her, but he was also troubled by the direction her thoughts were taking. "I thought you said he's got a gunfighter for a bodyguard."

"He does. Joe Buckhorn. I'd just have to take my chances with him."

"In other words, you'd wind up getting yourself killed for no good reason," Chance declared. "If you stop and think about it for a minute, you'll realize that."

She sighed. "I know. I just get so damn frustrated sometimes. It seems like there ought to be something we can do . . ."

"I know one thing we can do," Chance said as he moved closer and reached up, cupping his hand under her chin. When she didn't pull away but rather regarded him levelly, he went on. "We can do this." He leaned in and kissed her.

She didn't pull away. In fact, she slid her left arm around his neck and held him closer. She couldn't put both arms around him, because she was still holding the Winchester.

It was probably the first time he had ever kissed a woman who was toting a rifle, he thought, but things like that seemed to be pretty common where Emily Corcoran was concerned.

Her lips moved warmly against his. He rested his hands on her waist. Excitement grew within him as she surged against him.

Chance knew nothing more than a kiss was going to happen as long as Ace wasn't far away, up on top of that rock slab overlooking the trail, but the kiss certainly held the promise of more. . . .

The promise was broken as Ace slid down from the boulder, landed only a couple of feet from them, and whispered, "Somebody's moving around not far from here."

While the members of the posse from Bleak Creek were blundering around Palisade, looking in sheds and behind rain barrels for the fugitives and asking blustery questions of the citizens, Joe Buckhorn saddled his horse and rode to the back of the barn owned by the Corcoran Stage Line.

It took him only a few minutes to locate the fresh hoofprints he was looking for. It stood to reason that if Emily Corcoran and the Jensen boys knew Marshal Kaiser was in Palisade looking for them, they would do their best to get out of town.

Buckhorn was hunkered on his heels, studying the tracks and familiarizing himself with the distinctive marks left by the horseshoes—all horseshoes left distinctive marks if you knew what to look for—when a querulous voice cried, "Hey! What're you doin' back here, mister?"

He straightened and looked over his shoulder, moving casually and not getting in any hurry about it. The scrawny old man who worked as a hostler for the Corcorans stood glaring at him and holding a pitchfork in his gnarled hands.

"Take it easy, grandfather," Buckhorn said. "You don't want to tangle with me. This is none of your affair."

"I know you," Nate said as his eyes narrowed in anger and suspicion. "You're that 'breed gunfighter who works for Eagleton."

Buckhorn felt some anger of his own welling up. "Choose your words carefully, old man. I don't like to be insulted."

"Reckon it'd be hard to insult a fella who's already lowdown enough to work for a snake like Eagleton." The old man brandished the pitchfork. "And you ain't answered my question. Tell me what you're doin' back here 'fore I take this fork to you and let out some air."

Buckhorn ignored him and turned toward his horse. He wasn't going to waste a bullet on the old pelican. Besides, he had work to do. He wanted to get on the trail of his quarry before it got any colder.

"Hey!" Nate shouted as he came closer. "Don't you go turnin' your back on me—"

Buckhorn had reached the end of his patience. He turned quickly and his arm lashed out. The old man tried to thrust the pitchfork at him, but his movements were pathetically slow. Buckhorn knocked the sharp tines aside, reached out to grasp the tool's handle, and jerked it out of the hostler's grip.

The old man gasped and opened his mouth to sound a shout of alarm, but Buckhorn slammed the pitchfork handle against his head.

Nate staggered as the shout died in his throat. Buckhorn hit him again, and the old man went to the ground with blood seeping from the cut the pitchfork handle had opened. He groaned and scratched feebly at the dirt, but he didn't try to get up.

Grimacing in disgust, Buckhorn tossed the pitchfork aside. He muttered, "Mighty warrior, beating up on old men," then swung into the saddle. He turned the horse and rode away from the barn, following the tracks he had found. His own horse's hooves probably obliterated them, but that didn't really matter, Buckhorn thought. Those posse men were too stupid to ever find the trail in the first place.

The tracks led to the road that ran from Palisade to the Golden Dome mine. Buckhorn's lips quirked in a grim smile when he saw that. That was probably the girl's doing, he thought. Trying to head for a spot where the pursuers wouldn't expect them to go. The Jensens hadn't been around long enough to attempt something like that, while Emily Corcoran was a half-wild tomboy who, in some ways, had never grown up.

Of course, she was plenty grown up in other ways, Buckhorn amended, thinking of the blond beauty. As far as he was concerned, her looks paled in comparison to those of Rose Demarcus, but that didn't mean she wasn't pretty. He wondered if one of the Jensen boys was trying to court her. Wouldn't surprise him a bit.

The tracks didn't stay on the mine trail all the way to the Golden Dome. About halfway up, Buckhorn's keen eyes spotted a couple scratches left on the rocks by horseshoes where the riders had turned onto a smaller path. He paused a moment, thinking Emily was going to get trickier still.

He didn't know those mountain trails as well as he would have liked. He hadn't spent much time up there exploring them. Eagleton kept him close by nearly all the time, which made sense. He was the man's bodyguard, after all. He had accompanied the boss up to the mine a number of times and done a little prowling on the mountain, but it didn't take long for him to be lost as he followed the fugitives' tracks.

Well, he might not know where he was, he told himself, but he knew where he was going—after Emily and the Jensen brothers.

As he climbed higher on the mountain, his instincts told him that he was getting close.

Ace looked over at his brother and nodded. He could hear the horse approaching. The trail ran directly between the boulders where the Jensens crouched, waiting. When the man rode into view, Ace was going to leap from his perch and tackle him, with Chance jumping down right behind to help Ace subdue their pursuer. Emily was about twenty yards ahead, around a bend, and when she heard the scuffle she would run out into the open with the coach gun ready in case she needed it.

They all hoped that wouldn't be necessary. Gunfire would draw plenty of attention they didn't want.

It was a plan that had a very good chance of succeeding, Ace thought . . . if there was only one man for them to deal with. He had heard only one horse, but maybe that didn't mean anything.

Maybe that whole blasted posse was about to come down on top of them and cart them off to prison. Just the possibility of that was enough to make his heart thud painfully in his chest.

The horse's hooves clinked against the rocky trail as it continued to draw closer. Ace tensed and leaned forward as the horse's head came into view. He was poised to tackle the rider when the saddle appeared.

It was empty.

The realization hit Ace like a punch in the belly. The horse's reins were tied around the saddle horn, leaving it to plod along riderless. He had no idea how long it had been that way, but he knew it couldn't be good.

Across the trail from him on top of the other boulder, Chance had seen the same thing, and Ace knew from the stunned expression on his brother's face that Chance had reached the same conclusion. It was very bad.

Just how bad, they found out a moment later when a harsh voice called, "Hey, Jensens! Better come out with empty hands where I can see you if you don't want anything to happen to this pretty little girl!"

The cry of pain from Emily that followed those words stabbed into Ace and turned his blood cold.

Chapter Twenty-Four

"Don't keep me waiting, boys!" the voice called again.

Ace lifted his voice. "You come out where we can see you! I want to know that Emily's all right!"

"She is—for now! Tell them!"

Emily cried, "Ace! Chance! Don't cooperate with him—"

The sharp sound of a slap silenced her. Chance's face flushed with fury. He jerked the Lightning from under his coat and started to slide down off the boulder, ignoring Ace's gesture for him to stay where he was.

Ace went off his boulder the other way, dropping to the ground where the man who had captured Emily couldn't see him. He didn't know who the man was, possibly that gunfighter Buckhorn, but whoever he was, he was pretty canny, fooling them with the horse trick while he circled around and grabbed Emily.

If they surrendered to him, it would be all over. The man would take them back to Palisade as prisoners and turn them over to Marshal Kaiser. Surrounded by the posse from Bleak Creek, they would have no chance to escape. They would be facing years in prison.

And the Corcorans would be facing ruin. No

one else in Palisade was going to help them. The stage line would be crushed and swallowed up by the greedy maw of Samuel Eagleton.

Somewhere on the other side of the boulders, Chance shouted, "Come on out, damn you! If you hurt Emily, I'll kill you!"

Keep raising that racket, Ace thought as he began circling through the rocks. He didn't know if his brother was doing it deliberately to distract Emily's captor or if Chance was really just too scared and angry to think about anything else.

Either way, it was giving Ace the opportunity to move around without being heard. The odds against him would still be high . . . but the only other option was surrender.

For a Jensen, even one not named Smoke, that was just no option at all.

Chance struggled to get control of his emotions as he pressed himself against a little shoulder of rock and watched the bend in the trail where Emily had been hidden. He wanted to just blaze away as soon as he got a shot at the one who had captured her, but that was a good way to get her killed, and probably him, too.

They all had to stay alive. Ace hadn't come down with him, so that meant his brother was trying to get in position to turn the tables on their enemy. To give Ace that opportunity, Chance tried another tack. "Listen, mister. Step out so I can see that Emily's all right, and I'll throw down my gun! I give you my word on that. We'll cooperate. Just don't hurt her."

"What about your brother? Is he willing to make the same promise?"

"Sure he is," Chance said, mentally cursing even as he answered. He knew that next, Emily's captor would demand to hear Ace pledge to surrender, too.

The man surprised him. "Don't try anything funny. Miss Corcoran will be sorry if you do." With that, Buckhorn moved out into the open, holding Emily in front of him with his left arm looped around her neck and pressing cruelly against her throat. His right hand held a Colt so that the barrel dug into her side. The man seemed casual, but Chance figured he was anything but.

Over Emily's shoulder, he took in the bowler hat and the craggy, rough-hewn features of the gunslinger, Eagleton's own personal killer. The man had plenty of blood on his hands already. Spilling some of Emily's probably wouldn't bother him.

Buckhorn didn't seem surprised to see that Chance was alone. In fact, he chuckled at the sight. "Well, you didn't disappoint me, Jensen. I knew your brother wouldn't be here. Did he take off for the tall and uncut, or is he trying to sneak around and get behind me? You know damn well there's nothing he can do, don't you?"

Buckhorn's voice was loud enough to carry to Ace's ears somewhere in the rocks. He was trying to get Ace to give up, too.

"Look at the thumb on my gun hand, Jensen," Buckhorn went on. "By the way, which one are you?"

Chance's mouth was dry, but he managed to say, "I'm Chance."

"Look at my thumb, Chance. It's the only thing holding back the hammer on this gun. Your brother might be the best shot in the world. I don't know. He might be able to put a bullet in my head from wherever he is. But if he does, this gun's going off, too, and Miss Corcoran will get a slug through her guts. You don't want that, do you?"

Chance's jaw was too tight with rage for him to speak.

Buckhorn nodded. "Why don't we start by you throwing that gun down? Go ahead and do it now."

Chance's pulse pounded in his head. He had to play along with the gunfighter for the time being and stepped out from the rock and leaned over to set the Lightning on the rocky ground at his feet.

"Back away from it," Buckhorn ordered. "Got any hideout guns, knives, anything like that?"

"No," Chance managed to say. "That's the only weapon I carry."

"I don't know if I believe you, but it doesn't

really matter. Not as long as I've got this gun in Miss Corcoran's side."

"Did Eagleton send you after us?" Chance wanted to keep Buckhorn talking.

"Of course he did. Why else would I be here?"

"He sent you to kill us all, didn't he?"

Buckhorn sounded amused as he replied. "No. Actually, he sent me to kill just you and your brother. He told me to bring Emily back to him."

"What does he want with her? Does he want to kill her himself?"

Buckhorn frowned. "You've got it all wrong, Chance. Eagleton's not a killer. He's a businessman. He'll use Emily as leverage to force her father to sign the stage line over to him. That way he wins. I reckon that's what he cares about more than anything."

As his heart continued to slug hard in his chest, Chance said, "If you were supposed to kill me and Ace, why haven't you shot me?"

Buckhorn's voice hardened slightly. "Because Samuel Eagleton doesn't always have to get *everything* he wants. I'm thinking I'll take the two of you back to Palisade and turn you over to Marshal Kaiser. He'll see to it that you're convicted of whatever charges he's got against you and sent to prison. That'll get rid of you just as well as gunning you down."

Chance frowned. It almost sounded like Buckhorn didn't want any more killings on his conscience. Was that even possible? Could a cold-blooded hired killer ever reach the point where he didn't want to see any more men fall to his gun?

Was Buckhorn that sick of the smell of gun smoke?

It probably wouldn't be a good idea to put that theory to the test, not when Emily's life hung in the balance. But maybe somewhere along the line would come a moment when the tables could be turned, when Buckhorn might hesitate just for the split second that could change everything. . . .

It was about as slim a hope as any Chance had ever clung to, but it was better than nothing.

"All right, you've stalled long enough," Buckhorn said abruptly. "Ace Jensen, I know you can hear me! Come on out and throw your gun down, or I won't be responsible for what happens to Miss Corcoran!"

Ace slid out of a crack in the rock about fifteen feet behind Buckhorn. "Yes, you will." He aimed the Colt in his hand at the gunfighter's head. "And if anything—anything at all—happens to her, you'll be dead half a second later."

Ace wasn't bluffing. He would blow Buckhorn's brains out if the man hurt Emily. He didn't want it to come to that, though. "You don't want to die for Samuel Eagleton, Buckhorn. If you don't want to kill for him anymore, you sure as hell don't want to die."

"Who says I don't want to kill?" Buckhorn growled.

"If you wanted Chance dead, you could have shot him by now. You could have put a bullet through him as soon as he stepped out into the open."

"Good idea, reminding him of that," Chance muttered.

"I mean it," Ace said. "Your heart's not in it, Buckhorn. And why should it be? You probably know what kind of man Eagleton is better than anyone else."

"Maybe not anyone," Buckhorn said under his breath, but loud enough for Ace to hear it.

"You know he's power-mad, but really it's worse than that. He's not crazy, Buckhorn. He's smart. He knows he can make a fortune by taking over the stagecoach line."

"What the hell are you talking about?" Buckhorn sounded confused, and Ace could imagine the puzzled frown on the gunfighter's face. "The money Eagleton could make off the stage line is nothing compared to what he's taken out of the Golden Dome."

Ace took a deep breath. A lot of what he was about to say was still supposition on his part, but it made sense and explained why Eagleton was so anxious to get his hands on the Corcoran Stage

Line. "The Golden Dome is about to play out, but there's an even bigger gold mine down in the valley . . . the valley itself. But to make it pay off, Eagleton needs the stage line. Or to be more precise, he needs the *road*."

Chance's eyes widened as his keen brain grasped the implications of what his brother was saying. "It's the railroad! Tanner's going to build a spur line across the valley, and the stage road is the perfect route for it!"

"That's the way I've got it figured," Ace said. "Brian Corcoran owns the right-of-way on that land, and if he signed over the stagecoach company, Eagleton would get it. His silent partner Tanner will then use it to build a spur line across the valley to the new town that Eagleton establishes at the foot of Timberline Pass. I figure Eagleton already has other partners lined up to bring in cattle and start ranches in the valley. It'll boom, and so will Eagleton's new town. He'll build stockyards and make this a shipping center not only for the valley but for this whole part of the territory. It won't be as flashy as the riches from the mine, but it'll last longer and make more money in the end. The old Palisade up on the bench will be a ghost town."

Frowning, Buckhorn turned and backed against the rock so he could look back and forth at the Jensen brothers. Emily looked shocked by the things Ace had said, too.

"That's an interesting story, kid," Buckhorn said, "but I don't see how it changes anything. If you're right, Eagleton will wind up even richer than he already is. How's that supposed to make me turn against him?"

"You know Tanner's going to get a big cut of the money. So will the men who bring in the cattle. But you're still working for wages, aren't you, Buckhorn? Eagleton never offered to cut you in for a share, did he? If he had, you'd already know about all this, and I can tell that you didn't."

Buckhorn grimaced. "That doesn't matter. So I'm working for wages. That's what I've always done."

"Well, like you said," Ace shrugged, homing in on a comment Buckhorn had made earlier. "Eagleton gets everything. That's just the way life works, isn't it?"

Buckhorn turned his head to scowl at Ace, drifting the muzzle of the gun he held away from Emily's side. "You don't know what you're—"

Emily drove her elbow back and to the side to knock the gun farther away from her, jolting Buckhorn's thumb off the hammer. She threw her head backward and butted Buckhorn in the face, loosening his grip enough for her to tear free and dive forward, out of the line of fire, just as the shot blasted out.

At the same instant, Ace's Colt roared. The slug

smashed into Buckhorn's shoulder and knocked him back against the boulder behind him. His gun slipped from suddenly nerveless fingers and thudded to the ground.

Chance scooped up the Lightning and trained it on the wounded gunfighter.

With Buckhorn covered from two directions, there was nothing he could do except clutch his bloody shoulder with his other hand and snarl at the Jensens. "I'll kill you two," he vowed. "Whatever it takes, I'll kill you."

"Not today you won't," Chance said.

Emily scrambled to her feet. The palms of her hands were scraped a little from catching herself when she dived to the rocky ground, but other than that she seemed fine.

A great relief considering that a minute or so earlier she'd had a cold-blooded killer pressing a gun into her side, Ace thought.

She picked up the gun Buckhorn had dropped. "We have another problem now. Everybody down in Palisade will have heard those shots."

Ace said, "Which means—"

"Yeah," Emily broke in. "Marshal Kaiser and that posse of his will be on their way up here as soon as they can grab their horses."

Chance frowned at Buckhorn. "We need to get moving again—but what do we do with him?"

Chapter Twenty-Five

Emily said, "The simplest thing to do would be just to shoot him." The gun in her hand—Buckhorn's own that she had picked up—was already pointed in his general direction. "One more shot won't bring the posse down on us any faster."

Buckhorn sneered at her. "Trust me, girl, I know cold-blooded killers when I see them . . . and none of you three fit that description."

"He's right," Ace said. "We can't kill him. But we can do this." Without any more warning than that, he stepped forward, reversed the Colt in his hand, and slammed the butt against Buckhorn's head.

The gunfighter's knees buckled and he fell to the ground, stunned.

Ace holstered his gun and knelt to search inside Buckhorn's coat.

Emily frowned. "What are you doing? We need to get out of here!"

Ace found a handkerchief, balled it up, and thrust it into the bullet wound in Buckhorn's shoulder. "We can't leave him here unconscious without doing something to slow down the bleeding from that wound. Otherwise, he might die before anybody finds him. And I don't want him being able to tell the posse which way we went, so I had to knock him out."

"Well, I guess that makes sense, but when you get right down to it, there's only one way for us to go." She pointed. "Up."

"I'll get the horses." Chance headed in their direction.

She took off her bandanna and handed it to Ace. "Here, use this to tie that bandage in place. If we're going to save his life, we might as well do a decent job of it. But if it was up to me, after the way he stuck that gun in my side . . . I might've let him bleed to death."

"Don't think I didn't consider it," Ace said under his breath as he knotted the bandanna around Buckhorn's shoulder.

A moment later, the fugitives were all mounted and the brothers were following Emily up another of the twisting mountain trails. Soon they were in such a barren, rocky wasteland it might as well have been the surface of the moon.

Ace turned in the saddle and looked down the mountainside, but couldn't see where the pursuit was. That was a good thing, he told himself. It meant the posse couldn't see them, either. He and Chance had to trust Emily's instincts and her knowledge of the terrain. She hadn't let them down so far.

"We're higher than the entrance to the Golden Dome now," Emily told them when they stopped

266

to rest the mounts from the hard climb. "Do you really think it's about to play out, Ace?"

"That's just a guess on my part," he admitted, "but I'm confident I'm right about Eagleton wanting the right-of-way the stage road would give him to extend the spur line across the valley from Bleak Creek and Shoshone Gap." Ace leveled an arm and pointed out across the landscape far below them. "Look how perfectly it lines up. You can see it from here."

"Yeah, you can," Chance said. "I think you're right about the valley being good ranching land, too . . . although that's not something I'm really all that familiar with."

"Not many cattle inside saloons, are there?" Emily asked him with a smile.

"That's true."

She turned back to Ace. "Even if you're right about everything, what good does it do us to figure that out? What Eagleton's doing isn't any more illegal than it already was. The only difference is that now we know *why* he's been trying to take over the stage line. We still can't do anything to stop him."

"Tanner's bosses at the railroad might not like it if they knew he was scheming with Eagleton to ruin your father's business in order to take over that right-of-way. Sharp business is one thing, attempted murder is another. He's tried to have you and Bess killed more than once."

267

"So how do we let them know about it?" Chance asked.

"There's a telegraph office in Bleak Creek," Ace said. "I saw the poles and the wires. We can send a telegram to the home office of the railroad and tell them about what's going on here."

Emily said skeptically, "Do you really think they'd believe some stranger over what Tanner tells them? He's a trusted employee, after all, and a successful one, to boot. Would they even care if he's crooked?"

"I don't know," Ace replied honestly. "But I can't think of anything else we can do."

Chance scratched his jaw. "There's another problem. You'd have to go into Bleak Creek to send that wire. They don't like us there, remember?"

Emily shook her head. "No, Bess could do it."

Ace nodded slowly. "Yeah, if we could write the message and get it to Bess somehow, she could send it when she rides over there to get the mail in a couple days."

"Oh!" Emily ran her fingers through her hair in exasperation. "I forgot. We were going with her to make sure she got there and back safely. Kaiser's bound to think of that. He'll be watching Bess to make sure we don't meet up with her between Palisade and Bleak Creek."

"That's good," Chance said quickly. "Eagleton's men can't make any moves against her if she's got the law watching over her. Our problem will be getting the message to her so she can send it over the telegraph."

"I'll take it to her," Emily declared. "I'm the best one to do it. I know the back trails and you boys don't."

"You'd be the one running the risk of being arrested if Kaiser nabbed you," Chance said with a frown. "I don't like that idea."

"Well, that's too bad. It's not your decision to make." Emily nodded so vehemently it made her hair give a defiant toss. "We'll find a good place for the two of you to hide, then I'll head back down to Palisade tonight with the message for Bess."

"What if you're arrested?" Chance asked. "How will we know?"

"If I don't come back, you'll know," Emily said, adding grimly, "Either that or I'll be dead."

Buckhorn came to slowly. Before moving, he listened carefully. Hearing nothing, he opened his eyes and looked around, and then sat up and propped his back against one of the rocks. His wounded shoulder hurt like blazes. He'd lost enough blood that his head spun like one of the tops he had made, back when he was a kid.

He didn't think he'd been unconscious for very long, probably just a few minutes, but it was long enough for Emily Corcoran and those damn

Jensen boys to have gotten away from him. He didn't know which way they had gone, although he figured he might be able to pick up their trail again.

He glared and cursed under his breath. He didn't need to be thinking about his miserable childhood. The only thing on his mind ought to be Ace and Chance Jensen and how he was going to kill them when he found them again.

He turned his head and looked down at his shoulder. His own handkerchief was stuffed into the bullet wound to stop the bleeding, he realized, and it had been tied in place with Emily Corcoran's bandanna. A frown creased his forehead. He might well have bled to death if the three fugitives had just left him lying there unconscious. Instead, they had taken the time to bind up his wound and possibly save his life.

His frown deepened. Why the hell had they done that?

A better question was why hadn't he killed the Jensen brothers as Eagleton told him to do? It might have been tricky, but he was confident he could have done it. Those two could be lying right where he was, dead, and Emily would be his prisoner.

Instead, he had allowed his resentment over Eagleton's high-handed ways and his jealousy of the man over Rose Demarcus to cloud his judgment. He had decided to capture Ace and

Chance and turn them over to the law, knowing it would annoy Eagleton. In the end, that had been his undoing, along with his own momentary carelessness.

That was quite some yarn the kid had spun, Buckhorn thought. Was there any truth to it? He didn't know. Eagleton was cunning enough to have struck a secret deal with Jacob Tanner to bring a railroad spur across the valley to a new town at the foot of the mountain. Palisade existed in its current location simply because it was convenient to the mine—no other real reason for it to be where it was. If indeed the mine was played out, it might make sense to Eagleton to abandon Palisade and start over down in the valley, basing the new settlement around the cattle industry.

None of that mattered to Buckhorn. He wasn't a rancher any more than he was a miner. He was a hired gun. That was all.

It really was galling, though, to think about Samuel Eagleton sailing through life, always getting what he wanted. A lucrative gold mine, a new town when he didn't need the old one anymore, the most beautiful woman Joe Buckhorn had ever seen . . .

The sound of horses' hooves and men calling to each other broke into his bitter thoughts. He couldn't tell how far away the riders were, but if he could hear them, they could hear him. He lifted his head and bellowed, "Hey! Over here!"

The noises got louder. A couple minutes later, several men rode into sight along the twisting trail through the rocks. Buckhorn recognized the two marshals, Jed Kaiser from Bleak Creek and Claude Wheeler from Palisade. They had three posse members with them.

"Buckhorn!" Wheeler exclaimed as they rode up to him. "What are you doing here?"

"Doing your job for you," Buckhorn snapped. "I found the Jensen brothers and Emily Corcoran."

"Is that so?" Kaiser asked with his usual superior sneer. "I don't see them."

"Ace Jensen shot me and they got away, damn it," Buckhorn said. "But I had them. That's more than any of you can say."

Kaiser refuted it. "That's not true. Ace Jensen was locked up in my jail—"

"He's not now."

"Both of you take it easy," Wheeler said. "The important thing now is finding them. Did you see which way they went, Buckhorn?"

"Only one way they could have gone." The gunfighter started to lift his right arm so he could jerk his thumb over his shoulder, then paused and winced at the pain that caused. He lowered the arm carefully and used the other arm to complete the gesture, pointing up.

Wheeler frowned. "On up the mountain, you mean?"

Sarcastically, Buckhorn said, "You didn't meet them coming down, did you?"

"All right. We'll keep searching. How bad are you hurt?"

"Bad enough." Buckhorn didn't like to admit it, but he wasn't a big enough fool to deny the truth. "I need a sawbones."

Wheeler turned to the men behind him. "A couple of you boys find Buckhorn's horse and take him back down to town."

"Those are *my* posse men," Kaiser snapped. "You can't give them orders."

"Well, we're a lot closer to my town than to yours, so if anybody's got jurisdiction here, it's me," Wheeler said in a patient tone as if he were explaining something to a child. "I don't want to have to tell Samuel Eagleton that we left one of his most trusted men here on the mountainside to die."

"I'm not gonna die," Buckhorn muttered. "Just need some patching up."

"Oh, all right." Kaiser jerked his head at the men Wheeler had picked out. "Go ahead and help him."

"It's liable to be a mighty long chase," Wheeler said with a sigh. "All the way to the top of this damn mountain."

It seemed to Ace like they had climbed halfway to heaven. The snow that capped the top of the mountain didn't seem to be very far off, although he knew it was still several hundred feet above them. The wind was stronger and the air was colder, too. Chance wore a coat, but Ace had just his buckskin shirt over his denim trousers.

"I shot a bighorn sheep up here last fall. I have a coat lined with its hide back home." Emily shivered a little. "Wouldn't mind having it with me right now."

Chance said, "I'm not sure freezing to death is a lot better than taking our chances with that posse."

"You're not going to freeze to death," Emily told him. "It won't get that cold up here tonight. You'll just be a mite chilly, is all."

"I'm *already* a mite chilly."

"Do you have a place in mind for us to go?" Ace asked. "Or are we just looking for a good spot?"

"I have a place," she said. "I camped there before, too. It won't be much longer."

She was as good as her word.

A short time later, they followed a slanting trail up to a broad ledge with a great brow of rock looming above it. The overhang formed a cave-like area with plenty of room for several people and horses. A ring of stones had been arranged to form a fire circle, and a pile of dry branches and brush sat against the rear wall of the area.

Ace dismounted and looked around.

Emily slid off her horse, giving it a quick rest. "You can build a fire tonight without worrying about it being seen. There's nobody up high enough to see it for fifty or sixty miles, at least. So you ought to be warm enough, anyway."

"But hungry." Chance followed suit. They had been in such a hurry to get out of Palisade before the posse caught them that they hadn't had time to gather any supplies. He and Ace had a few strips of jerky they carried in their saddlebags, but that was all.

"You won't starve to death in one night," Emily said. "You have canteens, so you don't have to worry about water. I'll try to get back up here tomorrow with some provisions, since there's no telling how long you'll have to hide out here."

"What if you get caught in Palisade?" he asked.

She smiled at him. "Then I guess you and your brother will have to figure out which one of you is turning cannibal."

Chance grunted. "Very funny."

"You need to be careful getting that message to Bess," Ace told her. "I have some paper and a pencil in my saddlebags. We can go ahead and write it out before you start back down."

Emily nodded. "That's a good idea. It's your theory, Ace, so you ought to be the one to put it on paper."

Ace retrieved paper and pencil and sat on the

ledge. For the next half hour, he struggled to boil down the whole story into a telegraph message short enough to send quickly. When he finished, he folded the paper and slipped it into his pocket to give to Emily before she left.

It was a long shot, he thought, so the odds were against it working, but as far as he could see, it was the only shot they had.

It all depended on Emily dodging the posse searching on the mountain for them.

He stood and rejoined his fellow fugitives.

"I'll wait until it starts to get dark," she said. "I can find my way around on this mountain at night better than that blasted posse can."

"I hope you're right," Chance said. "There's an awful lot riding on you."

Sensing that his brother wanted a little more privacy to talk to her, Ace walked over to the edge of the cave-like area under the overhanging rock and peered out at the spectacular landscape stretching from horizon to horizon in front of him. Wyoming was a mighty big place, he thought as he heard their voices murmuring behind him.

He wondered what Bess was doing. She had to be worried sick over her sister, and their father probably felt that way, too. The whole thing hadn't had to come to this, he thought angrily. If Eagleton had simply gone to Brian Corcoran and made him a fair offer for the stage line, Corcoran might have taken it, especially if the mine owner had explained that he was going to build a railroad spur across the valley. That would have rendered stagecoach service obsolete. Corcoran could have taken the money, gone somewhere else, and started over. He wouldn't have had to give up his dream of owning a stagecoach line.

Instead, Eagleton had tried bullying tactics to get what he wanted, and when that didn't work he'd moved on to outright harassment and finally violence, even to the point of causing a stagecoach wreck that likely would have killed the Corcoran sisters. The man's lust for wealth and power ruled him until he couldn't think of anything else.

Shadows began to reach out from the mountains and spread across the landscape in front of Ace. He hadn't realized so much time had passed since they fled Palisade just ahead of the posse. Night would be falling soon and Emily would be heading back down the mountain to the settlement. It would be a dangerous trip in the dark under the best of circumstances.

With a bunch of trigger-happy posse men in her way, anything could happen.

Ace reached up and touched the pocket where he had put the message, feeling the paper crinkle as he pressed on it. He glanced over his shoulder and saw Chance and Emily standing with their heads close together, talking quietly. He didn't know what they were talking about, but it was none of his business anyway.

However, his brother's happiness was, and he knew that Chance would take it mighty hard if anything were to happen to her.

Ace made up his mind, and turned to his horse.

As he put his foot in the stirrup and swung up into the saddle, Chance called out from the other side of the cave, "Ace, what are you doing?"

He turned the horse. "Taking that message to Bess. I kept my eyes open while we were coming up here. I can find my way back down the mountain."

Emily took a step toward him and exclaimed, "That's crazy! I'm going to—"

"You're going to stay here with Chance," Ace told her. "Chance, take good care of her."

"Ace, you don't have to do this," Chance said. "I've been trying to talk her into letting me go—"

"You're *both* crazy!" Emily lunged toward Ace's horse and reached out to grab the reins, but Chance caught hold of her and pulled her back. As Ace started down the trail, she cried, "You're going to get yourself killed!"

"Maybe not," Ace called as he half-turned in the saddle to wave at his brother and Emily. "I've got the luck of the Jensens, after all."

Chapter Twenty-Six

Eagleton scowled at his bodyguard and said in a harsh voice, "Do you want to explain to me again why you didn't just go ahead and kill them when you had the chance? This is the third time you've let the Jensens get away, Buckhorn. What the hell am I paying you for?"

"You're paying me to keep you alive," Buckhorn answered bluntly. "You're still breathing."

His shoulder hurt like hell, and he was in no mood to put up with Eagleton browbeating him. The doctor had cleaned and bandaged the wound, which was a simple one—in and out of the shoulder without breaking any bones—and rigged a black silk sling for that arm.

He'd also given Buckhorn a small dose of laudanum, which dulled the pain slightly without making it go away and also made his brain feel fuzzy. Maybe he wasn't as careful as he should have been while talking to the boss.

"Nobody's tried to kill me," Eagleton said coldly. "It seems to me like you're not earning your money."

"Maybe they haven't tried to kill you because they know they'd have to get past me, and nobody wants to risk that." Buckhorn took a deep breath and told himself to stop being so combative, since it wasn't going to do any good. "Look, boss, the way it worked out, I probably couldn't have killed the Jensens without killing Emily Corcoran, too. You told me to bring her back here to you."

"You should've gone ahead and killed her, too," Eagleton snapped. "Shown some initiative."

Buckhorn kept a tight rein on his temper. "That would have meant going against your direct order. I didn't want to do that."

Eagleton waved a pudgy hand dismissively, turned toward the sideboard in his sitting room, and reached for the brandy decanter. "Well, it's over and done with now. Maybe Wheeler and Kaiser will get lucky and catch them. As for you, you're no good to me now with that busted wing—" He stopped short and his breath hissed between his teeth.

Buckhorn's left hand had dropped to the gun holstered on that hip and swept back up with the Colt in it, hammer cocked and ready to fall. The draw was fast, mighty fast, if not performed at quite the same blinding speed as he would have managed with an uninjured right arm. It was still slick enough to have beaten most men. "I wouldn't say I'm exactly useless," Buckhorn intoned flatly. "I'm pretty good with my left hand, too."

With the decanter in one hand, Eagleton picked up a glass and splashed brandy into it. "Fine.

You've made your point. Now put that gun away." Even though the revolver wasn't pointed in his direction, he looked a little nervous until Buckhorn pouched the iron.

Instead of sipping the brandy, Eagleton tossed it back.

It would have been easy just then, thought Buckhorn. He had the gun in his hand and Eagleton right there. All he had to do was squeeze the trigger. Rose would never have to submit to the man's brutish caresses again. She would be free, free to . . .

To do what, exactly? To take up with a half-breed gunfighter who would be a wanted murderer? He figured nobody in Palisade could stop him if he killed Eagleton, but the law would be after him from then on if he did. Rose wouldn't want to have anything to do with him in that case.

Or in any other case, he thought bitterly. He was just chasing a dream where she was concerned, a dream that would never come true.

"So you don't know where they are now?" Eagleton asked as if the momentary friction between the two men hadn't taken place.

"Still up on the mountain someplace would be my guess," Buckhorn said. "The posse hasn't come back as far as I know. They're still up there searching for the Jensens."

"Maybe luck will be with them," Eagleton said.

"Maybe by morning, those two troublemakers will be dead."

Buckhorn didn't say anything. He didn't know what to hope for. He wanted to see Ace and Chance Jensen dead just as much as Eagleton did.

He just wanted to do the killing himself.

Night fell like a gate crashing down, dropping darkness across the mountain with breathtaking speed. One minute Ace could see where he was going, the next he was practically blind.

He reined his chestnut to a halt and sat in the saddle for a long moment, letting his eyes adjust to the gloom. Once he had gotten used to the dark, the millions of stars in the sable sky arching over the mountains cast enough light for him to see his way.

He also used the pause to listen for any sounds of the posse searching the mountain for the fugitives. He didn't think Marshal Kaiser would give up just because night had fallen.

Not hearing anything, and confident that he could see where he was going again, Ace nudged the horse into motion. He kept the chestnut moving at a deliberate walk because of the thick shadows cloaking the trail and because he wanted to make as little noise as possible.

He had ridden another couple hundred yards when he heard something in front of him. He thought it was the rattle of bit chains, caused by a horse shaking its head. Definitely not any hoofbeats. The rider, whoever he was, was sitting still.

More than one of them, Ace realized a moment later when he heard a soft whisper. It was answered by an equally low-toned voice. He couldn't make out the words, but he knew the men were up ahead of him.

Moving as quietly as possible, he dismounted and left the chestnut's reins dangling so it would stay. He suspected the searchers had heard him coming and were waiting to ambush him. His best chance was to turn that around against them.

He slipped into the rocks, taking it slow. Being careful not to make any more noise than he had to, he hoped the night wind sighing around the mountain's flanks would help cover up any sounds he made. He'd been lucky to hear the ones that had warned him of the other men's presence.

He circled to the left, thinking the lurkers were on that side of the trail. The odds were bad if he encountered only two men. If half a dozen men were waiting to jump him, he'd have to back off and find another trail to take him down the mountain. He gave a shudder at that thought. It would be dangerous. He could wind up lost and wander around in circles.

Every couple steps, he stopped to listen. After several pauses, he heard another whisper and could understand what was being said.

"I thought he was fixin' to ride right past us. I'd have sworn I heard a horse comin'."

"So did I. He's out there, all right. Could be he stopped to rest his horse."

"You reckon it might not be one of the Jensens at all? Maybe it's one of the other fellas from the posse and he's lookin' for us. Maybe they already caught both those varmints."

"Don't you think we'd have heard the shootin'?"

"Maybe they didn't have to kill 'em."

The second man laughed quietly. "Jed Kaiser's so mad he's gonna grab any chance he can to fill those young fellas full of lead. If they show even the least sign of fight, they're dead if it's the marshal and the men with him who catch 'em."

Ace didn't doubt the truth of what he had just heard. Kaiser wanted them dead, and that prospect wouldn't disturb Claude Wheeler, either. A couple dead Jensens would work out well all around.

The two men fell silent as they continued to wait for Ace to show up.

He suspected they were volunteer members of the posse. Judging from their voices, they were on the other side of the massive rock next to him.

His eyes were fully adjusted to the darkness, and he could make out quite a bit by the starlight that filtered down from above. As he rounded the boulder, he spotted the two men standing and watching the trail, their horses behind them.

Scenting Ace, one of the horses spooked and tossed its head.

Its owner turned to quiet it, and the man spotted Ace sneaking up on them. He yelled, "Hey!" and clawed at the gun on his hip.

Ace lunged at the man, reaching out with his left hand to grab his wrist and keep him from drawing the gun. A shot could ruin everything. At the same time, Ace threw a punch with his right fist, putting as much power behind it as he could. The blow landed squarely on the man's nose, crushing it and sending blood spurting across Ace's knuckles. The man reeled back.

Since he was already going in that direction, Ace bulled into him and forced him to fall back against the other man. Their legs tangled and both went down. Despite that, the second man was able to get his gun out.

Ace saw starlight reflect from the barrel and lashed out with his right foot. The toe of his boot caught the man on the wrist and knocked the gun out of his hand. It went spinning away into the darkness. He aimed a second kick at the man's head, hoping to knock him unconscious, but the man reacted quickly, grabbing Ace's foot and heaving.

Ace couldn't catch himself. He went over backwards, rocks digging painfully into his back when he landed.

The man scrambled up and jumped on top of him. He locked his hands around Ace's throat and growled, "Damn you." It was obvious the man intended to choke the life out of him.

A good-sized young man, Ace bucked up from the ground but couldn't dislodge his attacker. The posse man was bigger.

Ace clubbed both hands together and shot them straight up between the man's arms and under his chin. The powerful blow rocked the man's head back and knocked his grip loose. Ace surged up from the ground and rolled the man to the side.

The man got a hand down and caught himself, but Ace swung his clubbed hands again, catching him on the jaw. The man sprawled to the side.

The first man let out a bubbling moan and tried to get up as blood leaked darkly from his flattened nose. Ace hit him on the jaw and stretched him out, as well.

On his knees and breathing hard, Ace waited to see if either man had any fight left in him.

It appeared they didn't.

Without even waiting to catch his breath, Ace moved quickly, using their belts to tie their hands behind their backs. He stuffed their bandannas in their mouths to keep them quiet when they woke up. He hoped the fella whose nose he had busted was still able to breathe well enough through it that he wouldn't suffocate, but he couldn't wait around to make sure of that.

He hurried around the boulder to get his horse, hoping that Kaiser and Wheeler had spread their men out across the mountain to watch all the trails. If he knew that for sure, he wouldn't have to be quite as careful as he descended. Unfortunately, he couldn't assume that, so he still proceeded cautiously.

Farther down the mountain, he looked to his left and saw lights on the same level about a mile away. That would be the Golden Dome mine, he thought, where men were working around the clock as usual to gouge riches out of the earth. If Ace's theory was right, Eagleton wouldn't need three shifts much longer. The payoff would be coming to an end.

Ace's only real interest in the mine was that it meant he had made it halfway down the mountain without getting killed or captured. He angled in the direction he thought the main trail lay. Once he reached it, he could make a dash for Palisade.

He had just ridden between two boulders and onto the larger trail when shots blasted out. Ace stiffened in the saddle, then realized the gunfire wasn't close by. The sound was drifting down from higher on the mountain. He reined in and turned to look up, seeing tiny flashes of light near the top of the peak, like deadly fireflies. Those were muzzle flashes, he knew, and they were in the area of the hideout where Chance and Emily had taken shelter.

A sick feeling filled Ace. There wasn't a damn thing he could do to help if his brother was up there fighting for his life. His mission was to deliver the telegraph message to Bess in the hope of keeping Chance and Emily safe, but that decision might have backfired. He might be the one who had somehow dodged trouble.

As Ace was sitting there feeling heartsick over what *might be* happening up above, four horsemen rode around a bend in the trail below him.

"Hey!" one of them shouted. "There's somebody up ahead by himself. We're all supposed to be in pairs or more!"

That was a good way of identifying somebody who wasn't a member of the posse, Ace thought as he jerked around toward the new threat. The only riders on the mountain were the posse men and the fugitives they sought.

"Get him!" another man shouted.

Ace hadn't recognized either of the voices as belonging to Kaiser or Wheeler, but that didn't matter. All were the enemy, no matter who they were. As the riders charged toward him, he bent over in the saddle, kicked the chestnut into a run, and drew his gun. Colt flame bloomed like crimson flowers in the darkness as the men opened fire on him.

Ace returned that fire, aiming a little high as he squeezed off several rounds. He didn't necessarily want to kill the men who believed they were hunting genuine lawbreakers, but he did want to scatter them so he could get through.

He accomplished that as the group broke apart in the face of the counterattack by a seeming madman. Ace leaned so far forward to make himself a smaller target, he was practically hugging the horse's neck as he flashed past the startled posse men. He didn't know where their bullets were going, but neither he nor the horse were hit and that was all he cared about.

The posse men shouted curses, continued shooting wildly, and wheeled their horses around to give chase. Ace knew they were behind him and urged the chestnut on to greater speed, calling on the valiant horse to give everything he had. He could see the lights of Palisade ahead and below him. All he had to do was follow the road down into the settlement, give his pursuers the slip, and make it to the stage line's head-quarters so he could talk to Bess and give her the message to send to the railroad. And stay alive while he was doing it.

That was all.

His thoughts were tortured by wondering what had happened to Chance and Emily, up near the top of the mountain.

Chapter Twenty-Seven

Emily was furious after Ace left the hideout. She twisted out of Chance's grip, stalked as far away from him as she could, and stood with her arms crossed over her chest, glaring and fuming. "The two of you shouldn't have done that. By letting Ace make what he thought was a noble gesture, you've probably ruined everything!"

Chance stayed where he was. "I wouldn't be so sure of that. If I've learned one thing over the years, it's not to underestimate my brother. Ace has pulled our fat out of the fire more times than I can remember, and usually when the odds were against him."

"It'll be a miracle if he makes it to town without getting killed or caught. Things already looked pretty bad. Now they're just worse." She looked away and wouldn't talk to him.

Chance tried several times to get her to engage in conversation, then gave up. He started arranging some wood in the fire circle, taking advantage of the last of the fading light to see what he was doing.

When he had the firewood laid out, he used some shavings as tinder and snapped a lucifer to life, held the flame to the curling pieces of bark until they caught, blazed up, and the fire took hold in the branches he had arranged carefully.

As the chilly wind whipped around and through the area under the overhang, he hunkered next to the flames for a while, watching Emily's stiff back as she looked out at the gathering night.

Finally, as if drawn by the heat, she turned and walked over to the fire. Her face was still taut and angry in its reddish light.

No less beautiful for that, Chance thought, staying silent until she spoke first.

"I came damn close to getting on my horse and going after Ace and leaving you here. You know that, don't you?"

He nodded. "It doesn't surprise me."

"I don't need anybody doing anything gallant for me. I can take care of myself *and* my family."

"I know you can. Nobody's saying otherwise."

"I'm surprised you let him go. I would have thought you'd be fighting each other to see who got to make the big sacrifice."

Chance warmed his hands. "That's the thing of it . . . Ace isn't planning to make any sacrifice. He figures he'll make it through and get that message to Bess without being caught. In something like this, he feels the same way I do every time I sit down at a poker table. I plan on winning."

"But you don't win every single time, do you?" Emily asked quietly.

Chance hesitated before answering. "Often enough, I do."

"But not always. And losing this game might mean that Ace dies."

"Believe me. You're not telling me anything I haven't already thought about."

They were quiet for a while after that.

Emily sat down on the other side of the fire and warmed up. "You mentioned something about having some jerky . . ."

"I'll get it." Chance went to fetch the strips of dried beef from his saddlebags.

He was standing next to the horse when he heard what sounded like a boot sole scraping on rock. His head whipped around as he looked to see if Emily was approaching him, but she was still sitting by the fire.

He bit back a curse and looked down the trail, then cursed again as he realized he had spent too much time looking into the flames. His night vision was poor. He knew better than to stare into a fire, but he wasn't much of a frontiersman so he had forgotten.

He didn't have any trouble seeing the spurt of flame from a gun muzzle, though. The blast echoed through the cave-like area and slammed against his eardrums. The bullet hit the rock wall and whined off into the darkness. Men charged toward the hideout, boots slapping against the trail.

The Lightning leaped into his hand, triggering several shots at the attackers as he backed toward the fire—and Emily. His slugs whipped around the men and drove them back. They retreated down the trail a short distance, using the curving shoulder of the mountain for cover.

"Jensen!" The shout that floated up the trail came from Marshal Jed Kaiser. "We have you trapped up there, Jensen! You might as well surrender!"

Emily was up and on her feet, the revolver she had taken from Joe Buckhorn gripped in her hand. As Chance reached her side, he kicked the fire apart, quickly extinguishing it except for a few glowing embers. They backed away from the glow and into the deeper shadows.

"How did they find us so quickly?" Emily whispered. "I didn't think they'd get this high on the mountain tonight."

"Kaiser's half loco. He must've pushed those posse men on instead of letting them make camp for the night. Maybe one of them has been up here before and knew about this place."

She sighed. "I don't guess it matters. He's right, we're trapped up here."

"There's no other way out?"

"Not that a horse could take. A person could climb up higher, I suppose, but what's the point? Do we just keep climbing higher and higher until there's nowhere else to go?"

"If we let Kaiser take us in, it probably means prison for both of us. I don't know about you, but I couldn't stand being locked up."

"No," Emily said quietly. "No, neither could I."

"The last card hasn't been dealt." Chance felt a smile tug at his lips. "Let's see how the hand plays out."

Emily surprised him then. She was the one to put her hand on the back of his neck and lean in to press her mouth to his. Carefully, because of the guns they were holding, they embraced in the shadows, and for a long moment neither of them knew anything except the warmth they were sharing.

Emily broke the kiss. "Yes, let's see how the hand plays out."

They put their guns away and she gripped his hand, leading him onto a narrow ledge that twisted upward, higher on the mountain. Behind them, Kaiser continued his blustery shouts until he finally ordered the men with him to charge the hideout again.

Guns roaring and muzzle flashes ripping through the blackness, they advanced, but it was too late.

Chance and Emily were gone.

It looked like every building in Palisade was lit up. Fires burned in smudge barrels in the street as if the town was expecting an attack by an army.

He was only one man, Ace thought as he studied the situation from a vantage point in the trees up the slope from the settlement, but he hoped to bring down the boss of Palisade anyway. He watched rifle-toting guards patrol the streets. He had no doubt they were Eagleton's men.

Several were posted in front of the hotel, which wasn't really a problem. Ace had no interest in going there. Several more had taken up positions in front of the stage line office and barn, and that presented a problem. He needed to get to Bess so he could give her the message to take to the telegraph office in Bleak Creek. He didn't see any way he could do that without being caught.

Unless . . .

He studied the barn. The back of the barn had no windows, and the doors were closed and probably barred on the inside. A tree grew near the building, its branches reaching out toward the high roof but falling several feet short.

As far as he could tell from where he was, no guards were behind the barn—probably because it had no easy entrance. Not much of the light from the street reached back there, either.

It was his only avenue of approach, he decided. He didn't know if it was possible, but when everything else was *impossible* . . .

He dismounted, noticing grass on the hill, and patted the chestnut on the shoulder. "I'll come back and get you later if I can, fella. If I can't . . .

you've been a mighty good trail partner, and I'll miss you." With that said, he stole down the slope toward the settlement. The chestnut could graze for a while, and if Ace didn't come back someone would find the horse sooner or later. Still, it wasn't easy leaving the animal.

Using every bit of cover he could find, Ace made his way toward the back of the barn. Reaching the tree growing behind it, he saw that it was an aspen, which wasn't his first choice for what he had to do. Climbing it would make the branches and leaves shake, causing noise as they brushed together.

It couldn't be helped. It was his only option.

Growing up mostly in saloons, Ace and Chance hadn't had many opportunities to climb trees. The urge to do so seemed to be in the blood of every boy, however, so on those rare occasions when they were around trees, they'd shinnied up the trunks like boys instinctively do.

Ace hadn't forgotten those childhood lessons. He hugged the aspen's trunk and worked his way up slowly but surely until he could reach up and grasp one of the lower branches. After that, it got easier. He climbed slowly and carefully, making as little noise as he could, until he was level with the top of the barn next to the stage line office.

Things got even riskier. He located the thickest, sturdiest looking branch and crawled out onto it. Close to the trunk, it didn't sag under his weight, but the farther out he went, it began to bend.

He looked to the end of the branch about four feet from the edge of the roof. Holding his breath, he reached above him, got hold of another branch, and used it to brace himself as he worked his feet under him and stood up gingerly. He slid his boot soles along the branch an inch or two at a time, one hand gripping the higher branch while his other arm stuck out at his side to balance him. With each step, the branch he was standing on bounced slightly as it bent more and more.

Finally, he had to let go of the higher branch and balance precariously as he moved out the last few inches. He had never felt quite so unsteady in all his life.

Light came over the building from the street, making the back edge of the barn roof fairly easy to see. He fixed his eyes on that goal and took a deep breath. If he dared lean forward, he could almost reach out and touch it, but the branch would bend too much and he would plummet to the ground.

Instead, he leaped.

His pulse hammered wildly in his head and his breath froze in his throat as he seemed to hang in midair for a split second that was infinitely longer. Then his reaching hands slapped the rough wood shingles on the barn roof and caught hold. Ace desperately tightened his grip as his body swung down against the barn, the impact making his fingers slip. He dug in harder with them.

After a moment, he realized he wasn't falling. The muscles in his arms, shoulders, and back bunched as he began pulling himself up. The strain on his fingers was terrific, but he withstood the pain until he was high enough that he could swing a leg up and hook it over the edge of the roof.

Rolling onto the top of the barn a few seconds later, he was safe . . . at least for a while. He lay just below the roof's peak for a minute or two with his muscles trembling.

Funny how he never had realized he was afraid of heights, he thought, but a leap like that was enough to make anybody scared of falling.

Gathering his wits and his breath, he rolled over onto his hands and knees and crawled along the peak until he neared the front of the barn. On his belly, he wriggled the last foot or so, until he could see down into the street.

The guards were still in front of the barn and the office and living quarters next door. They weren't looking up, of course—they didn't expect any threats to come from above—but if he tried to swing down into the opening for the hayloft, which was right below him, they would probably hear him.

He crawled backward to the rear of the barn

again, felt around until he found a partially loose shingle, and wrenched it free. The nails squealed a little, but he didn't think the sound was likely to be heard in the street. He took the shingle with him and crawled back to the front of the barn.

Twisting around, he flung the shingle into the darkness. It landed with a clatter behind the stage line office. The guards heard it, called to each other, and hurried around the barn to see what had caused the noise.

Quickly, Ace turned, slid off the roof, hung by his hands again, and kicked his legs to start himself swinging. After a couple times back and forth, he let go and landed just inside the open hayloft door.

He grabbed the edge of the opening to keep from toppling backward out of it and pulled himself forward, landing on his hands and knees again. The darkness inside the barn swallowed him up.

He had made it, confident Eagleton's guards at the stage line property hadn't seen him, but it was possible others along the street had. Ace scrambled quickly toward the ladder leading down from the loft, easily finding it in the dark, since he and Chance had spent a couple nights up there.

A minute later, his boots hit the hard-packed dirt inside the barn, and it felt mighty good.

He cat-footed across the aisle toward Nate's

sleeping quarters next to the tack room. Pausing outside the door, Ace called in a whisper, "Nate! Nate, are you in there?"

The door jerked open and he heard a startled voice gasp, "Ace?" Arms wrapped around his neck and a trembling body pressed against him.

As Ace instinctively wrapped his own arms around that slender but shapely form, he knew good and well he wasn't hugging the old, stove-up former jehu turned hostler.

Chapter Twenty-Eight

Buckhorn sat in a wing chair with his right ankle cocked on his left knee, wondering if Rose was going to show up, or if Eagleton had sent word for her not to come to the hotel seeing as he was well on his way to being drunk, having guzzled down the brandy at a pretty rapid pace.

The gunslinger shook his head just slightly. He couldn't very well ask the boss, he thought, not without possibly making his boss wonder why he was so interested in Rose's plans.

Eagleton was still muttering about the Jensens and the Corcorans as he paced, drank, and smoked. He stopped short when a knock sounded on the door.

Rose, Buckhorn thought, then realized the knock was curt and peremptory, not feminine at all. He was already getting to his feet when Eagleton jerked his head toward the door.

Buckhorn put his left hand on the butt of his gun, then realized that with his right arm in the sling, he couldn't hold the gun with one hand and open the door with the other. He asked harshly through the panel, "Who is it?"

The answer came back, "Jacob Tanner."

Buckhorn turned his head to look at Eagleton and raised an eyebrow inquiringly. Eagleton made a curt gesture indicating that the gunfighter should open the door.

He holstered his gun and did so, stepping back so the railroad man could come in.

Tanner brushed past him with barely a glance and confronted Eagleton, asking with a glare, "What the hell is going on over here in Palisade, Sam?"

Buckhorn quietly shut the door behind the railroad man.

"What do you mean?" Eagleton responded with a menacing rasp in his voice.

"I mean, you were supposed to have everything under control. This is your town, isn't it? You said you wouldn't have any trouble taking over the stagecoach line and getting that right-of-way, but Corcoran's still holding out and causing trouble."

Eagleton glanced at Buckhorn as if he thought Tanner was saying too much for the gunfighter to overhear.

Buckhorn kept his face bland and expressionless as if Tanner's angry words meant nothing to him. Inside, though, Buckhorn was thinking that the Jensen kid's wild story was true . . . or at least had some basis in fact. Eagleton wanted the stage line because of the right-of-way along the road across the valley. He wouldn't need that unless he planned to continue operating the line himself . . . or shut it down and build a railroad spur.

"Everything is under control," Eagleton assured Tanner. "Corcoran's only stagecoach is in Bleak Creek, so he can't make the next mail run. I have connections in Washington ready to move and strip him of the contract as soon as he fails to deliver the mail in a timely manner. In a couple days, Corcoran will be ruined and will have no choice but to sign over the line to me for whatever he can get." A vicious smile touched Eagleton's lips. "It'll be a pittance, I can assure you of that."

Tanner took out a thin black cigarillo, clamped it between his teeth, and grated out, "Maybe you should have just had him killed." He waved a hand at Buckhorn. "The Indian could have handled it."

Buckhorn stiffened. Eagleton caught his eye and gave a tiny shake of his head. Buckhorn forced himself to relax, but his dislike for Tanner wasn't disappearing anytime soon.

"Outright violence is dangerous," Eagleton

said. "I still have to live here, and in the new town, as well. I've tried to make it appear that any moves I've made against the Corcorans were accidents." An edge crept into his voice as he went on. "I'm not the one who tried to bushwhack the Jensen brothers in Shoshone Gap. Really, Jacob, you should have known better. You're a businessman, a builder, not a killer."

Tanner chewed on the unlit cigarillo. "I know. I lost my head when I saw the stagecoach coming after you'd promised it would be wrecked. I didn't know who the Jensens were then, but I knew I didn't want Corcoran getting any more help." He sighed. "I came close to ending our problems with them right then and there, before they ever really got started."

Buckhorn couldn't contain himself. "Close doesn't count for much in an ambush."

Tanner glared at him and looked surprised that Buckhorn would speak up.

Eagleton said smoothly, "All right. Let's not worry about what's already happened. Where do we stand going forward?"

"Marshals Kaiser and Wheeler are still up on the mountain with the posse, searching for the Jensens and Emily Corcoran." Tanner's lip curled in a disdainful sneer. "I don't have a lot of confidence in those two, but at least they're keeping the Jensens busy. They can't cause any more trouble for us as long as they're dodging the law.

Bess Corcoran and her father are still here in town, but I don't see what they can do to hurt us. Like you said, they don't even have a stagecoach anymore."

Buckhorn asked, "What if they deliver the mail by horseback?"

Eagleton and Tanner turned to stare at him.

The mining magnate frowned. "What are you talking about, Joe?"

"They brought the mail back from Bleak Creek by horseback last time." As he put the idea that had just sprung into his head into words, Buckhorn saw that it made sense. "There's nothing stopping Bess from riding over there tomorrow, taking the mail from here with her, and bringing back whatever's at the depot. That would fulfill the terms of the mail contract, wouldn't it? It probably doesn't say anything about *how* they have to deliver the mail."

Tanner took the cigarillo out of his mouth and used the other hand to scrub his face wearily. "My God. Does this travesty ever end? Every time we think we've got Corcoran backed into a corner, he finds some way out."

"We don't know that's what they'll do," Eagleton stalled.

"Nothing else makes sense." Buckhorn enjoyed the way those two self-styled titans of industry were listening to him, a lowly half-breed gunfighter.

Tanner said, "He's right. We need to get hold of Corcoran and his daughter and bring them here so they can't do that."

A worried frown creased Eagleton's forehead. "That would be kidnapping. I told you, I've been trying to avoid acting in the open."

"Bring them in the back, keep them up here until it's too late for them to carry that mail to Bleak Creek, and it'll be your word against theirs," Tanner argued. "Who do you think people are going to believe? The disgruntled owner of a failed business and his spiteful daughter, or the man who holds the future of this entire area in the palm of his hand?"

Buckhorn saw acceptance appear in Eagleton's eyes. The boss might not like Tanner's plan all that much, but he was willing to go along with it.

Eagleton nodded. "All right." He turned to Buckhorn and went on. "Take two men with you. Go over to Corcoran's and bring him and the girl back here. Bring them in the back, though, and be sure you're not seen."

With his arm hurting as bad as it was, Buckhorn would have preferred taking some more laudanum, going to bed, and sleeping for a couple days. But maybe if he did what Eagleton said, it would put an end to the standoff, he thought. "All right, boss. I'll get 'em." He opened the door once again and left the suite.

• • •

Ace stepped back and rested his hands on her shoulders. "Bess."

She came up on her toes and pressed her mouth to his for a long moment. When she broke the kiss, she whispered, "I was afraid I'd never see you again, Ace." She looked around in the shadowy barn illuminated only by light from the street seeping in through the cracks around the double doors. "Where are Emily and Chance? They came back with you, didn't they?"

Ace hesitated, which caused Bess to gasp. "They're not—"

"They're still up on the mountain. They were fine the last time I saw them. They're hiding from that posse, but I came back down to find you." He frowned in the darkness. "What are you doing out here in the barn?"

"I was worried, and it makes me feel better to be around the horses. It always has. Nate's sleeping on the sofa in the stage line office."

"That's good. I expected to find him in here, but I was going to get him to carry a message to you." Ace slipped the paper from his pocket and pressed it into her hand. "It's a telegram. You need to send it to the home office of the railroad when you carry the mail to Bleak Creek tomorrow."

"The railroad . . . I don't understand."

His hands still resting on her shoulders felt good as he explained the theory he had come up with concerning Samuel Eagleton's true motive for trying to take over the stagecoach line.

Bess nodded. "That all makes sense, I suppose. Do you think it'll do any good, alerting the railroad to what Eagleton and Tanner are doing?"

"I don't know," Ace replied honestly. "Railroads have been known to bend a few rules to get what they want. They may prefer to look the other way about the whole thing. But it seems to be the only chance we have."

"All right." Bess slipped the paper into her own pocket. "I'll take this with me. Do you think Eagleton will let me get through to Bleak Creek?"

"I reckon so. If the posse doesn't catch Emily and Chance tonight, I think Kaiser and Wheeler will be watching you tomorrow, to make sure we don't try to rendezvous with you somewhere in the valley. I'm not sure Eagleton would risk sending gunmen after you under those circumstances."

She laughed, but it had a slightly hollow sound to it. "You sure do know how to make a girl feel confident, Ace. What are you going to do?"

"I thought I'd slip back out of town and wait somewhere close by. If the posse comes back down, I'll head up the mountain to find Chance and Emily. We'll have to keep dodging the law until we find out whether or not that telegram is going to do any good."

"That's awfully risky," Bess said as she slid her

hand up his arm. "Marshal Kaiser is a little crazy where you and Chance are concerned. He's not going to give up looking for you."

"Well, we'll just have to steer clear of him—" He stopped short as they heard loud, angry words coming from somewhere nearby.

Eagleton had told him to take two men with him, so Buckhorn went over to the saloon, found Starkey and Byers playing poker, and told them to come with him.

Both men thought about arguing, but they could tell from the look in his eyes that he was in no mood for it. They threw in their cards and stood up.

"What's going on?" Starkey asked as they left the saloon and stepped out into the street.

"The boss has got a job for us," Buckhorn answered curtly.

"And he put you in charge, Joe?" Byers drawled. "Hell, you've been shot."

"I still have one good arm," Buckhorn growled. "And it's better than either of yours."

Both men bristled. Men who made their livings with their guns had to have a lot of pride in order to go about their business knowing that someday they would run into someone who was faster on the draw.

And on that day, more than likely, they would die.

"You can get your dander up later," Buckhorn went on. "We don't have time for it now. Eagleton wants us to grab Brian Corcoran and his daughter and take them to his suite without anybody seeing."

Starkey let out a low whistle of surprise. "So he's tired of messin' around, is he? Gonna just kill both of 'em and be done with it?"

"That'd be a shame," Byers said. "Bess Corcoran's not as pretty as her sister, but she's still a nice piece of woman flesh. You reckon the boss 'd let us have a little fun with her before we finish 'em off?"

Buckhorn swallowed the bitter taste that climbed up his throat as he listened to Byers. "The plan isn't to kill them. We're just going to hold them until Corcoran fails to deliver the mail to Bleak Creek. That'll cost him his government contract and finish the job of ruining him. He won't be able to hold out against the boss after that."

Byers made a face. "Good Lord. Times have changed, haven't they? I remember when if somebody was standin' in your way, you just hired fellas like us to wipe 'em out. Sure was a hell of a lot simpler back then."

"I don't think the boss has got the guts to do that," Starkey said. "He'll stoop to outright murder, but he doesn't want to get his own hands dirty doin' it."

That was sure right, Buckhorn thought. And he was liking it less and less.

They reached the stage line office. The men standing guard out front nodded, and Buckhorn asked them, "Everything quiet?"

"Yeah, pretty much," one of the gunmen replied. "We heard a noise behind the buildings a while ago, but when we looked there was nothin' back there. Could've been a dog or a cat, some critter like that."

Buckhorn frowned. Anything out of the ordinary was a potential problem, and he would have preferred it if the men had found what caused the noise. But logically, they were right. It was probably just some night-roaming animal.

"You're liable to hear some other ruckus in a few minutes," he warned the men. "The boss has sent us to fetch Corcoran and his daughter to the hotel. You'd damn well better keep that under your hats, though."

"Sure thing, Joe," the man agreed readily. "We don't question the boss's orders. The girl's not in there, though. I saw her go into the barn earlier this evening, and I'm pretty sure she hasn't come back out."

Buckhorn's frown deepened. Again, something unusual. He didn't like it. It left them no choice but to deal with it as best they could.

"Fine. We'll grab the old man first. The girl

won't give us any trouble, if she doesn't want anything to happen to her pa."

"You need help?" the guard asked.

Buckhorn snorted. "I think we can handle one old man."

"The hostler's in there, too, I think."

"All right, two old men." Buckhorn jerked his head at Starkey and Byers. "Come on."

When they reached the shadows behind the office, they drew their guns. Buckhorn figured they could kick the back door open, rush in, and grab Brian Corcoran before he knew what was happening. If Nate tried to stop them, that would just be too bad for the old-timer.

Buckhorn had just put his foot on the bottom step leading up to the back porch when the door swung open without warning and Brian Corcoran shouted, "Get out of here right now or I'll blast you!" He punctuated the threat by thrusting the twin barrels of a coach gun out the door.

"Look out!" Byers yelled. "I'll get him!"

Flame flashed from the muzzle of his gun.

Chapter Twenty-Nine

Bess's fingers tightened on Ace's arm as she exclaimed, "That's Pa! It sounds like trouble!" She and Ace turned as one and charged toward the rear barn doors.

Ace lifted the bar from the brackets on the rear doors, still cautious about showing himself on the streets of Palisade. Too many of Eagleton's gunmen were lurking around to risk that. Hearing a gunshot followed by the heavy boom of a shotgun changed that.

Bess cried out in alarm at the sounds. Ace threw the bar aside and yanked one of the doors open. More shots blasted as he and Bess charged out of the barn.

Ace spotted the muzzle flashes right away and pulled his gun. Three men were spread out around the back door of the building that housed the stage line office and the Corcoran family's living quarters. They crouched and fired six-guns toward the building's rear door in a fierce barrage.

Risking the storm of lead, a figure popped up and unleashed one barrel of a coach gun. The blast caused one of the attackers to buckle. Ace barely had time to recognize Brian Corcoran's face in the back-flash from the scattergun before Corcoran jerked back and collapsed, evidently struck by one of the slugs flying around.

"Pa!" Bess screamed.

Ace fired his Colt as one of the gunmen twisted toward him. The man's revolver spouted flame, but Ace's bullet had already ripped through his body and twisted him halfway around. His shot went wild.

312

Over the racketing gun thunder, Ace heard men shouting somewhere nearby. A second later, several of Eagleton's men charged around the corner of the barn and ran toward the gunfight at the rear of the buildings. As they opened fire, Ace grabbed Bess and pulled her behind him, shielding her with his body. He triggered more rounds toward the men joining the battle and one of the guards spilled off his feet.

A rifle cracked from inside the building.

Probably Nate joining the fight, Ace thought. He was convinced Corcoran had been wounded and was out of action. Ace backed toward the barn, still trying to stay in front of Bess as bullets screamed around them and kicked up dust at their feet.

What felt like a red-hot poker suddenly raked across his right forearm. He grunted in pain as his arm and hand spasmed and the Colt slipped out of his fingers. He knew a bullet had just burned across his arm.

Another slug whined past his head from the right. He glanced in that direction and recognized Joe Buckhorn, crouching behind a barrel and taking aim at him again. Obviously the half-breed gunfighter could use his left hand almost as well as his right when it came to gunplay.

Bess cried out. Ace turned toward her in alarm and saw blood on her sleeve. He couldn't tell how badly she was hurt, and as he reached for her, a hammer blow crashed against his head. He staggered and tried to stiffen his legs but couldn't keep his knees from buckling.

He heard Bess screaming as he hit the ground, but there was nothing he could do to help her. A black wave had him in its grip, and it washed him away.

Buckhorn's heart pounded as he straightened behind the barrel. He kept his gun trained on Ace Jensen even though the young man had fallen to the ground, either dead or passed out. Buckhorn thought his last shot had struck Ace in the head, but he wasn't sure about that.

Starkey and Byers were both dead, Starkey with half his head blown away by the first load of buckshot from Corcoran's coach gun, Byers shot through the body by Ace.

Bess struggled in the grip of two of the guards Eagleton had posted all around town. As Buckhorn stalked toward them, he gestured with his gun toward the office building and told the others, "Get in there and grab Corcoran. Be careful. That old hostler is in there, and he may still have some fight in him."

They had to hurry. The people of Palisade were, by and large, scared little sheep who would draw their curtains closed tighter and huddle in their beds when they heard gunshots and screams, but a few might be curious enough to investigate the ruckus. Eagleton had made it clear that he didn't want any witnesses to the abduction of Brian Corcoran and his daughter.

Ace Jensen had fallen on his side. Buckhorn dug a boot toe into the young man's shoulder and rolled him onto his back. A bloody welt showed in Ace's thick dark hair above his left ear but no bullet hole. His chest rose and fell, so Buckhorn knew Ace was still alive. The graze on his head had knocked him out.

The gunslinger looked back to Bess. She was wounded. Blood seeped between the fingers of her right hand as she clutched her left arm.

The injury didn't look too bad, Buckhorn thought. Certainly not fatal.

"Let me go!" she shrieked. As he approached, she cried, "Stay away from me, you monster!"

He holstered his gun, then his left hand flashed up and cracked across her face with enough force to jerk her head to the side and stun her into silence. "Take her to Eagleton's suite in the hotel," he told the men holding her, barking the order. "Go in the back door and don't let anybody see you."

"Sure, Joe," one of the men said.

Bess sagged in their grip, so they half-dragged, half-carried her toward the rear of the hotel.

Buckhorn swung back around toward the stage line office as several more shots roared. He put his hand on the butt of his gun in readiness as he waited to see who would emerge from the building.

A couple of Eagleton's men came out carrying Brian Corcoran's senseless form.

Buckhorn couldn't tell if the man was alive. He moved closer and asked, "Is he still breathing?"

"For now," one of the gunmen replied. "Looks like he got a slug through the side. Can't really tell how bad it is."

Buckhorn repeated the same order he had given concerning Bess and turned to the two gunnies who came out of the building "What happened with the hostler?"

"The old pelican put up a fight. We had to ventilate him."

"Dead?"

"Dead as can be."

Buckhorn grimaced. He didn't care about the old man, but his death seemed sort of senseless. The gunman had never cared about that before. If whoever paid his wages wanted somebody dead, that had always been motivation enough.

For some reason, the rampant bloodshed struck him as a waste. It all should have been handled in some other way, he thought. Eagleton had allowed the whole situation to deteriorate until it was just a mess.

One way or another, it would be finished soon, the gunfighter sensed. Brian Corcoran was wounded, maybe seriously, and Bess had caught a slug, too. Emily was somewhere up on the mountain above the Golden Dome, hiding out from the law along with Chance Jensen. They couldn't do anything to stop Eagleton's plans any longer.

And Ace Jensen was out cold from that bullet graze.

Buckhorn looked down at the young man for a moment, then waved two guards over and gave the same order again. "Pick him up and take him to the hotel. Be sure to go in the back and haul him up to Eagleton's suite."

The simplest thing would be to cut Ace's throat and be done with it, but Buckhorn held off, deciding that Eagleton ought to have to deal with his victims. He shouldn't be able to shield himself from all the results of his ruthless scheming.

Let the man who would gain the most get a little of the blood on his own hands for a change, Buckhorn thought grimly.

Several hundred yards above where he and Emily had had the brief gun battle with Marshal Kaiser and several members of the posse, Chance blew on his hands to keep them warm as he sat on a rock and watched her pace back and forth on the little ledge where they had paused to rest. He could see her fairly well in the starlight, especially her mane of blond curls. "You might want to stop moving around so much," he cautioned. "That'll just make it easier for some-body down below to spot you."

"Right now, I'm so mad I don't hardly care. Anyway, that trail is only wide enough for one person at a time to come at us, so I reckon we can hold them off."

"Yeah, well, what if they break out their rifles and start blazing away at us from down there? There's only so much lead we can dodge if it starts bouncing around this ledge."

She stopped her pacing and looked at him, then sighed. "You're right. The last thing we need is that damn posse taking potshots at us . . . pardon my language."

Chance grinned. "It's understandable, after everything that Eagleton and his bunch have put you and your family through."

"We've got a mighty big score to settle with him, that's for sure."

The climb had been hard and precarious. A missed handhold or a slippery foothold meant a disastrous plunge down the slope. Chance wasn't sure how much higher they could go. It seemed like they ought to be pretty close to the top of the mountain. Just them and the bighorn sheep, he thought wryly before turning his thoughts to what would happen next. It was even money what would happen first, he supposed—he and Emily would fall off the mountain, they would freeze to death, or the posse would catch up to them and they would have a fight on their hands again.

He got an answer to that conundrum sooner than he expected. While he was sitting there trying futilely to warm up a little, he heard a clatter somewhere nearby and recognized it as the sound of a falling rock.

And it came from *above* him and Emily.

Chance shot to his feet and twisted around as alarm bells clamored in his brain. Maybe one of those sheep he'd been thinking about had kicked a rock loose, he told himself wildly. Reality quickly replaced his wild thinking as he realized if any members of the posse had gotten above them somehow, they were in real trouble—caught between the two prongs of a trap.

The next second, a shape hurtled down out of the darkness and crashed into him. The impact drove him off his feet.

He felt the ledge gouge painfully into his back just below his shoulders when he landed, making his head dangle above hundreds of feet of empty air.

The weight of the man pinned Chance to the ledge. He tried to heave himself up and throw his attacker off, but he couldn't get any leverage. The man slammed a fist into his face.

Somewhere nearby, Emily yelled a curse and then screamed, "Let go of me! Oh!" The sounds of a frantic struggle followed her cries.

Spurred by her desperation, Chance threw a punch of his own at the dark shape above him and connected solidly. He grabbed the front of his attacker's shirt as the man rocked back, using it to haul himself up. He lowered his head and drove it into the man's face.

Grappling with each other, the two of them rolled away from the brink. Chance flattened the palm of his hand against the man's face and tried to dig hooked fingers into his eyes, but the man jerked back. The side of his hand slashed across Chance's throat, making him gag.

Gasping for breath, he writhed free of the man's flailing arms, surged halfway to his feet, and launched a roundhouse punch that crashed into the man's jaw with enough force to drive him back against the rock wall behind him.

Chance stood all the way up and looked around for Emily. His heart stopped as he saw Marshal Jed Kaiser standing at the edge of the path, his left arm around Emily's waist and his right clamped over her mouth. She struggled against his cruel grip, but Kaiser's feet were well-planted and she couldn't gain any traction against him.

Chance took a step toward them, but Kaiser called out in a clear, arrogant voice, "Stop right there, Jensen! If you come any closer, you might cause me to lose my grip on this young lady, and you wouldn't want that!"

"You leave her alone! If you hurt her, I'll kill you!"

"Threatening an officer of the law . . . I'm afraid that's one more mark against you, son. One more crime you'll have to answer for."

"I haven't committed any crimes," Chance raged. Aware that several other members of the posse had slid down onto the ledge from somewhere above them, he figured one of the men was familiar with the mountain, had figured out where they were going, and knew a way to get around them.

"That'll be up to a judge to decide," Kaiser said. "My job is to bring in the lawbreakers and let the court deal with them. Where's that brother of yours?"

"I don't know," Chance answered honestly. "You don't see him here, do you?"

Kaiser frowned. "We'll catch up with him later. Right now, we're going to take you back to Palisade and put you behind bars where you belong. I'm sure Marshal Wheeler will be glad to have you as a guest in his jail until we can round up your brother."

Generally, Chance was cool-headed in times of trouble and not given to panic. As he looked around at the grim-faced posse men surrounding him, he felt like his nerves were stretched so tight they were going to snap. With the odds so high against him, especially in a precarious location like the ledge, he didn't see any way out. Certainly not one that would allow him to free Emily, too.

"We've wasted enough time," Kaiser said abruptly. "Take him!"

Men leaped at Chance. He tried to dart away, but one grabbed his arm and jerked him around. Another tackled him around the waist. A third slashed at his head with a gun.

Chance couldn't get out of the way of the vicious blow. It landed solidly and set off bright red explosions in his brain. He sagged in the grip of the men who held him, and they forced him to the ground.

Fists and feet slammed into him for what seemed like a long time before Kaiser called, "That's enough. Get him up and tie his hands behind him. Justice has prevailed!"

Chapter Thirty

Consciousness seeped back into Ace's brain. His head hurt. It felt like someone had taken a sledgehammer to his skull. He opened his eyes and realized he was moving, but his legs weren't working.

Time wasn't flowing in its normal manner, either. The strong hands gripping him dragged him along for what seemed like hours, then suddenly released him. Something jumped up and smacked him in the face.

He closed his eyes and tried to think. That

wasn't it. He had fallen when they let go of him. Painful though it was, his thoughts were beginning to arrange themselves in their proper order.

A voice echoed in Ace's ears like its owner was shouting into an empty rain barrel. It demanded, "What the hell did you bring *him* here for?"

"Because Buckhorn told us to," answered a voice that also sounded distorted to Ace. It gradually became more normal, however, as the man went on. "I'm sorry, boss, but we didn't want to argue with that crazy 'breed. You know how he can be when he's riled up."

"Indeed I do," the first man muttered. "Well, I suppose you can take him back downstairs, carry him out in the alley, and cut his throat. Just dispose of the body somewhere it won't be found anytime soon."

"No!"

That anguished cry came from a woman's throat, Ace thought. A young woman. *Bess*.

The last time he'd seen her, she had been bleeding from a bullet wound in her arm. Fear for her drove the last of the fog from his brain. He opened his eyes and lifted his head.

"Damn it," snapped the man with the echoing voice. "He woke up and he's seen me now."

That was true enough, although Ace had no idea who he was looking at. The man looming over him was just a thick-bodied, middle-aged man with a mostly bald head and a brutal face. He wore what appeared to be an expensive suit.

Ace realized it was probably Samuel Eagleton. The mine owner had caused an incredible amount of trouble for the Jensen brothers, but he had done so without either of them ever laying eyes on him.

Worry about Bess overrode Ace's curiosity about their enemy. He looked around and spotted her kneeling beside the unconscious body of her father. At least, he hoped Brian Corcoran was only unconscious. He could see a lot of blood on Corcoran's shirt.

Bess had a rag tied around her wounded arm as a makeshift bandage. The wound didn't appear to be too serious, but Ace sensed they were all in deep trouble and might wind up dead anyway.

"Get on with it," Eagleton barked, making a curt gesture to the men who had brought Ace to him.

Ace assumed he was in Eagleton's suite. He had become aware that he was lying on a thick rug, and the furniture he could see appeared to be comfortable and expensive.

"Wait a minute," a new voice said.

Eagleton bristled. "I didn't know you were giving the orders around here, Joe."

Buckhorn sauntered into Ace's line of sight. "I'm not giving orders, boss, just making a suggestion. You've almost got everything lined up the way you want it. All you have to do is keep these folks here until tomorrow night. By that time, the mail won't have reached Bleak Creek when it's supposed to, and Corcoran's stage line will be busted. Dump Jensen's body tonight and somebody's liable to find it. That'll just muddy up the waters."

"I suppose," Eagleton said with a dubious frown.

A man Ace recognized as Jacob Tanner stepped up and declared, "I don't like this waiting around. Jensen has caused us trouble again and again. You'd better get rid of him while you've got the chance."

Ace would have smiled at that if his head didn't hurt so much. Tanner's words reminded him that Chance was still on the loose somewhere. It would be just like him to show up out of nowhere and turn the tables on the ruthless, greedy—

A knock sounded on the door.

Buckhorn turned sharply toward it, his hand going to his gun.

Tanner leaned closer to Eagleton and asked quietly, "Were you expecting anyone else?"

"No." Eagleton nodded toward the door. "Find out who it is, Joe."

Buckhorn went to the door with his hand still resting on the butt of his gun. "Who's out there?"

"It's Marshal Wheeler," came the reply.

Eagleton visibly relaxed. He nodded. "Let him in. It doesn't matter what Claude sees. He's one of us."

Tanner looked worried about that, Ace thought.

Buckhorn did what Eagleton told him and swung the door open. The burly figure of Marshal Claude Wheeler came into the suite's sitting room. He looked worried, too.

"What is it, Claude?" Eagleton asked.

"I thought you'd want to know that Jed Kaiser just brought in a couple prisoners and locked them up in my jail—Emily Corcoran and Chance Jensen."

Bess cried out at the mention of her sister's name. Despair threatened to fill Ace when he heard that his brother had been captured. So much for the idea of him swooping in and saving the day. He was just one more prisoner with a mighty limited life expectancy.

A frown creased Eagleton's forehead. "What sort of shape are they in?"

"They're all right. The girl is fine. Jensen was knocked out when the posse captured him, but he's conscious now and none the worse for wear, as far as I can tell. Should I leave them locked up?"

Eagleton's frown deepened as he considered the question. He glanced at Buckhorn, but the enigmatic gunfighter didn't offer any guidance. Finally, Eagleton said, "No, bring them over here. I want everyone in one place where we can keep an eye on them." He paused. "Not here in the suite, though. I'm, ah, going to be entertaining a guest later. Take them to the room next door. It's kept empty. Buckhorn can see that the others are taken over there while you're fetching your two prisoners."

Wheeler nodded. "All right, Mr. Eagleton. I reckon you'd prefer that my deputies and I be discreet about it?"

"Of course."

Wheeler left the room.

Buckhorn's thoughts took a turn. Originally, he had been hired as a bodyguard. At his suggestion, the room next door was kept empty, and for good reason. That way, nobody could fire a gun through the wall into the suite. And since the suite was at the end of the hallway there wasn't a room on the other side of it. All strategy to keep Eagleton safe.

Returning to the task at hand, Buckhorn said flatly, "I'll get some of the boys to carry Corcoran and this Jensen next door."

"Good. Oh, and Joe, see if you can do something about the blood on the rugs, too. I don't want anyone being upset by the sight of it."

Buckhorn was seething inside as he supervised the transfer of the prisoners from Eagleton's suite into the room next door. He knew good and well the identity of the visitor Eagleton was expecting later—Rose Demarcus—but he wasn't sure why that bothered him as much as it did.

Maybe it was because Eagleton was going to be carrying on his affair while the victims of his scheming were locked up only a thin wall away. It brought all his sordidness too close to her and threatened to soil her with it.

Well, that was rich, he thought wryly. A half-breed gunfighter with an ocean of blood on his hands worrying about a cathouse owner's reputation.

Eagleton had always been careful to keep the truth from her, but would she really care if she found out? He was just trying to make more money, after all. In her line of work, Rose ought to understand.

But maybe that wouldn't be the case, Buckhorn told himself. Despite her profession, Rose had something fine about her, something that would draw the line at kidnapping, intimidation, and murder. The boss was doing the right thing by keeping all that away from her.

The right thing for *him,* anyway. Buckhorn suddenly wondered how she might feel about everything if she knew the truth. Would it make a difference?

The question gnawed at him and wouldn't let go.

Ace's legs worked again as two gunmen hauled him to his feet. It was a relief, since he hadn't been sure. He'd been worried that he was paralyzed.

As he walked into the empty room and sat next to Bess on the floor, he was also glad to be able to talk to her again and make sure she wasn't injured too badly.

As soon as the door shut behind the guards, she told him, "The bullet just plowed a little furrow in my arm. It hurt worse than anything I've ever felt before, but it didn't bleed all that much. I'm sure it'll be fine. I'm a lot more worried about Pa."

Brian Corcoran was stretched out on the floor next to her, still unconscious.

At Buckhorn's order, the gunmen had torn strips off the bed and bound them around Corcoran's torso. That had stopped the bleeding.

Bess was worried that her father had already lost too much blood, though, and Ace shared that concern. Corcoran's face was pale, and his breathing was shallow.

"He's still alive, and so are we," Ace told her.

They couldn't give up hope. Although it certainly looked like Eagleton was on the verge of victory, maybe they would get an opportunity to change that.

Leaning against the door, Buckhorn watched them with an unreadable expression on his face. After a while he said, "I haven't forgotten about you shooting me, Jensen. This shoulder hurts like hell."

"I'd say I'm sorry," Ace replied, "but I'm not. You shouldn't have thrown in with a snake like

Eagleton and agreed to do all his dirty work for him."

Buckhorn didn't say anything in response to that, but Ace thought he saw something in the gunfighter's eyes, maybe the faintest flicker of agreement. Ace thought again that it might be possible to drive a wedge between Buckhorn and his employer.

Before he could say anything else, someone knocked on the door. Buckhorn straightened and put his hand on his gun. "Yeah?"

"It's Marshal Wheeler."

Buckhorn let go of the gun, opened the door, and stepped back.

Wheeler went in first, carrying a shotgun, then turned to cover the doorway as Emily entered the room next, then Chance, followed by a couple of Wheeler's deputies with drawn revolvers.

Emily exclaimed, "Bess!" and ran to her sister, who leaped to her feet to meet her. None of the men tried to stop them as they embraced.

Ace stood up, too, and nodded to Chance. Their reunion was less visibly emotional, but Ace was mighty glad to see his brother again and knew Chance felt the same way.

Of course, it would have been even better if one or both of them had been free.

"It wasn't easy getting over here without anyone noticing," Wheeler said to Buckhorn. "The whole town's still in an uproar over all that shooting earlier. Nobody's quite sure what happened, but they know some sort of ruckus occurred around the stage line building."

"They won't find anything," the gunfighter said. "I had the old man's body taken out of town."

Emily turned sharply toward him and repeated, "The old man?"

Bess put a hand on her sister's arm and said in a choked voice, "Nate's dead, Emily. He tried to protect Pa after he was shot, and Eagleton's men killed him."

Emily's eyes widened. In a voice shaking with rage, she said, "He was just an old man!"

"An old man with a rifle," Buckhorn said. "For what it's worth, I wish he'd thrown it down when he saw the odds were against him."

"Nate would have never done that," Emily snapped. "He was always loyal to Pa. I don't want your phony sympathy. I just want you to die."

"You'll get your wish sooner or later," Buckhorn said with a shrug. "I don't know if you'll be around to see it, though."

With a worried tone in his voice, Wheeler said, "I sure hope the boss knows what he's doing. Shooting people, holding them prisoner, getting rid of bodies . . . I'm supposed to be a lawman, you know. This is getting a mite hard to swallow."

"You're an employee of the Golden Dome Mining Corporation, just like me," Buckhorn said. "Your only job is to do what the boss wants done." He paused, then repeated under his breath, "Just like me."

Wheeler tucked the shotgun under his arm. "Well, Mr. Eagleton told me to stay here and help you keep an eye on them, so I reckon that's what I'll do."

Buckhorn was incensed. "I don't need any help."

Wheeler shrugged beefy shoulders. "Doesn't matter. That's what the boss said."

"Fine." Buckhorn clearly didn't like the idea of having the marshal for company, but he wasn't going to argue. "Where's Kaiser?"

"He and the other men from the posse are here in the hotel. They've got rooms downstairs. The boss said he'd put them up for the night, as late as it is."

"So just about everybody's here," Buckhorn mused.

"Yeah, I suppose you could look at it like that."

Once again, Ace thought something more was going on in the gunfighter's brain than was readily apparent.

Wheeler's deputies left, but not long after that someone else knocked quietly on the door. The marshal opened it to admit Jacob Tanner.

"Eagleton's kicked me out of his suite, too."

The railroad man had one of his stogies clenched between his teeth and seemed angry as he stalked in. "I'm starting to think he doesn't appreciate everything the rest of us have done to help him accomplish his goals. He'd be a rich man without us because of that mine, I suppose . . . but he wouldn't be well on his way to being the richest, most influential man in the whole territory. You wouldn't know that from the high-handed way he acts."

"The man who has the money makes the rules," Wheeler said. "That's the way it's always been in this world. I reckon that's the way it'll always be."

"Doesn't mean it's right," Tanner growled.

Buckhorn laughed.

They all looked at him in surprise, even the prisoners.

Ace thought Tanner and Wheeler acted like they had never heard Buckhorn laugh before, maybe hadn't entertained the notion that the gunfighter even *could* laugh.

"That's where you're making your mistake," Buckhorn said. "Thinking that this world has anything to do with right and wrong. Thinking that life should be fair, at least every now and then. It never has been and it never will be, so what the hell does it matter?"

Obviously irritated, Tanner snapped, "What in blazes are you talking about, Indian?"

"This." The Colt on Buckhorn's left hip seemed to leap into his hand with blinding speed, and before any of the people in the room had a clue what he was doing, he crashed the gun against Tanner's head and sent the railroad man sprawling to the floor.

Chapter Thirty-One

Ace and Chance were as stunned as any of the others by Buckhorn's sudden action, but they recovered first and lunged toward Wheeler while the crooked lawman was still staring at Buckhorn. If they could get their hands on Wheeler's shotgun, it could change everything.

Buckhorn was too fast for all of them. He leveled the Colt at Wheeler before the lawman recovered from his shock and could lift his weapon far enough to use. The gun was also pointed in the general direction of the Jensen brothers.

"All of you just hold it," Buckhorn ordered. "Claude, I don't want to kill you. I don't have anything against you except your choice of employer, and hell, I made the same mistake. Toss that Greener onto the bed."

"Joe, what in the Sam Hill are you doing?" Wheeler asked.

"Trying to make the world a little more fair, I reckon. Now do what I told you."

Wheeler sighed and threw the shotgun onto the bed.

"Now your pistol, too, and be careful how you take it out of the holster."

Wheeler drew the handgun carefully and tossed it onto the bed next to the shotgun, then backed off when Buckhorn motioned for him to do so.

"I've got a hunch you're gonna be really sorry about doin' this," Wheeler said with a sigh.

"You may be right about that. Sometimes a man just has to do something, even though he knows it's futile."

"No offense, but you're just about the damn oddest half-breed hired gun I've ever come across."

Buckhorn laughed again. "None taken, Claude."

Ace asked, "What *are* you going to do, Buckhorn? Are you double-crossing Eagleton?"

"Don't get your hopes up," Buckhorn replied with a sneer. "I told you, I haven't forgotten it was you who shot me, or that you two have caused me a lot of trouble. But I finally realized I don't really give a damn about that stage line or the railroad that Eagleton wants to build or the fact that he wants to set himself up as the tinpot dictator of this whole end of the territory. I just want the truth to come out for the first time in this whole miserable business."

Ace could make no sense of that. "The truth . . . ?"

"I want one woman to see Eagleton for what he really is. I won't rest until I find out what she thinks of him after that."

Ace and Chance glanced at each other. Neither of them had any idea what Buckhorn was talking about, but clearly, it was important to the gunfighter. Since it offered them their only shred of hope, they were willing to play along with it.

"Listen to me, Buckhorn." Ace held out a hand toward the man. "Let me and my brother get those guns on the bed, and we'll back your play, whatever it is."

"That's right," Chance added. "As long as it's not going to hurt Emily and Bess and their pa any more than they already are."

Bess took a step forward. "Please, Mr. Buckhorn. My father needs a doctor. If he's kept prisoner here until tomorrow night and Mr. Eagleton won't let anyone help him, he'll die. I'm sure of it."

Buckhorn looked at Emily. "What about you, girl? You going to beg, too?"

"Hell, no. But if you do the right thing for once in your miserable life, I might not kill you."

Buckhorn shook his head. "I admire you, Miss Corcoran. You might not have much sense sometimes, but you're not short on sand, I'll say that."

He frowned in thought for a couple seconds, then reached a decision. "You boys pick up those guns and keep Wheeler and Tanner covered while I'm gone. Don't try anything funny, though. Neither of you is fast enough to stop me from killing you if you do. And don't double-cross me. Even if you think you've gotten away with it, I'll hunt you down and make you sorry."

"We're not interested in a double cross," Ace said as he moved warily toward the bed. "Just in protecting the Corcorans."

Chance added, "Whatever problem you've got with Eagleton is your business."

Ace picked up the shotgun, Chance scooped Wheeler's Colt off the bed, and they backed off to cover Wheeler and the still stunned Tanner.

Ace asked Buckhorn, "Where are you going, anyway?"

"This room's fixing to be a little more crowded," the gunfighter replied. "We're gonna have us a little come-to-Jesus meeting."

Buckhorn locked the door behind him when he left. Emily turned immediately to the window and said, "We can get out of here—"

"Wait," Ace told her. "You heard Buckhorn. If you want this thing with Eagleton to end, your best bet might be to play along with him. He's gone down a path where he can't turn back."

"I agree," Chance said. "We talked before about

letting the hand play out, Emily. My gut tells me this is the time to do it."

She glared at them, then sighed. "All right. You may both be loco, but you've had pretty good ideas so far. Just don't make me regret it."

Buckhorn tried the knob on the door of Eagleton's suite, turning it carefully so that it made no noise. The door was locked. That didn't matter. He had a key, although Eagleton didn't know that. The gunslinger had always figured that in order to properly do his job as the man's bodyguard, he ought to be able to get into the suite any time, day or night.

He slipped the key into the lock and turned it slowly enough that the tumblers made only the faintest click as they came free.

When he swung the door open, the two people in the sitting room had no warning that he was there until he said, "Hello, boss. Rose."

No more Miss Demarcus.

They were drinking brandy by the sideboard. Eagleton spilled some of his as he jerked around and roared, "Buckhorn! What are you doing here? Get back over there with those—" He stopped abruptly and glanced at Rose.

As usual, she was much more cool and self-possessed. If she was surprised by Buckhorn's entrance, she wasn't going to show it.

"With those what, boss?" Buckhorn asked

mockingly. "Those people you had kidnapped when trying to kill them over and over didn't work?"

"Shut up," Eagleton said, scowling. "You don't know what you're talking about."

"*I* don't know what he's talking about," Rose said, "but I'd like to. Joe, does this have something to do with all that shooting in town earlier this evening?"

"It has everything to do with it," Buckhorn said. "You two are coming with me. You can see for yourself, Rose. You can see what Eagleton's been doing and what sort of man he really is."

Spittle flew from Eagleton's mouth as he roared, "You're fired, you filthy redskin!"

"Too late for that," Buckhorn said, smiling thinly. "I've already quit." He motioned with the gun in his hand. "Now come on, both of you."

"You don't need the gun for me," Rose murmured. "I very much want to know what this is all about."

Buckhorn backed through the open door into the hall and gestured for them to follow him. As they did, Buckhorn saw something from the corner of his eye.

At the landing where the stairs from the lobby ended, Marshal Jed Kaiser from Bleak Creek had just appeared. The lawman stopped in his tracks, his eyes widening as he saw Buckhorn holding the gun on Eagleton.

"Marshal, stop this Indian!" Eagleton cried. "He's gone crazy!"

Kaiser fumbled, trying to sweep his coat aside and claw his gun from its holster. He had no chance before he was looking down the barrel of Buckhorn's Colt.

"Don't do it, Marshal," Buckhorn warned. "I'll kill you if I have to." A thought occurred to him. "Anyway, you ought to come with us. Somebody's about to confess to a crime. A whole heap of crimes, in fact."

"What are you talking about?" Kaiser had moved his hand away from his gun.

Buckhorn pointed at Eagleton with his chin. "He's got a lot he wants to get off his chest."

Eagleton growled curses.

Buckhorn ignored him. He turned so that he could cover both Eagleton and Kaiser and backed toward the door of the next room. "All of you come with me," he ordered.

Desperately, Eagleton said to Rose, "Don't believe a word this man says. He's insane, I tell you."

"I think I can judge that for myself, Samuel," she replied, still cool and deliberate.

Buckhorn reached the door and said, "Marshal, come over here and take the key out of my pocket and unlock this door. Please don't try any tricks."

"I don't believe I will," Kaiser said in his usual stuffed-shirt manner. "I'm as curious as this . . .

young woman here . . . to find out what this is all about."

Buckhorn didn't like the disapproving tone in the marshal's voice when he mentioned Rose, but he was willing to let that pass.

Kaiser was true to his word. He didn't try anything as he took the key from Buckhorn's coat pocket and unlocked the door.

Buckhorn stepped back and motioned with the revolver's barrel for the others to go first. "It's going to be a little crowded in there, but this shouldn't take long."

Ace heard what Buckhorn said, and the gunfighter was right. With eleven people in the room, the place was cramped. Brian Corcoran lay on the rug, still unconscious, as did Jacob Tanner, and that cut down on the available space.

With guns in their hands, the Jensen brothers stood in front of Bess and Emily, in the far corner next to the bed. Wheeler was on the other side of the bed.

The first man through the door was Kaiser, who paused and exclaimed, "My prisoners! My God, Marshal Wheeler, you released them? I trusted you!"

Wheeler shrugged. "You might have made a mistake there, Jed."

Eagleton was next, red-faced and seething, followed by a very attractive brunette in a bottle-green gown that flattered her figure.

Buckhorn came last and heeled the door closed behind him. "All right. All the players involved in this little drama are assembled at last."

Always the bold one, Emily said, "Except for poor Nate. You killed him and had his body dumped out of town, remember?"

"What?" Kaiser exclaimed.

Buckhorn signed, but kept his gun ready. "Just let me tell this."

Over the next few minutes, as he laid out the affair from start to finish, it became apparent just who he was telling it *to*. He directed all of it to the brunette, who listened with her lovely face remaining impassive. He didn't know all the details because he hadn't been around for all of it, but the gunfighter did a pretty good job of sketching in the big picture . . . and left no doubt where the blame for everything in his story fell— squarely at the feet of Samuel Eagleton, who was growing more and more apoplectic as Buckhorn talked.

Finally, Buckhorn said, "Now you know what sort of man Eagleton really is, Rose."

"Is that why you've done all this, Joe?" she asked quietly. "To show me the truth?"

"That's right. I thought maybe if you knew about all the blood on his hands you'd feel differently about him. I thought maybe you . . . that you . . ."

"That I'd have feelings for you, instead?"

Buckhorn didn't answer, just stared at her.

"Joe, I already knew what sort of man Samuel is." She leaned forward. "He's a rich man. And he's going to be even richer. Why do you think I got involved with him in the first place? As for hoping that I might turn on him and take you instead . . . you stupid 'breed. I was never doing anything but making fun of you." Her hand came up from a fold in her dress and flame spat from the muzzle of the little derringer as she fired it into Buckhorn's chest at close range.

At the same time, Jacob Tanner surged up from the floor, having regained consciousness without anyone noticing while Buckhorn was talking. Tanner clubbed a fist into Kaiser's face and snatched the marshal's gun from its holster. He whirled toward the Jensen brothers and fired. The slug whipped between Ace and Chance and shattered the window behind them.

Moving with surprising speed and grace for a big man, Wheeler bounded onto the bed and leaped across it, tackling Ace. The shotgun Ace held boomed as it discharged one of its barrels into the ceiling and he and the marshal fell into the narrow space between the bed and the wall as they struggled.

Chance crouched and fired at Tanner before the railroad man could get off a second shot. The slug lanced into Tanner's chest and turned him half-way around, but he managed to pull the trigger again, striking Rose Demarcus between the shoulder blades, making her arch her back and cry out.

Eagleton shouted, "Rose!"

Chance fired again, drilling Tanner in the forehead. The man's head jerked back as the bullet bored through his brain and exploded out the back of his skull. He dropped, dead before he hit the floor.

On top of Ace, pinning him to the floor with his weight, Wheeler tried to wrestle the shotgun away. The weapon still had one shell in it.

With limited space to maneuver, Ace twisted the barrels until both of them were shoved up under Wheeler's chin and fumbled for the trigger.

Realizing that he was about to get his head blown completely off his shoulders, Wheeler cried out in panic and jerked away.

That brought him within reach of Emily Corcoran, who grabbed the empty chamber pot from under the bed and smashed it down on his head. Ace followed that with a stroke from the shotgun's stock. The butt crashed into Wheeler's jaw, breaking the bone and knocking him out cold. He fell forward onto Ace again.

"Get him off me!" Ace shouted, his voice muffled by Wheeler's chest pressed into his face.

Chance and Emily grabbed the back of Wheeler's coat and hauled the unconscious lawman up, then let him sprawl on the floor. Ace scrambled to his feet in time to see Eagleton swinging up the gun that Buckhorn had dropped when Rose shot him.

"She's dead!" the mining magnate screamed. "She's dead and it's all your fault!" He jerked the trigger and the bullet would have hit Emily if Bess hadn't grabbed her just in time and dived out of the line of fire.

Eagleton was about to fire again when Ace touched off the shotgun's second barrel. The load of buckshot tore into Eagleton's chest, picked him up, and threw him back against the door. He hung there for a moment, his vitals shredded, and then slowly slid down to a sitting position, leaving a gory smear on the door behind him.

Left standing were only Ace, Chance, and Marshal Kaiser, who had stood the whole time with a stunned expression on his face, somehow untouched by all the lead that had been flying around the room.

As the echoes of the blast died away, Kaiser opened his mouth to say something but couldn't find any words. His jaw hung open slackly.

Ace and Chance heard someone sobbing. They moved over where they could see Joe Buckhorn slumped over the body of Rose Demarcus, his back heaving as he cried. She had shot him, maybe mortally wounded him, yet he was grieving over her.

If life ever made complete sense, Ace thought, it would be for the first time.

They had other things to worry about. He looked at Kaiser. "Marshal, you claim to be a protector of law and order. Palisade's going to need somebody to take charge. Eagleton's hired guns will still need to be dealt with. Are you going to step up and do the right thing?"

Kaiser looked a little like a fish out of water. "I . . . I . . . I ought to arrest you . . ."

Chance stepped in. "You know who was really in the wrong here. You heard the whole story, and Eagleton didn't deny a bit of it. What you need to do is go round up your posse and let the rest of those gunmen know they'd better light a shuck while they still can." He shrugged. "It's a sure bet they won't be getting any more fighting wages from Eagleton."

"Yes, y-you're right," Kaiser stammered. He squared his shoulders. "Somebody's got to be the law here, since Claude Wheeler is clearly as much a criminal as any of these others. And I'm the only one who has a badge."

"That's right, Marshal," Ace said, smiling. "You're the only one who has a badge."

Chapter Thirty-Two

Brian Corcoran's wound was serious. He had lost a lot of blood, but the doctor believed he would pull through, especially if he got plenty of rest for the next few months.

Bess stayed at her father's bedside, but Ace, Chance, and Emily delivered the mail pouch to Bleak Creek the next day. After sending the wire to the home office of the railroad informing them that Jacob Tanner was dead and revealing the scheme he had entered into with Samuel Eagleton, they picked up the stagecoach and brought it back to Palisade.

Marshal Kaiser and his posse hadn't had to run any of Eagleton's remaining men out of town. With no more payoffs ahead of them, they had pulled up stakes and drifted out in a hurry to look for more gun work elsewhere.

The response from the railroad was swift. The captains of industry who ran it were canny men and saw right away the merits of Eagleton's plan . . . as long as it didn't involve murder. Executives of the railroad, including one of the owners, a woman named Vivian Browning, arrived in Palisade less than two weeks later— coming in by stagecoach with Ace at the reins and Chance riding shotgun—to offer a recuperating

Brian Corcoran a small fortune for the right-of-way across the valley. They also suggested that by the time the depot was built—the depot that would be the centerpiece of a new settlement—he might want the job of running it.

"I don't know anything about running a damn train station!" Corcoran protested to his daughters when they discussed the situation.

"But you always said that you enjoyed a challenge," Bess pointed out.

"Sounds like it would be a challenge to me," Emily added.

"Aye, I have been known to say that," Corcoran agreed grudgingly. "I'll give it some thought, but that's as far as I'll go right now."

"That's enough, Pa," Emily said, patting his hand. "You've got time to think about it."

Time was something that was weighing on the heads of Ace and Chance. They had been in Palisade for weeks, and no matter how fond they had grown of Bess and Emily, their nature was such that it wouldn't let them stay in one place for too long.

One day they looked at each other, knew what the other was thinking, and nodded.

Messy good-byes were something they didn't care for. Before dawn the next morning, they saddled their horses and rode out of Palisade, leaving behind notes for the Corcoran sisters that tried to explain why they were leaving, although they doubted that Bess and Emily would ever fully understand.

"Those two are going to be mighty angry with us," Chance commented as he and Ace rode through Timberline Pass and started down the mountain road where their adventure had begun.

"I'm sure they will," Ace agreed. "But they're going to have their hands full helping their father with that railroad station. You know they'll both pitch right in."

Chance chuckled. "Shoot, I wouldn't be surprised if those two wind up *running* that railroad in a few years."

Ace couldn't argue with that.

They reached the valley and started north, not knowing where it led but well aware they didn't want to head east toward Shoshone Gap and Bleak Creek. Several times, they had seen Marshal Kaiser eyeing them as if he still thought he ought to arrest them, even though all the charges against them had been dropped.

No point in tempting the lawman, they thought.

They hadn't gone very far when a rider spurred out from a clump of trees and blocked the trail. Both brothers tensed and moved their hands toward their guns as they recognized the man in the dawn light.

"Take it easy," Joe Buckhorn said. "I'm not looking for a gunfight."

The man was gaunt, and his skin still had a

pallor under its reddish hue. He had almost died from being shot by Rose Demarcus. That would have saved the law the trouble of hanging him. Even though he hadn't killed Nate Sawyer, he'd been there when the old hostler was gunned down and had ordered the men who did the killing into the building.

Just like Claude Wheeler, Buckhorn would have been put on trial when he recovered—if he recovered—but he'd escaped from the doctor's house by taking the deputy guarding him by surprise and knocking the man out.

Ace and Chance had figured the gunfighter was long gone from the area, so seeing him so close to Palisade was a shock.

"What *are* you doing here?" Ace asked.

"I've been waiting for the two of you. I figured you were too fiddle-footed to hang around forever, so I've been watching the pass. I wanted to tell you a couple things."

"All right," Chance said warily. He watched Buckhorn closely with narrowed, suspicious eyes. "Go ahead."

"First of all, I want to say I'm sorry about that old man."

"You mean Nate?" Ace asked.

"Yeah. He shouldn't have died."

"Damn right he shouldn't have," Chance snapped.

"Well, I can't bring him back," Buckhorn said,

irritation rasping his voice. "No more than I can bring back all the other folks who shouldn't have died but did because of me. But I *am* sorry. For what good it does."

"Damn little," Chance muttered.

"What's the other thing you want to say?" Ace asked.

Buckhorn leaned forward in the saddle. "That I haven't forgotten about you shooting me, Jensen. I don't bear you any ill will, but I haven't forgotten. Might be wise if the two of you never crossed trails with me again."

"Believe me, mister," Chance said, "that's just about the last thing we want."

"Just so we understand each other." Buckhorn gave them a curt nod, turned his horse, and rode off into the trees.

When he was gone, Chance said, "You reckon he's waiting to ambush us?"

"No," Ace said. "I think he's a man who means what he says. We don't have anything to worry about where he's concerned . . . unless we happen to meet up with him again."

"And if we do?"

"Then everybody had better watch out," Ace said as he heeled his horse into motion. Chance followed suit.

They had ridden about a hundred yards when Chance said, "What do you reckon Smoke Jensen would have done just then?"

"Smoke?" Ace smiled. "Oh, Smoke would have shot him. Buckhorn would have tried to draw on him, and Smoke would have blown him right out of the saddle."

"But . . . neither of us is Smoke Jensen."

"Nope," Ace said, shaking his head. "We're not."

Chance looked over at his brother and grinned. "But one of these days, you might grow up to be *just* like him."

J. A. Johnstone on William W. Johnstone
"Print the Legend"

William W. Johnstone was born in southern Missouri, the youngest of four children. He was raised with strong moral and family values by his minister father, and tutored by his schoolteacher mother. Despite this, he quit school at age fifteen.

"I have the highest respect for education," he says, "but such is the folly of youth, and wanting to see the world beyond the four walls and the blackboard."

True to this vow, Bill attempted to enlist in the French Foreign Legion ("I saw Gary Cooper in *Beau Geste* when I was a kid and I thought the French Foreign Legion would be fun") but was rejected, thankfully, for being underage. Instead, he joined a traveling carnival and did all kinds of odd jobs. It was listening to the veteran carny folk, some of whom had been on the circuit since the late 1800s, telling amazing tales about their experiences, that planted the storytelling seed in Bill's imagination.

"They were mostly honest people, despite the bad reputation traveling carny shows had back then," Bill remembers. "Of course, there were exceptions. There was one guy named Picky, who got that name because he was a master pickpocket. He could steal a man's socks right off his feet without him knowing. Believe me, Picky got us chased out of more than a few towns."

After a few months of this grueling existence, Bill returned home and finished high school. Next came stints as a deputy sheriff in the Tallulah, Louisiana, Sheriff's Department, followed by a hitch in the U.S. Army. Then he began a career in radio broadcasting at KTLD in Tallulah, which would last sixteen years. It was there that he fine-tuned his storytelling skills. He turned to writing in 1970, but it wouldn't be until 1979 that his first novel, *The Devil's Kiss*, was published. Thus began the full-time writing career of William W. Johnstone. He wrote horror (*The Uninvited*), thrillers (*The Last of the Dog Team*), even a romance novel or two. Then, in February 1983, *Out of the Ashes* was published. Searching for his missing family in a postapocalyptic America, rebel mercenary and patriot Ben Raines is united with the civilians of the Resistance forces and moves to the forefront of a revolution for the nation's future.

Out of the Ashes was a smash. The series would continue for the next twenty years, winning Bill three generations of fans all over the world. The series was often imitated but never duplicated. "We all tried to copy the Ashes series," said one publishing executive, "but Bill's uncanny ability, both then and now, to predict in which direction the political winds were blowing brought a certain immediacy to the table no one else could capture." The Ashes series would end its run with more than thirty-four books and twenty million copies in print, making it one of the most successful men's action series in American book publishing. (The Ashes series also, Bill notes with a touch of pride, got him on the FBI's Watch List for its less than flattering portrayal of spineless politicians and the growing power of big government over our lives, among other things. In that respect, I often find myself saying, "Bill was years ahead of his time.")

Always steps ahead of the political curve, Bill's recent thrillers, written with myself, include *Vengeance Is Mine, Invasion USA, Border War, Jackknife, Remember the Alamo, Home Invasion, Phoenix Rising, The Blood of Patriots, The Bleeding Edge*, and the upcoming *Suicide Mission.*

It is with the western, though, that Bill found his greatest success. His westerns propelled him onto both the *USA Today* and the *New York Times* bestseller lists.

Bill's western series include *Matt Jensen, the Last Mountain Man, Preacher, the First Mountain Man, The Family Jensen, Luke Jensen, Bounty Hunter, Eagles, MacCallister* (an Eagles spin-off), *Sidewinders, The Brothers O'Brien, Sixkiller, Blood Bond, The Last Gunfighter*, and the new series *Flintlock* and *The Trail West*. May 2013 saw the hardcover western *Butch Cassidy: The Lost Years*.

"The western," Bill says, "is one of the few true art forms that is one hundred percent American. I liken the Western as America's version of England's Arthurian legends, like the Knights of the Round Table, or Robin Hood and his Merry Men. Starting with the 1902 publication of *The Virginian* by Owen Wister, and followed by the greats like Zane Grey, Max Brand, Ernest Haycox, and of course Louis L'Amour, the western has helped to shape the cultural landscape of America.

"I'm no goggle-eyed college academic, so when my fans ask me why the western is as popular now as it was a century ago, I don't offer a 200-page thesis. Instead, I can only offer this: The western is honest. In this great country, which is suffering under the yoke of political correctness, the western harks back to an era when justice was sure and swift. Steal a man's horse, rustle his cattle, rob a bank, a stagecoach, or a train, you were hunted down and fitted with a hangman's noose. One size fit all.

"Sure, we westerners are prone to a little embellishment and exaggeration and, I admit it, occasionally play a little fast and loose with the facts. But we do so for a very good reason—to enhance the enjoyment of readers.

"It was Owen Wister, in *The Virginian*, who first coined the phrase 'When you call me that, smile.' Legend has it that Wister actually heard those words spoken by a deputy sheriff in Medicine Bow, Wyoming, when another poker player called him a son of a bitch.

"Did it really happen, or is it one of those myths that have passed down from one generation to the next? I honestly don't know. But there's a line in one of my favorite westerns of all time, *The Man Who Shot Liberty Valance*, where the newspaper editor tells the young reporter, 'When the truth becomes legend, print the legend.'

"These are the words I live by."

Center Point Large Print
600 Brooks Road / PO Box 1
Thorndike, ME 04986-0001 USA

(207) 568-3717

US & Canada:
1 800 929-9108
www.centerpointlargeprint.com